Capulet Close

Suzy Edney

Thank you to all of my family and friends who have read my writing and encouraged me to publish my book.

Also thank you to the Rugby Café Writers who have inspired me to write regularly.

Special thanks to Jan Finch who spent a lot of time editing my work and to Terry, my husband who has been endlessly patient and came up with a great book cover design for Capulet Close.

Chapter 1

He looked at his watch for the third time. She was usually here by now...ah, there she was. His eyes followed the slim, attractive woman dressed in a work uniform; hurrying along the supermarket aisles, consulting her list and adding items to her trolley. Her shiny brown hair was cut in a choppy bob, and although preoccupied, she had a half-smile on her lips which had been what had attracted him to her the first time he had seen her all those years ago. He felt a twinge of regret when he thought back to those early years, both full of hope and ambition and very much in love. He sighed; he'd made his choice. Regret was useless; they both had new lives now.

'Julia'

A voice, which she recognised with a painful jolt, was Steve's. What was he doing here?

'I can't stop, just getting some shopping for Mum in my lunch hour.'

'I was hoping you might have time for a coffee.'

He sounded like a disappointed little boy. Julia waved as she turned away and headed for the checkout. Steve had never liked being thwarted. He was his parents' golden boy, the darling of the design company where he had worked for the past four years, and Julia's now ex-husband. He had traded her in for a younger model, and it still hurt.

She was running late. Pushing all thoughts of Steve from her mind, she quickly finished the shopping and headed over to her mum's. As she unloaded the bags and stowed everything away in the small compact kitchen, she couldn't help but wonder what it was that Steve had wanted.

They were married for fifteen years and divorced now for nearly four. The marriage in many ways had been successful. They had built up a design company from scratch. Every penny had been ploughed back into the business. In the early years, Julia did everything: advertising, pricing jobs, choosing materials, keeping the accounts and leaving Steve to do what he did best which was designing interiors. On reflection, Julia mused there weren't many public spaces where Steve's work couldn't be seen. Interiors of shops, offices hotels and restaurants, you name it, he had had his hand in it. Julia turned her attention to lunch.

'Mum, chicken or ham in your salad?'

As they ate, Julia filled her mum in on her day, when she got to the meeting with Steve her mum put down her knife and fork and snorted 'cheeky so-and-so! After the way he treated you, he's lucky you even give him the time of day.'

Julia smiled across at her mum. She was in her seventies, a small neat lady; but the chronic arthritis that plagued her in recent years had taken a toll. Her poor hands were stiff and her joints were swollen. Today was a good day but sometimes she couldn't even cut up her food.

Julia did her shopping and tried to have lunch with her as often as she could during the week. She had good friends who called in regularly and took her out if she was up to it. If not, they visited just to keep her company. She always did what she could, and Julia thanked the universe every day for her mum's optimism. She willingly tried every new diet, suggestions from the doctor anything that might improve her condition. She never complained, apart from mourning her lack of stylish footwear.

Julia remembered her mum never being without her fabulous high-heeled shoes. In fact, one of her favourite child hood memories was playing dress up in front of her mum's full-length mirror and wearing a pair of high heeled shoes, nowadays her mum was reduced to buying shoes for comfort rather than style as the arthritis distorted her feet, making them look out of proportion for her small frame.

Julia quickly cleared away the lunch things, her mind already on her next job. Making sure her mum had everything to hand and was able to manage, they said their goodbyes and Julia was off.

'Don't work too hard, love.'

The rest of the afternoon passed in a flurry of cleaning, messages about the next day's jobs and persistent unwelcome thoughts of Steve. Knowing him, there would be an ulterior motive for the coffee invitation. The split had been devastating. She still found it hard to believe sometimes. Even though she had come out of the relationship financially secure, her emotions and her confidence had been at rock bottom, and really she was only just getting her confidence back.

Chapter 2

At 5.30pm, Julia walked up the path, feeling the familiar frisson of irritation as she glanced up at her neighbour's front window shrouded in ivy.

I really must talk to Dave about that, it looks so seedy.

Immediately she put her key in the door of 2 Capulet Close, the feeling passed. She had returned to her sanctuary, the oasis of calm that she called home. As she looked around this small cosy space that she had created, Julia felt a sense of wellbeing. She had bought every stick of furniture and decorated every single room herself. The furniture wasn't all new, but she had an eye for colour and had mixed textures and fabrics to create a comfortable, stylish home. A home that could never be taken from her and one that was bought and paid for with her own money.

Julia knew it wasn't just her mum who wanted to see her dating again. Her friends also thought she should get out there. Angie had suggested speed dating. She had considered it and had even gone as far as looking into it, but had chickened out at the last minute. The girls understood that it was something they couldn't help her with. They included her socially; lunch dates, theatre trips and parties but often she was the odd woman out because their friends like themselves were often other couples.

Kicking off her shoes, she headed upstairs. No cooking tonight, she was due at her friend Ali's house for a girls' night in. They had been at school together, and Ali's neighbour Angie had also become a good friend since they all began getting together regularly over twenty years ago. The two of them had seen her through some difficult times.

Financially, things were tough for her and Steve in those early years. They both made sacrifices in order to grow the business. Sometimes after a hard week, the get-together with the girls having a laugh, commiserating and celebrating together made everything OK again.

Just as she was getting changed, she heard her mobile ring.

That's typical!

She dashed down the stairs. Scrabbling through her bag, she saw Steve's name flash up on the screen. With a sinking heart, she was beginning to realise that the meeting in the supermarket hadn't been a coincidence after all.

What could he possibly want after all this time?

She would have to tell the girls. Whatever their response, she knew that it would be fiercely protective. Grabbing a bottle of wine from the fridge, she locked the front door and headed out. Ali was a brilliant cook, and although they all took turns hosting their weekly meet-ups, she knew that tonight the food would be especially good.

They had a lovely evening. Ali's husband Simon was always tactful about their Monday nights. He left them to it, and even Jake, Ali's teenage son, would grunt a hello; then nip off to his room, or sit watching a film or a football match with his dad.

Julia smiled across at Jake. She had known him all of his life, and he had always loved her visits. As an energetic toddler, she alone could persuade him to sit still as she read him his favourite stories. 'You're so patient with him,' marvelled Ali, 'how do you do it?'

'Ah, it's good practice,' she had smiled, gently kissing the top of Jake's head and looking forward to a time when she and Steve could start their own family.

Remembering this made her think sadly of the past. It was never the right time. The business needed expanding; we need a better house; a bigger car. How would we manage with a baby now? This project needs your expertise. I can't do it without you. All excuses that she loyally went along with.

Realising she was miles away, she turned her attention to Angie, who was telling them a funny story about her three-year-old granddaughter Ruby. Angie was so proud of her, but they lived in Australia, so she had to be content with

FaceTime calls. Last time they called, it was morning in Australia but a cold winter's evening here. Ruby kept asking why the lights were on, and giggled when she was told that it was night-time. She kept asking them to show her the night, and then became convinced that Granddad had used his magic to make it night-time. Granddad does magic tricks, so Ruby made that connection herself.

They were still laughing at Angie's story as Ali served the dessert. Julia looked at her friends, raised her glass and said, 'To Monday nights!'

'To Monday nights!' they echoed.

Eventually, the chat turned to work. Ali asked her when she was going to leave Clean & Easy.

'You did say it was just a temporary job until you got your place finished,' said Angie.

'I know, I know; it's just making that leap, I suppose.'

'What you should be doing is concentrating on children's bedrooms and playrooms, you know as well as I do that people will always spend money on their kids even if they have nothing for themselves.'

This was Ali. They all chuckled as they remembered the money that Ali and Simon had spent on Jake's bedroom. At four months old, he had a beautiful nursery full of expensive matching furniture and built in wardrobes. They had even commissioned Julia to paint a mural of nursery rhyme characters all over one wall. All of this for a tiny baby, and the two of them were still sleeping in a bedroom thrown back to the 1950s complete with Simon's Gran's utility furniture.

'We must have been mad.'

Ali recalled how it had taken four years of scrimping and saving to finish the house and get it exactly how they wanted it, and then Simon had changed his job.

'We ended up moving here, some other baby is enjoying Jake's mural now, I'm sure.'

They all laughed as Angie commented dryly that Jake would hardly want the mural now so it would have been long gone had they stayed in the house.

'Talking of designing, I saw Steve today. He wanted to buy me a coffee.'

'What could he possibly have to say after all this time?' demanded Ali.

Julia explained that she was furious with him, but curious as to why he was even in the supermarket.

'Oh, and he tried to call earlier too,' she explained about the missed call. 'I didn't want to spoil my evening getting into a discussion with Steve, but I can't deny I'm curious.'

'Trouble in paradise, maybe,' suggested Angie with a cheeky grin, referring to Steve's much younger partner. (The newer model, as Julia referred to Stacey).

Geed on by the girls, Julia pulled out her phone and scrolled through the voice messages. Steve's breezy voice clicked in.

'Hi Julia, I really do need to speak to you, please give me a call as soon as you get this message.'

They all looked at one another.

Ali said slowly, 'Well, he sounds troubled, but not distraught. So it's probably not an emergency.'

Angie frowned, she wondered if Steve might be going to offer her some work. Julia dismissed that idea immediately. There were things about the business sale that the girls were not fully aware of, but any work linked to the new company would never be coming her way. Of that much, she was certain.

'I hate to say it, but there's only one way to find out what he wants.'

This was Angie.

Ali suggested she just bite the bullet and give him a call.

'At least you'll know then.'

Julia agreed, saying she would do it tomorrow. They made their farewells, agreeing to meet the following Monday when Julia would be hosting the evening.

**

As Julia hurried around the corner, she was thankful it was a mild evening. Capulet Close was well lit, and as she paused to get her key out of her pocket, she noticed Dave from number four getting out of his van.

'Dave.'

He looked over and smiled.

'I just wanted to ask if you could cut back some of that ivy when you get a minute, it's starting to grow over my wall.

Dave agreed, he said he would try to do it over the weekend. Thanking him, she headed up the path. As she put her key in the door, her phone started to ring. As usual, it was in the bottom of her bag; and by the time she had got indoors and turned the lights on, the ringing had stopped.

Bloody hell, Steve again, he really does want to speak to me!

The call had gone to voicemail.

'Julia, I really do need to speak with you. I'm outside, can I come in? I promise not to stay long.'

Her heart sank. She told everyone she was over Steve, but really, she was finding it very difficult to move on. Seeing him today brought back all those feelings of insecurity, and now she was certain that the meeting in the supermarket was no coincidence.

She left it a few minutes, and after sipping a glass of water and taking a couple of deep breaths, texted back,

Ok, 5 minutes

Chapter 3

They were in the kitchen. Julia hadn't felt inclined to show Steve into her comfortable living room with the big squashy sofa. Instead, she had invited him into the square kitchen. They sat awkwardly either side of the scrubbed pine table, Steve looked round admiringly.

'I like…' He was about to tell her how much he liked what she had done to the kitchen, but the stony look she gave him pulled him up.

'Come on Steve, you don't usually have a problem getting to the point. What is it this time?'

Julia remembered with a sick feeling in the pit of her stomach the last time her and Steve had been in a similar situation in the beautiful sitting room in Rose Cottage; the sitting room that she had helped to design and renovate. In the house that was supposed to be their forever home, she could feel tears prick her eyelids just thinking about it.

Looking at him now, she could see this was causing him some difficulty. He couldn't even meet her gaze.

'Well, um, the thing is, Julia. It's really hard for me to tell you this. It's Stacey, she's pregnant.'

Julia froze, her throat seemed to be closing up and she couldn't speak. Steve was talking but she was unable to process what he was saying. She was aware that his mouth was moving but nothing made sense. Waves of nausea hit her and she got up from the table.

'Good grief Julia, I thought you'd prefer to hear it from me.'

She was throwing up in the cloakroom as she heard the front door slam behind him.

Typical; buggering off when the going gets tough.

She was sobbing as she washed her hands and splashed her face with cold water.

Looking at the clock as she emerged from the toilet, she couldn't believe that it was only 11pm. An hour ago, she was laughing with her friends, but now it felt that her whole world had crashed for the second time. She felt like an old woman as she mechanically prepared her overnight oats, turned off lights and made sure her clothes were ready for the morning.

Only when she was lying in bed did she allow her thoughts to return to the past. Was she being unreasonable, unrealistic even? Stacey was a young woman; why was it so surprising that she would want a baby? Then it dawned on her, the unfairness of the situation. She had given her life to the business and their marriage. She had put her longing for a family on the back burner in order to please Steve and help with expanding the business.

Indeed, thanks to both their efforts, the business was such a success that it attracted a massive buy out from another design company. Although Julia ran everything in the background, it was Steve who had been lured by the big bucks and the offer of a top job.

Julia was reluctant. As her mum had said, 'You need your career too, Julia. What will you do?'

Julia held out for as long as she could. But every argument she came up with, Steve had a counter argument. Her main worry was that there was no job offer for her in the new company.

Chapter 4

It was just a few weeks later that Steve succeeded in talking her into accepting the terms of the buyout. He had all of the answers. When she worried that there was no job for her, he said, 'You deserve a break, why don't you organise the renovation of the new house? You know your talent is in designing personal spaces, and we can afford it now.'

He had kissed her jubilantly. 'We can make it a real family home. It's all worked out brilliantly, hasn't it?'

Julia still had her reservations, but she took Steve at his word. She knew at the age of thirty-seven it might take a while to get pregnant, so she stopped taking her contraception and threw herself into the renovation and furnishing of Rose Cottage. Her mum chuckled when she saw it.

'Hardly a cottage, it's got four bedrooms! And once your kitchen extension is built, it'll be more like a manor house.'

They moved in straight away and at first just lived in the two downstairs rooms. Luckily, with the money from the business and Steve's eye wateringly generous salary, Julia had free reign with budget, fixtures fittings and furnishings. Within a year, they had their dream home. Sadly, Julia still wasn't pregnant.

'We've been trying for nearly a year. Do you think there might be something wrong with one of us?'

Her friends thought it wouldn't hurt to get some tests done. They reasoned that if there was a problem with one of them, at least they would know.

Steve didn't seem concerned. He trotted out the much told tale of his own mother. Married at thirty-three and waited ten years until they were blessed with the arrival of Steve.

When the tale was repeated to her friends, Ali raised her eyebrows and muttered, 'No wonder he's such a golden boy, then. Only child, older parents….'

Julia had laughed with them at the time, feeling a little disloyal. After all, Steve's parents were good to them, and she was glad he had had such a good upbringing. He would make a great dad.

Thumping the pillow, she glanced at the bedside clock.

Midnight, it's useless. I'll never sleep now, not with all this crap running through my head.

Then, as if to add insult to injury, she could hear an intermittent tap on the window.

Not now, Dave and his bloody ivy.

Shoving her feet into her slippers and slipping her arms into her dressing gown, she went back downstairs. Julia grabbed a blanket off the back of the sofa and curled up in the corner tucking her feet under her and wrapping the blanket around her. Once she was comfortably cuddled up, she allowed her thoughts to drift back to the last months of her marriage.

It was only when she began fretting about becoming pregnant that she realised how distant Steve had become. In truth, it wasn't surprising she hadn't conceived. They hardly made love any more. She bit her lip as she remembered confiding in Ali and asking her how long it had taken her to get pregnant with Jake.

'Oh, at least a year but it was fun trying,' she had replied with a cheeky grin.

Julia remembered that sinking feeling when she realised how little physical contact her and Steve had since moving into Rose Cottage. They seemed to lead separate lives. He was busy with his new job, he never wanted to discuss it with her and once the renovations to the house were done she had felt like a spare part.

Julia had forced herself in spite of her embarrassment to ask Ali how often even after all these years she thought it was normal to make love with your husband. Although very good friends, they never discussed their sex lives; it didn't feel right somehow. But Julia was scared that things were not normal. Steve's actions were not those of a man with a desire to start a family.

In fact, thought Julia with a dawning sense of embarrassment, *since I gave up work I feel like a member of staff. Renovating his house, doing the laundry, making sure he has nice meals. And in exchange I get a decent salary, a nice car to drive; and if I'm lucky, a bit of absent-minded affection.*

Julia remembered Ali looking at her and finding it a really difficult question.

'Well, it's different for everyone.' Ali had replied, colour rising in her cheeks, 'We're still very affectionate, and even with work I'd say several times a week. When we were first together though, blimey we couldn't keep our hands off each other; you know what that's like.'

Realising how distressed Julia was, Ali caught hold of her hands.

'Julia, you must speak to Steve, he isn't being fair. I don't want to know about personal stuff, and I know how hard it was for you to ask me those things. But if I'm honest, he strikes me as a bit of a cold fish. You always put him first, and that secrecy about the takeover, I'm sure he's conned you somewhere.'

She went on to voice her concerns, saying that she thought Julia had shared the work, and the success of the business was as much hers as Steve's, but now he appeared to have the best deal and hadn't even noticed how upset and worried she was. 'The thing is, you might have a fabulous house but you're not enjoying it together.'

Chapter 5

After confiding in Ali, Julia decided she would have it out with Steve, talk to him about their future and let him know exactly how she had been feeling. She set the scene carefully, preparing a nice meal, buying his favourite wine and making sure the table was set beautifully. The patio doors were left open showing the colourful pots on the patio and allowing the fragrance of the night scented stock to float into the house.

***

The evening was progressing nicely. Steve had arrived home on time for once. He had even bought her favourite flowers, freesias and roses which she had arranged in her crystal vase.

They lingered over the meal, talking of this and that and for a while it seemed like old times. Julia had decided not to mention her worries yet and had planned a surprise for Steve. She had thought about it after Ali had mentioned her love life. Maybe it was up to her to instigate their love making for a change.

He was lounging in the love seat with his coffee. For once, he didn't have his I Pad or mobile to hand and he looked totally relaxed. Music was playing in the background, and even after all this time she could remember the track; One of their favourite songs, Carole King's 'You Make Me Feel like a Natural Woman.' She remembered going over and dropping a light kiss on his hair.

'I won't be a minute,' she had whispered. 'I've got something for you.'

'Don't be long then, I want to talk to you.'

Julia remembered the flutter of excitement she felt as she carefully unpacked the ridiculously expensive silk underwear she had bought on line. Wearing the delicate bra and wispy lace and silk pants, she was grateful for the beautiful elegant wrap that made the whole outfit sexy but tasteful. She timed her entrance to coincide with the end of the track.

She could still remember feeling the butterflies in her stomach and the dry feeling in her throat as she recalled sliding the door open and making her entrance.

'Here I am, Steve.'

Without looking up, he said irritably, 'Come over here, Julia. It's getting late and I…..'

Too late, she was already moving closer and he was turning his head. Their eyes met, her cheeks burnt with humiliation, eyes heavy with unshed tears.

What a bloody farce.

She turned and stumbled from the room. She could hear Steve calling her name as she ran to the bathroom. She felt like a hooker luring him to bed, what was she thinking? It had become clear that their problems ran deeper than that. One night of passion couldn't put things right.

Sobbing under her breath, she slowly took off the beautiful silk underwear and packed it away. Then she showered, found her plainest white cotton nightie and left the bathroom looking more like a maiden aunt than the alluring woman she had hoped to portray.

Not sure where she should sleep, she had reluctantly made her way to the bedroom and peeped around the door. There was Steve, still fully clothed and stretched out on the bed. He beckoned her over.

'What the hell was that all about, Julia? I had something really important that I wanted to say to you and you go and pull a stunt like that.'

She remembered yelling at him; 'Stunt! That was no stunt I'm desperate; we never really talk! I gave up work to start a family, how the fuck that's gonna happen when we rarely go to bed at the same time, leave alone have sex? You tell me, Steve!'

She remembered his horrified face and his look of helplessness when she began sobbing.

Steve patted her back, trying to calm her down. Eventually as her sobs subsided he made tea and bought a cup to her.

Well, that hasn't happened in a while.

Julia realised that Steve, even in the early years of their marriage, rarely made a meal or drinks. She definitely was and always had been the giver in their relationship.

As they drank their tea, he falteringly came to the point. Just as she had wanted to discuss their relationship, Steve wanted to confess something. He didn't want a family. He had always seen it as if it did happen, it would be something that would happen a long way in the future, and it wasn't something he wanted now. Not with the new job and all.

Julia looked at him, aghast.

'So you lied, I'd never have agreed to the takeover if I'd known you didn't mean it. I thought you wanted it as much as I did. What the hell am I supposed to do now?'

What came next was the biggest blow of all. Steve said slowly, 'Well, as I see it, there are two choices. We can carry on as we are, you don't have to work you can enjoy the house. Spend a bit more time with your mum. Do what you're so good at, look after the house and garden, entertain my clients, maybe do a bit of voluntary work.' Seeing her stricken expression, he said,

'Or if you really want a family more than this good life we have now, well, I understand that too. You might want to cut loose and find someone else. After all, you don't have as much time on your side as me.'

Unable to meet her steely gaze, he merely shrugged.

At least he had the good grace to sleep in the spare room. Julia didn't get much rest that night. She had plenty of food for thought, but of one thing she was certain. She couldn't stay with Steve after this, she just couldn't.

He doesn't even love me enough to want me to stay, she had thought with a heavy heart.

Chapter 6

Now she had begun to process this shocking news, Julia was feeling more angry than upset. It felt so unfair that Steve, who wasn't bothered about a family, had strung her along for all that time. He obviously hadn't loved her enough to let her have what she so desperately wanted, but was now all set to play happy families with Stacey.

She had come to terms with the fact it probably wouldn't happen for her now, she could go down the single parent route. Lots of career women did, but honestly, that went against all of her instincts. She believed that children needed two parents. Remembering her own childhood with a mum and a dad, and recalling how devastating it had been for her mum coping alone with a young teenager after the premature death of Julia's dad. No, single parenthood definitely wouldn't be her choice.

Glancing at the clock, she realised it was gone 2am. She had work tomorrow and plenty of food for thought after

Steve's news. Weariness overcame her, and she took herself back to bed, hoping for at least a few hours rest before the alarm went off. Sleep when it eventually came was intermittent at best, and all too soon the alarm rang. Grabbing her dressing gown, she stormed down the stairs.

Before I do anything else I have got to get to that bloody ivy.

With that, Julia grabbed a large pair of decorating scissors from under the kitchen sink. Leaning out of the bedroom window, she leaned across to Dave's side of the house and cut the offending pieces of ivy off with a satisfied snap.

***

Later that morning as Julia headed to the car, her neighbour Freda hurried over.

'Hi, you couldn't drop me in town, could you? I've a dentist appointment at nine, no bloody taxis and I hate getting the bus this time of day. Full of kids....'

Once Freda got started, she could moan for England. And although Julia's hackles rose at the thought of chauffeuring her lazy neighbour to an appointment that she could easily get to by bus or even walk it.

A bit of exercise might do her some good, came Julia's uncharitable thought, she really couldn't be bothered to assert herself, and she knew Freda would do all of the talking,

It might even be a distraction, who knows?

'You wouldn't believe the morning I've had, that noisy bloody dog; he's had my toe up his arse more than once this morning. Bark, the little so-and-so knows when I'm busy. He's like a kid looking for attention all the time.'

It went on for the whole ten minutes. Her son Blake was selfish. He never brought the children to see her. Her friend had promised to take her shopping but she had ended up working.

'I haven't seen a soul all week.'

Julia nodded and smiled in what she hoped were all the right places, and eventually dropped Freda off at her dentist.

'Thank you, you're a life saver.'

Throwing Julia a smile, she gathered her bags and disappeared through the door of the dentist's surgery.

Whew! Thought Julia as a welcome silence enveloped her. *Somebody shoot me if I ever become as big a moaner as that woman.*

Later that day, Julia popped in to see her mum.

'I can't stop today, Mum, but I'll make your lunch.'

Maria called cheerfully from the living room,

'You certainly are stopping. I feel great today, I made us some potato and parsnip soup. You sit down and let me look after you for once.'

Julia sank down in one of the comfy dining chairs and they ate their soup in a companionable silence for a few minutes.

'Mum, this is lovely. It reminds me of when I'd come home from school when I was about eleven or twelve, feeling hard done by. And we'd sit in the warm with tea and cake, or in the winter, soup. Eventually I'd tell you all about it.'

Her mum laughed, 'Oh yes, it'd all come tumbling out. The teacher who gave you lines for talking, the girl who didn't invite you to her party, the boy you fancied but asked your friend out...'

Julia put down her spoon and looked at her mum.

'I feel like that today, Steve called in last night.....'

With that, Julia told her mum the whole story about Stacy being pregnant, and how devastated she felt. Her mum as ever didn't advise, counsel or interrupt. She just waited until Julia had finished her story.

'Mmm, that must have been hard to take, knowing that Steve had said he didn't want children. But he did tell you himself. So that's a point in his favour.'

'Only just, Mum, the baby's due at the beginning of August. I feel as though he only told me as an afterthought.'

Julia went on to tell her mum that she had been doing a lot of thinking since she found out.

'I know I jokingly refer to Steve trading me in for a younger model, but that's not strictly true. He did get together with her quite quickly but only after he admitted to not wanting children. He made me feel like he was doing me a favour by offering me the option of staying with him.'

Maria listened sadly as Julia recounted that terrible night, her cheeks flushed with embarrassment as she recalled Steve's calculated summing up of his two choices for their future.

The day after Steve's announcement, Julia had gone straight to a solicitor to start divorce proceedings citing irretrievable breakdown of their marriage.

Steve had accepted her decision very practically. In fact, ever the businessman he took steps to buy her out of Rose Cottage, leaving her with enough money to buy her own house in Capulet Close.

It was only once the house was finished, money was getting tight and she began looking for work that Julia realised with dismay that Ali was right. She had been conned again in a manner of speaking

Chapter 7

After toting her portfolio around to different design companies for several weeks, Julia couldn't understand the lack of response. She was happy to work for someone else, and thought she could also take on freelance work.

She had photographed every project that she had completed, and even had before-and-after photos of her own house. The problem was that because they had built the business together, she really didn't have much experience of job hunting. So when the offers didn't materialise, she thought it must be her fault so kept tweaking her CV and trying again.

Eventually, Steve had called her.

'Julia, I heard from Christie and Browns that you applied for a job in the design studio.'

Immediately her hackles were up. 'Yes, well I've got to earn a living, Steve. The divorce settlement won't keep me going forever, and now the house is finished I need to earn some money.'

That was when he dropped more devastating news.

As part of the buyout, not only was Julia not offered a job, but Steve thought it was OK to agree a clause that prevented her from accepting a job from a rival company *or* setting up a business within a twenty mile radius for two years. That distance was impossible to cover every day. She could travel that far occasionally, but she really needed to be near enough to her mum to be able to pop in every day.

Julia was shocked at his duplicity! Not only had he talked her into the buyout with the promise of starting a family, but when he snatched that hope from her, he had tried to talk her into staying in a loveless marriage. Probably thinking he could string her along until the clause was spent.

She remembered looking over the contracts. Stupidly, she had trusted Steve and let him negotiate terms and conditions. And yes, she had signed everything, so all legal and above board there. The contract was watertight. Her solicitor advised her to sit it out.

'You only have about eight months to run, so get yourself a temporary job for now. And then once the two years are up, the choice is yours. You could even start your own business again.'

He shook her hand and wished her well for the future.

That was how she had ended up surprising her family and friends by taking the job with Clean & Easy. She had told

Ali and Angie that she didn't have the confidence to set up on her own yet. She would do a few freelance jobs and build it up slowly.

She had felt stupid, almost like those people who are victims of a scam, not wanting to admit that she had been conned. It was one thing after another, and she felt almost ashamed that because she was so naïve, Steve had been able to manipulate every situation to his own advantage.

At first she believed her own story she really did intend it to be a temporary job. But the truth was by the time the two years were up and she was legally able to look for design work, she felt settled for the first time in a while. The clients were lovely, the hours were regular, the money wasn't great but her expenses were low. Steve had at least made sure she had enough of a settlement to buy the house. 'Conscience money,' she had called it.....And best of all, she could be there for her mum.

The other thing that she liked was living in the Close. It was only small, six houses in a tiny cul-de-sac. The nice thing was though, that for the first time in her adult life, she actually knew all of her neighbours. Another good thing was that she lived so close to the girls, just a five minute walk away.

Chapter 8

Dave came out of the front door of number four, lost in thought. Out of the corner of his eye he could see Freda from number eight standing on her doorstep wearing fleece leggings and sweatshirt. She resembled an over stuffed teddy bear. He smiled as he made the analogy. He could talk he was hardly what you would call a snappy dresser.

He chided himself for his uncharitable thoughts. In fairness, Freda scrubbed up very well. She was always immaculate when she left the house, hair, clothes, nails, make-up; the lot. She would probably be mortified if she realised she had been spotted without her war paint.

That was one of his dad's sayings, he really must be careful. Comments that were acceptable in his dad's day were always on the tip of his tongue, and sometimes they just slipped out.

The trouble was he had been on his own too long. Diane, his ex-wife, had never let him get away with anything. She was always challenging what she called his 'sexist attitude.'

He had already been unofficially reprimanded at work for calling one of the managers 'love.' She had even recommended that he go on a diversity awareness course. If only she knew how diverse he could be. Dave chuckled as he climbed into his van.

As he was pulling away, his heart sank. Julia was waving to him. He did think about pretending he hadn't noticed, but he liked Julia, and he did feel guilty as he still hadn't done anything about the ivy. He stopped the van and lowered the window.

'Hi, Julia, I'm sorry. I did mean to do the ivy but something came up.'

Glimpsing at Julia's irritated expression Dave felt a stab of discomfort. Assertively, she got right to the point.

'It's getting out of hand; it's tapping on my window. I ended up having to lean across to cut some back the other morning. It was stopping me sleeping.'

He was just thinking smugly that however independent women thought they were, there had always been what his dad liked to coin pink jobs and blue jobs, and the blue jobs were best left to the men. Dave was not expecting the response that came next. Julia smiled and handed him a business card.

'Gardening isn't for everyone, Dave. If you don't fancy going up the ladder yourself, you can get these to do the ivy.'

Perfectly pleasant and reasonable but irritating nonetheless. There was no way he was paying someone to do the ivy. He would do it, but in his own good time.

Later that evening, Julia was tidying up her front garden when Valerie from number ten stopped for a chat.

***

Julia, your baskets and pots always look so lovely and colourful.' She lowered her voice as she glanced across at Dave's.

'Doesn't that get on your nerves, growing all over your side of the house?'

Julia grimaced and filled Valerie in on her earlier conversation with Dave. Valerie roared with laughter.

'He's a nice man, but really doesn't see the benefit of looking after his property. He's been on his own for quite a while now, but I don't think he's had the windows cleaned since his wife left.'

Julia invited Valerie in for a glass of wine and they spent a pleasant hour catching up on the news from the street. Valerie was delighted that the house next to hers that had been empty for some time had at last been sold. She went on to tell Julia that they were a retired couple, and she had met them briefly when they viewed the property.

'I really warmed to them. I think they love the idea that we're a little community. They live in a big town right on a main road, so they'll find this very cosy.'

Reluctantly, Valerie put down her wine glass and hugged Julia goodbye.

'Must get back, I've a load of sports gear to wash for Florence and we're watching a film later.' Noticing Julia's smile, she hastened to explain ruefully,

'No, not a chick flick, it's a Shakespeare play that Florence needs to watch as she's got an essay to do on Henry V. I'd far rather be watching *Fifty Shades of Grey*, but thought I'd share her pain and watch it with her.'

They were both still laughing as she left Julia's to walk home.

***

Saturday was a lovely bright sunny day, and Dave had decided that he ought to at least get the ivy cut back from Julia's side of the house. He couldn't understand what the fuss was about. He quite liked the overgrown shrubbery at the front; it gave him another layer of privacy. The ivy shrouding the windows reminded him of his childhood home, and he hadn't even considered that it might become a nuisance to his neighbour.

As he worked, he was aware of the comings and goings in the street. James and Gary at number six were cleaning their cars. Dave grinned to himself as he heard

'Workin' in the Car Wash;' playing. James was belting out the lyrics as he danced along to the music.

Gary, much quieter than his partner, methodically cleaned the windows, content with humming along to the music. Occasionally they exchanged smiles, or James would say something and Gary would laugh. They both spotted Dave and gave him a wave.

'You can come and do ours when you're done,' called James.

Dave was about to go over and explain that he really didn't have the time when he paused to think.

Dave, you pillock, he was joking! Diane would have been so cross with him.

'You take everything literally, Dave, for heaven's sake.'

He took a deep breath, waved across and smiled, turning his attention immediately back to the job in hand.

His eye was drawn to number eight. Freda had a visitor, her friend Maisie. Dave recognised her she worked in the local supermarket. Julia came out, casually dressed. She was off to take her mum out for lunch. Before getting in the car, she walked over to the gate.

'You decided to brave the ladder then, Dave? Thank you, that tapping was beginning to annoy me.'

'That's OK, I was always going to do it but I've just been busy with work and the band, that's all.'

He smiled down at her and continued to clear the ivy from Julia's side of the house. He briefly considered getting

36

the lawnmower out and doing the front lawn, but once Julia had driven off, he quickly tidied up and put the tools away. He had more important things to do. Dave had to organise a venue for band practise.

Just as he was going through a list of likely venues for the band to rehearse, unbeknown to him, he was the subject of discussion at number eight. Earlier that day Freda had called a state of emergency. She was in the middle of her online shop, and at the point of paying, something had gone wrong.

Fortunately, her friend Maisie was on hand to sort it. She was tech savvy, whereas Freda - like a lot of people always presumed that when things went wrong it was her own fault. As a result, at the first hint of a blip, she would throw in the towel and call for help.

In this instance, it *was* her mistake. She was doing her online shop, but used the wrong account details. Never mind, it was all sorted. The order had gone through, and they were sitting in the kitchen drinking gin, and having a good catch-up.

'What do you make of him at number four, then?' Freda gave a sly grin. They had been watching Dave beavering away up the ladder. Freda had made a couple of salacious remarks about his rear end; he was quite a neat chap, slight and not very tall. Although not fit, he certainly wasn't overweight. However, he didn't help his image; the idea of personal grooming had passed him by. With his poor haircut and in sore need of a shave, he looked every one of his fifty-eight years. Crumpled T-shirts, a wide brimmed hat and creased combats were his weekend garb. He only looked slightly tidier on a work day when this was exchanged for black jeans and a polo shirt.

Maisie said jokingly, 'Well, he's got a full head of hair and all his own teeth, it could be worse.'

Freda was scathing.

'I couldn't get involved with him, ugh! I nursed old men and they haven't got anything down there, I bet it'd be like a shrivelled walnut. That's no good to me.'

Maisie laughed heartily, 'Now that's ridiculous, he's no Hugh Jackman but I bet he's younger than us.'

'Well, he looks old and he acts old. Mind you, I bet he wouldn't say no to me. He's always giving me the eye.'

Maisie gave her a playful punch on the arm.

'Go girl, you could do worse, somebody at work knows him. He's in a band! He could kick start your singing career. Let's find out where they're playing, we could be his groupies.'

They clinked glasses and giggled.

Later, as Freda showed Maisie out, she couldn't help glancing over at Gary, who was vigorously polishing the body of the car. 'Now,' she breathed, 'that's more like it! He could give me a good rub down any time.'

'Freda! He's young enough to be your son.'

Unabashed, Freda called over to Gary,

'Hi there, lovely day for it

Maisie covered her face hardly daring to look at Gary.

She even managed to make a simple greeting sound suggestive.

Gary looked up and gave a wave, but quickly gathered his things together and headed inside.

Freda looked at her friend, saying, 'He's gorgeous. I think there might be a spark there, he's a bit shy, but I'm sure he fancies me.'

Maisie laughed, 'Scared to death more like, you need to look at someone nearer your own age.'

Freda was not happy and shut her front door with a slam leaving Maisie bemused. Freda was a good friend but she had some funny ideas, why on earth would a young handsome man like Gary be interested in a woman old enough to be his mother?

***

Meanwhile, Dave hadn't been idle. He had been phoning around local pubs and had found a venue willing to let a local swing band rehearse for free for two hours on a Tuesday night.

They were all good players, but sadly youth wasn't on their side. They were what Diane had unkindly coined, 'the oldest swingers in town'. The thing was Dave's dad had started the band some years before. The drummer was still going strong but he was ninety-two, and although they were musically accurate, they were simply anodyne. Their name belied this, however; Dave in a fit of optimism had named them the Soar Valley Stompers.

The following Monday, Dave had popped in to have lunch with his dad.

'I was thinking I'd ask the neighbours along to the practice tomorrow night, Dad. If we can bring in some customers, they might give us a gig, what do you think?'

'Good thinking, son. I'll ask Jim and June next door. I think Harry will bring his wife and her friend too.'

Dave went back to work full of enthusiasm and canvassed some of his work colleagues to come along too. He planned to call in on all of his neighbours after work and invite them along personally.

Diane would be impressed. I'm engaging with people.

It simply didn't occur to Dave that if he had made as much effort with Diane as he was now making for the band maybe he and Diane would still be together.

Chapter 9

Julia hummed to herself as she selected a playlist for the girls. Ironically, the first song that played was the song from *South Pacific*, her favourite musical. 'I'm Gonna Wash That Man Right out of My Hair.' She sang along to it as she put the finishing touches to the table, and had just poured herself a glass of wine when the bell rang.   Taking off her apron and checking her hair in the mirror, Julia opened the door, greeting Ali with a wide smile.

'Wow!' Ali couldn't keep the surprise out of her voice when she saw her. 'You look amazing, not that you don't always look....'

'OK, Ali, you can stop digging now!' laughed Julia. 'I've got a lot to tell you, but let's wait for Angie and I can fill you both in then.'

As she was pouring Ali a drink, Angie arrived, and soon they were settled at the big kitchen table with their food and glasses of chilled white wine.

'Mmm, this chicken's delicious. I've some serious competition here,' teased Ali. 'Come on Julia, don't keep us in suspense! Is this anything to do with Steve? Or is it that you've met someone? Or did you win the lottery? Those jeans look amazing, they really fit well and they definitely didn't come from Primark. Your hair looks fabulous too.'

Angie just sat quietly looking from one to the other sipping her drink. When Ali eventually drew breath, Angie put her hand over Ali's, saying:

'Give the girl a chance she can't get a word in. Let her tell us what's been happening, she doesn't need interrogating.'

At this point, they all burst out laughing.

'Sorry,' said Ali sheepishly, 'it's just that after last week and all that business with Steve we couldn't help but worry.'

They ate the last of the Spanish chicken; it was delicious, aromatic and went with the crisp chill of the wine perfectly. Julia had already told them the reason that Steve had been trying to contact her and that he had been waiting for her on Monday night.

They were both furious on her behalf and as they sat drinking their wine, they made her howl with laughter as they listed all of the things they would like to do to him if they could get their hands on him.

One suggestion was to feed him contraceptive pills for a month. How they would do this wasn't in the plan but it did seem extremely funny especially when Angie said, completely deadpan,

'It won't do him any long term damage; he'll just put on a bit of weight and grow boobs. Stacey wouldn't find him so attractive then.'

They all ended up laughing uproariously at the thought of slim handsome Steve with curves and boobs. Then Ali suggested that she get someone to hack into his computer and steal some of his clients.

'Girls, girls, that's enough!' screeched Julia, holding her sides and almost crying with laughter. 'I'm not a bunny boiler.'

That started them all off again.

Julia served up the sticky toffee pudding that she had made for dessert, and poured them all a cup of coffee. She explained that she had done a lot of thinking since Steve's visit. She had decided to put herself first and move on with her life. Steve had his life with Stacy; she could complain and bitch about it but couldn't change what had happened.

She explained that when she had given Freda a lift last week, she was in the car for ten minutes, but she was so negative. Moaning about the dog, her son and her friend, lazy so-and-so wouldn't get the bus.

'When I saw Mum at lunchtime struggling to make a meal with her arthritis and staying so cheerful it made me think. I've got a lot going for me - good friends, a lovely mum, a nice house. Anyway, I gave myself a good talking to and took myself shopping. I hadn't bought clothes since the divorce, so I treated myself. And yes Ali, you're quite right, not one thing was from Primark.'

They all laughed; self-consciously Julia touched her hair.

'What about the colour?'

They both nodded enthusiastically.

'It's perfect, that shade of caramel really suits you,' responded Angie.

'You do know though, don't you, that even in your darkest days you could never be a Freda?' remarked Ali. Her and Angie exchanged glances. They had met Freda a few times but hadn't really taken to her. They considered her a bit of a joy sucker.

'Thanks, girls, but I could feel myself being pulled into a negative spiral. That's why our Mondays have been so good for me. We celebrate successes, but we commiserate too. Anyway, let's not get too sentimental,' she smiled inwardly as she noticed Ali making the sick bucket sign. The three of them could be scathing if they witnessed excessive displays of emotion.

Julia continued, 'I've got some more good news. I was thinking about what you said last week Ali; you know, designing children's bedrooms.' She went on to explain that one of the couples she had been cleaning for were expecting their first baby and wanted the small room decorating.

'You'll never guess what they want…..'

'A nursery rhyme mural,' they said in unison.

44

Excitedly, she told them how much they had loved the pictures of the one she did for Jake.

'They've their own ideas too, so I'm going round on Friday with a design board and costings.'

Julia took out her phone and showed her friends the spec that the couple had sent her. It was only a small room but one of the things that they wanted was for it to be gender neutral.

'Very twenty-first century, well I daresay that'll become more the norm. And a great first job to get your teeth into.'

That was Ali, she was always the more excitable of the two, but Julia could see that Angie was pleased for her too.

Reluctantly, at ten-thirty they called it a night. As they were chatting at the door, Julia spotted a note on the mat. It was from Dave inviting her to come and listen to the band practising the following night.

'What do you think, girls, do you fancy it?'

They both agreed it would be nice to listen to some live music for a change and decided to meet on the corner and walk to the Half Moon.

'If it's raining, I'll get Simon to drop us off,' offered Ali, waving goodbye.

As Julia switched off the lights and locked up, she realised that she was doing what she should have done after the divorce. She was saying a final goodbye to Steve.

Chapter 10

Dave was first to arrive on Tuesday night. The landlady, Sharon, was a friendly soul. She greeted him with a smile.

'A bit of live music is just what this place needs,' she said cheerily.

She felt a bit doubtful as the ninety-two-year-old drummer arrived and Dave helped him onto his drum throne. Oh well, she wasn't paying them, and if they weren't any good she needn't invite them again.

When the rest of the band arrived and they began tuning up, she was reassured. They could all definitely play but would a group of men whose collective ages add up to three hundred and eighty really be able to swing?

The poor old drummer could barely walk unaided, and the saxophone player didn't look as though he had the strength to lift his own instrument. When Dave had proudly introduced them as the Soar Valley Stompers, she could barely conceal her amusement. However, she liked what she had seen of Dave so far. His enthusiasm for the band was endearing, and he had told her when they did get gigs, most of what they earned went to charity.

They certainly weren't in it for the money.

They were playing in a small room at the back which normally remained empty during the week.

Dave wondered if inviting his neighbours along would turn out to be a good idea. He had to admit their individual responses had been lukewarm to say the least. When he popped round to Julia's, he could hear laughter and music, and rather than knock he dropped a note through her door. Gary and James from number six said that they might pop in but couldn't promise. Then he had seen Valerie at number ten, she was just on her way to take her daughter to her music lesson.

Valerie was a lovely woman, larger than life. He had to confess her enthusiasm and the sheer physicality of her unnerved him at times.

She's just so loud and, well, tactile, he shuddered.
Roger, her husband, was much quieter and calm in comparison. He worked away and came back a couple of weekends a month. They seemed very happy, and Roger clearly adored his wife and daughter.

Valerie was one of life's huggers, which made Dave very uncomfortable.

Apart from his wife when they were together, and his daughter when she was small, Dave had avoided physical contact with others as much as possible. On this occasion, he

47

avoided being crushed to Valerie's ample bosom by waiting until she was safely in the car before going over to her and saying anything.

'Ooh, music, yes! Can I bring Florence along for an hour? She plays and would love to see a live band, wouldn't you, Florence?'

'Yeah, course, it'll be great to have a musician in the audience," he smiled across at Florence. 'I hear you playing your violin in the mornings when I'm in the garden; you're good.'

Florence accepted the compliment with a smile as Valerie drove away.

He had invited Freda when she had popped over with a parcel she had taken in for him. She must have been looking out for him as he had just got back from work as she knocked on the door.

She had responded to his invitation with,

'I might come, but only if I can get a lift. Have you invited the others? I might go with one of them.' Freda continued, 'I never did learn to drive and I don't suppose my son would take me, that boy's a selfish so-and-so....'

Dave made the mistake of saying,

'It's only the Half Moon; you could walk it in fifteen minutes. Then if you don't fancy walking back in the dark, you could get a taxi.'

In return, he was treated to a litany of her aches and pains and reasons as to why she couldn't possibly walk anywhere. Eager to get on, he asked about her friend Maisie.

'Good thinking, I'll ask her, she won't mind driving. I love music, I'm a bit of a vocalist myself, you know.'

Dave was saved from having to comment as her mobile rang.

'I'll have to go, can't stand around talking all night.'

Phew, talk about saved by the bell.

He hurried back into his fusty living room to open his parcel. It hadn't occurred to Dave as he set about opening the small package that Diane would be saddened if she could see the neglected state of the living room.

She had always kept everything bright, clean and cosy. Unfortunately, from the moment she moved out, Dave had gone into old man mode. He kept his electric keyboard out all of the time, the sheet music was piled up all over the floor, the beautiful oak dining table was covered in a thick rubber pad to protect the top and his laptop was a permanent fixture on the table.

He kept a small space clear for eating and he even left the condiments on the table giving the place the appearance of a transport café. The thing was he just didn't seem to notice the seediness of the room so didn't see the need to clean it regularly.

Later as Dave was eating his meal, he mused over the contents of the parcels. He kept glancing over to the sofa as he thought about what he would be doing for the rest of the evening.

Chapter 11

As it turned out, Dave's idea to invite people along to the rehearsal was a good one. His dad's friends had arrived and were already sitting with their drinks. By the time the band had started to tune up, he had spotted Julia looking very smart, standing at the bar with two women, one of whom looked familiar. Ali, he thought her name might be. He was sure she worked with Diane at the Town Hall.

Then there was a bit of a kerfuffle as he heard Freda's strident voice telling her friend to get the drinks, 'I'll pay but you'll have to get them, my back's been terrible all day.' Obediently, Maisie went to the bar, and Freda settled herself into the seats right in front of the band. There was almost a party atmosphere as they all settled down to enjoy the music.

As Julia and her friends sipped their drinks, she smiled across at Freda. Julia needn't have worried that Freda would want to muscle in on their company she had spotted James just heading for the bar. To her friend's amusement, the woman who couldn't possibly carry a drink five minutes ago was out of her seat, and with the speed of a gazelle had taken her place beside James. Maisie saw her buy some crisps before gesturing to James to come and join them.

Ali was looking closely at the band and said, 'I've just realised where I know your neighbour Dave from.' She went on to explain that she worked with Diane, Dave's former wife.

'I don't think she was there when I moved in, it probably explains why the house looks so neglected.' Julia made them laugh when she told them that she had to shame him into cutting back the ivy.

'Funny really, I always thought they were an unlikely pair,' mused Ali and went on to explain that Diane was always so smart, but on the odd occasion she saw them together, Dave would always come along looking like the odd job man.

Rather than accept Freda's invitation to join her and her friend over by the band, James opted to stay at the bar sipping a beer and chatting to a couple of Dave's work colleagues. Freda made her way back to Maisie.

'Gary couldn't make it, working late.'

'You're shameless.'

Covering her mouth with her hand, Maisie sniggered.

'Just being neighbourly, I didn't want him to feel out of it,' responded Freda, winking at her friend.

As they launched into their first set, Dave was feeling pleased with himself. Not only had he got the venue for free, but the guys were doing a great job. While the place wasn't exactly rocking, the audience were certainly tapping their toes and they were showing their appreciation by clapping and singing along. Glancing over at his dad's neighbours, he thought,

Blimey, we've even got them up dancing!

Jim and June were jiving to Duke Ellington's classic, 'It Don't Mean a Thing If It Ain't Got That Swing.' To the admiration of the audience, Jim was in the zone. He might be in his eighties, but he could still move, and he was finding the pedestrian pace of what should have been a jive tune a bit disappointing.

'Crank it up, guys,' he yelled as the drummer tapped away gently.

Just as the first set was coming to an end, the door burst open and Valerie arrived. Dressed in linen trousers with a colourful pashmina flung around her shoulders, she made quite the entrance. She caught sight of Julia and waved, indicating that she would join them in a minute. Julia introduced Florence to her friends and invited her to sit with them, while Valerie got them a drink.

They all exchanged amused glances as they saw Valerie launching herself enthusiastically at Dave, enveloping his reluctant body in a big hug. As Valerie joined them, she apologised for being late. 'We forgot which pub, didn't we, Florence?'

Catching Julia's eye and smiling, she said, 'Well, *you* did, Mum. We've been down the road in The Seven Stars for the last half an hour,' and raised her eyebrows good-naturedly, indicating that it was par for the course. Everyone laughed, especially when Valerie pointed out that it was the astronomy link. Moon, stars, she had just got confused, that was all.

Dave, delighted by the support being shown by his neighbours, made a big effort to greet each of them individually. He smiled across at Julia and her friends.

'You seem to be enjoying the music, thanks for coming.'
He went on to explain about the band, how his dad had started it and they did get paid but most of the money went to charity.

Julia looked around the room.

'It's a good turnout from Capulet Close, couldn't your friend come?'

Dave looked puzzled.

'Friend, some friends from work have arrived.'
He pointed to the two men at the bar chatting to James.

Julia laughed. 'No, I mean the lady who was at your house last night. I popped the note round to say that I was coming tonight, and I saw her in the living room.'

Dave smiled, mumbled something and moved around the table. He hadn't spotted the note and he hadn't picked the post up either. As was his habit, he just stepped over it until the pile of paper prevented him from opening the door.

Damn, I must remember to draw those curtains.

Ali looked at Julia as her eyes followed Dave. 'Now that's a bit odd, I wonder why he didn't say who she was?' Angie pointed out that it could be a new relationship or simply a one night stand.

'Mind you, he's not exactly a new man, is he? I bet he doesn't moisturise.'

They all smothered a giggle, and Ali pointed out that Dave might not want to reveal too much of his personal life as he may have remembered that she worked with Diane.

'Not that she'd mind, she's been with her new chap for a couple of years now. They're always off somewhere, theatre, meals out and holidays. They have a lovely time.'

***

Freda was feeling bored, it wasn't really her kind of music.

'Swing without the swing', she had muttered to Maisie.

Maisie had laughed. 'Well they're a bit ancient, bless 'em. I suppose it's impressive that they still get out there and play. It's nice that Dave supports his dad too.' She looked up as he walked towards them.

'Great band, Dave, thanks for inviting us.'

Ever supportive and keen to improve Freda's mood, she said, 'Freda can sing, you know, maybe she could get up and let you hear her vocals.'

Dave shook his head. 'Sorry, the guys are a bit set in their ways; they have to rehearse everything, got to go. Second set;' and he was off.

Freda scowled at her friend. 'Why did you say that? I wouldn't want to sing with that load of geriatrics anyway.'

Maisie shrugged, she suspected that Freda was feeling miffed that James hadn't joined them when he left the bar. Instead, he had joined Valerie and Florence, and judging by the animated looks and the gales of laughter coming from that end of the table during the interval, he was keeping them well entertained.

To Maisie's amusement, Freda was looking daggers at them, but as everyone quietened down and the music started to play, Freda's ears pricked up as she heard Dave giving the backstory to the next song.

'This next number was written for the show Porgy and Bess in 1934 (when my dad was still young.)' The audience and the band members laughed obligingly as Dave introduced Gershwin's 'Summertime'.

The band's more sedate style suited the song, and Jim certainly didn't need to ask them to 'crank it up'. Freda couldn't resist singing along quietly at first until soon she was singing her heart out from her table.

Everyone turned to look at her admiringly, and as she came to the end of the song, to her delight everyone was clapping and cheering.

'Wow,' said Valerie. 'You've got yourself a voice there girl.'

Julia leaned across and complimented her, and Ali and Angie gave her the thumbs up. James, bless him, made her night and kissed her on the cheek, saying, 'Gary missed a good night.' Freda loved the attention especially when at the end of the set Dave thanked everyone for coming but gave Freda a special thank you.

'You still won't let me get up and sing though will you,' she muttered under her breath.'

Valerie heard her and said encouragingly, 'There are other bands, Freda, open mics even. You shouldn't keep that voice hidden, you know.'

Later, as everyone was heading off, Florence stood at the side of the stage talking to Dave. To his surprise, at the age of fifteen, not only was she a brilliant cello player but she was a grade six violinist and could play the piano too.

As they chatted, he espied Valerie marching over like a woman on a mission. Dave looked up warily; he couldn't face another hug from Valerie. He had endured one rib crushing embrace today, he couldn't face another. With remarkable dexterity he hurriedly said goodbye to Florence and dropped to the floor calling, 'Thank you for coming, Valerie, I can't get up. I must get these leads packed away.'

Valerie smiled to herself. She was a bad woman and thoroughly enjoyed taking Dave out of his comfort zone. Roger was her greatest fan and he would love the story of Dave cowering on the floor to avoid her embrace.

She looked forward to telling him about the evening later on when they had their nightly FaceTime chat. As Valerie left the room, she asked Dave to let her know next time the band would be playing locally, and she would bring Roger along. 'Will do,' agreed Dave. He liked Roger and he always felt easier in Valerie's company when he was around.

Chapter 12

Sitting in Maisie's car outside Freda's house, they were discussing the evening. Freda was on cloud nine, she had been congratulated on her singing. And she had loved the attention and the applause. Her only disappointment was that Gary hadn't been there to hear her.

'I meant to tell you that Dave and I had quite a chat when I took his parcel round.'

Maisie nudged her. 'Ooh, you said he was giving you the eye! Now he's heard your voice, he might make a move.'

'I've told you I'm not interested, he's nice enough but dull and dirty, the state of his teeth and as for his clothes.'

Maisie did agree with her there.

'Maybe he just needs taking in hand.' She giggled and nudged her friend, who in spite of herself had to chuckle.

'I did notice he'd made more of an effort tonight, he was clean shaven for a change. It takes years off him, he's a puzzle though; I'm always taking parcels in for him three last week, two this week, and it's only Tuesday.'

Freda went on to say that she had thought he was buying clothes. 'It can't be that though; He always looks the same.'

They looked at each other and chorused.

'That bloody hat!' followed by a paroxysm of laughter.

As they said their goodbyes, Freda said seriously, 'I'm going to do something about my singing, you know. Dave's lot might not want to give me a chance, but you heard what Valerie said. She's a nice woman, she is, and she told me not to waste my talent.'

***

In the living room of number six, James was pouring Gary a glass of wine and filling him in on the evening. 'Freda was asking about you,' he said slyly.

'Oh please,' said Gary. 'She's so suggestive every time she talks to me. Even when we were cleaning the cars, she said; 'nice day for it.'

James burst out laughing. 'Well, it was! I'm sure she didn't mean anything by it, she lives next door. We can't keep ignoring her.'

Gary gave him a look as if to say, 'I can.' James changed the subject, saying that he had particularly enjoyed Valerie's company, and suggested that they have a curry night next time Roger was home, and invite a few of the neighbours over.

Gary smiled, he loved James' exuberance. He could and did talk to everyone and anyone, he was so outgoing.

They say opposites attract and it's true, he thought, leaning across to give James a hug.

'Great idea, James, lets party. I'll do my famous vegetable curry, and you can be in charge of cocktails on arrival, and posh coffee to finish the evening,'

***

Back home at number four, Dave unloaded the gear and stowed it safely in the garage. The keyboard, his pride and joy, came straight back into the living room and was soon sitting on the carpet in the customary dust-free space.

Thinking about his brief conversation with Julia, he went out to the porch and picked up the post. He went through takeaway leaflets, charity bags, junk mail. And in amongst the Avon Catalogue and his last two bank statements, he found Julia's note.

Maybe I should be a bit more on the ball with correspondence, he thought ruefully. He stacked the post on the side, poured himself a beer and promptly forgot all about it as he settled down to reflect on his successful evening.

***

Sharon, the landlady, had really enjoyed the music. True, they were a bit sedate, but you would hardly want a rock band blaring out in a village pub on a Tuesday night. The people Dave had invited were all good spenders too, probably because they were locals and lived within walking distance the pub had actually taken some money for a change.

She would speak to the owners but she was thinking of booking the Soar Valley Stompers for an event she was putting on to raise money for a children's charity that she was involved in.

***

The next day at work, Dave felt pleased with the response from his colleagues. Pete and Jed asked if it would be a regular Tuesday night thing. He was certainly hoping so. He explained that he was waiting to hear back from Sharon but he would certainly keep them posted. They told him they were impressed that he was in a band, but both winked and said he was a dark horse. Nice but dim Dave missed the innuendo so Jed had to spell it out for him.

'Man, you managed to fill the place with some gorgeous women, where did you find them? The lady sitting at the front, she could sing, couldn't she?'

Dave accepted their admiration willingly enough, but he had to grin to himself. He was unintentionally getting himself a reputation as a bloke who attracted women. In truth, he wasn't interested, it was just too difficult. Women were an enigma to Dave. He hadn't really ever understood Diane. He had loved her, but couldn't give her the affirmation or the attention that she deserved. In the end, he reflected they had been living separate lives.

Chapter 13

Dave was eating his evening meal when he saw Freda walking her little Dachshund past the gate. As his eyes followed her, he felt a twinge of regret that he hadn't given her a bit more encouragement with her singing. He was telling the truth though when he had told her that the guys couldn't have played for her. They really did have to rehearse everything. A shame really, she did have a good voice.

Once he had eaten, he mechanically cleared his small space at the table, and put his plate and cutlery in the sink. He ran some hot water on the day's dishes, added a squirt of washing up liquid and returned to his favourite armchair in his grubby living room. In truth, it was the only seat that wasn't covered with papers, sheet music or clothes.

It was a good job he rarely had guests, he would have had to clear a space, he mused. Or worse still, tidy up. Dave grimaced at the thought. How on earth would he ever find anything if he had to put his things away? His place may look untidy, but he could put his hand on anything he needed in a second. It was his own fool proof filing cabinet, he thought smugly.

Later that evening Dave was in the spare room going through the contents of the parcels that Freda had been taking in for him. Five parcels in just over a week. Dave wasn't usually a big spender; his van was seven years old. And since he had been on his own, he paid the bills on the house and did a few rudimentary repairs. He certainly hadn't spent any money on furnishings, and he had no intention of doing so either.

He did, however, like to treat himself to the latest music gear. His big purchase this year had been his new Yamaha top of the range keyboard; he had wanted it as soon as he had seen it and knew as soon as he touched the keys that it was worth every penny. The sound was beautiful and he felt up there with the performing greats as he played.

Back in the spare room, Dave looked critically at himself in the mirror. He felt a bit nervous, he could almost imagine what those people felt like in the makeover shows that Diane had loved so much. He couldn't understand it at the time and used to scoff at their delighted reaction when they saw their reflection for the first time. Surely they weren't so stupid that they couldn't buy themselves some new clothes, he just hadn't got it at the time, much to Diane's annoyance.

First things first, let's find some undies.

As he began putting his legs into the brand new pants, he felt a sensation of pure pleasure at the feel of the material against his skin. His purchases were usually five pairs of boxer shorts from Asda for a tenner, and he washed and wore them until the seams began to give way. And then he would replace them. This underwear was something else, fine seams and beautiful material; silk and cotton, no less.

When he was fully dressed, he stood in front of the only full length mirror in the house and marvelled at his reflection. He looked so different. He remembered his old Mum's saying.

'Clothes, maketh the man, David.'
Diane and his mum got on well and she always used to qualify the saying with,

'Or woman Mum, or woman.'

It never failed to amuse the two of them. Sadly, his mum had passed away five years ago now, and he still missed her.

'You wouldn't recognise me in this get up, would you, Mum?' he said aloud as he looked at himself in the mirror. *Very different to my usual style*, he thought as he turned to look at the back of his reflection.

The black leather shoes would need breaking in, they felt a bit tight. However, he realised that was probably because he usually wore soft comfortable trainers, he would get used to them. He could see that the colour suited him too; shades of blue with touches of white. He so rarely wore anything but black that he had forgotten that blue was his colour.

Dave felt a frisson of shame when he recalled how he had resisted Diane's attempts to smarten him up. One year for his birthday, she had bought him a beautiful blue sweater made of soft knitted cotton. When he opened his other gifts, he realised she had conspired with the rest of the family so that his collective gifts made up a whole coordinated outfit.

His parents had bought him two good quality shirts. His brother and sister-in-law had bought jeans. And his daughter's gift (bought by Diane, of course) had been some smart leather trainers. He had thanked each and every one of them for the gifts, he genuinely liked and appreciated them, but he had worn the items separately.

He took a sly pleasure from seeing Diane's irritation every time he wore one of the items teamed with something unsuitable. He regretted it now, of course, it was petty. And he could see why some of his actions during their marriage had contributed to his wife's decision to leave.

Looking at the clock, Dave realised that it was gone midnight, and he had been faffing around for over an hour. He had to be up for work in the morning. He carefully undressed hanging each item in his wardrobe and putting the new underwear in the wash basket.

Chapter 14

The next time Dave and his dad got together, it was Sunday. They were in his dad's local, The Bell, having a lunchtime pint. They always tried to get together at some time after a band practice so they could have what they liked to call their *post-mortem*, where they would discuss any new songs they wanted to learn and what they could improve on. Dave had some good news for his dad.

'Sharon was pleased we brought all of those people in, Dad.' He went on to explain that she had asked if they would like the back room every first Tuesday of the month. 'If we do what we did last week and go through our set, bring people in, she won't charge us. If we want to rehearse new material and we just want use of the room, she charges £25, which is only a fiver each. And we can probably fund it out of subs anyway. Oh, and another thing, she's planning a fundraiser in the summer! She's keen to involve us in that too. She says she'll be back with a date once she's spoken to the owner of the pub.'

His dad was tickled pink. 'Well done you, that was a great result all round. Jim and June are still talking about it;

hopefully next month we can rally the troops again, your neighbours seem a friendly bunch, especially the tall black lady.' He looked at Dave with a cheeky grin. 'She likes you.'

Dave pulled a face. 'Yes, she likes everyone, that's Valerie; larger than life and a bit scary to be honest.' He shivered. 'I develop a bit of a twitch when she's around; you never know when she's going to hug you.'

'Mmm, I can tell.' His dad chuckled as he sipped his pint.

***

During the evening, Freda was walking her little dog. She didn't take him far, just around the close and along the road to her friend Maisie's house. If she was lucky, Maisie would invite her in. She had a favour to ask.

'Bugger,' her timing was all wrong. Maisie was just getting into her car. She waved, calling, 'Hold fire, before you go, I want to ask you something. Don't feel you've got to say yes.'

Maisie looked wary she was used to Freda's requests.

'Will you come to the open mic with me on Friday? It's in town, I might not even get to sing and I'll have to ask someone to play for me. But at least I'll get to see how these nights work.'

Maisie agreed reluctantly. 'I'll take you, but remember I work Saturdays, so I don't want to be out too late.'

Freda had stopped listening; she had got the answer she wanted. She could persuade Maisie to stay later once they were there, and hopefully she would get to sing in front of an audience again. Valerie was right, she shouldn't hide her voice. She didn't want to be a bedroom singer she wanted to recapture the feeling of excitement that singing in front of an audience gave her. There was nothing like it.

As she walked Freddie back home, she glanced over at Dave's house. As usual, the curtains hadn't been pulled properly and everything looked dark, grubby and dismal. She was tempted to knock and tell him about the open mic, thinking that he could return the compliment and come and listen to her singing. That would show him.

Distracted momentarily, she caught a glimpse of long dark hair and a shapely silhouette of a woman drawing the curtains.

Wait until I tell Maisie, our Dave has hidden depths, she thought, grinning to herself.

***

Dave had seen Freda walking by, he hoped she wasn't going to call in today of all days. He really didn't want his neighbours knowing about his personal life. He held his breath but she only paused at the gate before heading to her front door. Phew, although it was still light he took advantage of the empty street and pulled his living room curtains closed so that no chink of light could be seen from the outside.

Eagerly, he returned to the spare room pausing briefly, impressed by what he saw. A pleasant, middle-aged woman with mid-length chestnut hair looked back at him shyly. She wore a smart striped blue linen dress that came to just below the knee and sheer tights. Her shoes were black patent with chunky heels. On the back of the chair hung a fluffy, sparkly blue cardigan which she flung around her shoulders….

Dave thought she looked lovely. *The only thing that might improve her appearance was some makeup. Well, that would have to wait until another day.*

He smiled, looked in the mirror and said,

'Hello Kandy pleased to meet you.'

Chapter 15

Gary woke slowly, gradually becoming aware of the light filtering in through the curtains and hearing the sounds of the house coming to life.

Reluctantly he got out of bed and made his way into the bathroom. He had always been the same, his mum used to despair trying to shift him in time for school. He grinned as he compared himself to James who, judging by the delicious aroma of coffee wafting up the stairs and the insistent beat of Bruno Mars' 'Uptown Funk' through the floorboards, was already well into his morning routine.

James was a great fan of productivity books, written by successful people who make the most of their time. His latest find was a publication called *Productivity in Life*. The author suggests that the most successful people have good time management skills. So scatty disorganised James; to Gary's amusement had adopted an efficient routine.

Rather than becoming overwhelmed with tasks as Gary was apt to be, James eschewed multi-tasking, saying that he preferred to do one thing at a time, enjoy completing each task and do it well. Gary agreed with him in principle, but with work expectations, he felt it was an unrealistic goal for himself.

It made things a lot calmer in the mornings, although James had always been an early riser he was in the habit of sitting around thinking he had loads of time, and then they would be dashing around trying to use the bathroom, make lunch, and inevitably they would both leave the house stressed and irritable.

It seems we're both reaping the benefits of James' new regime, thought Gary thankfully as he got ready.

Fifteen minutes later, Gary; shaved, showered and dressed in freshly ironed shirt and smart trousers joined James at the kitchen table. James greeted him with a lazy smile and pushed a steaming cup of coffee towards him.

'Looking good, Gazza, what's the special occasion?' They both burst out laughing.

'Cheeky,' Gary grinned. Gazza was such an unlikely nickname for the formal preppie looking Gary, but James had a great sense of fun, and he loved to hear Gary laugh. He could be so serious at times. As Gary sipped his coffee and nibbled some toast, he said;

'Remember I'm in court today. So I've got to look the part.'

Pouring him another cup of coffee, James said,

'Ah, I remember the exploitation case. That's caused you some sleepless nights, hasn't it?'

He squeezed Gary's shoulder sympathetically.

Gary thought of his star witness Jakub, a young man caught stealing food. Something had made Gary investigate further; why did anyone need to steal food if they were working? He uncovered a whole group of young men who were being exploited. Gary hoped that the meticulous gathering of evidence by his team would end in convictions for the unscrupulous gang who had preyed on these vulnerable young men.

Gary finished his coffee, put his cup and plate in the dishwasher, gathered up his briefcase and laptop and briefly glanced back at James. He had his back to Gary as he wiped the kitchen table and loaded the dishwasher.

'Bye, see you later, I shouldn't be late tonight. The judiciary are notoriously precious when it comes to their weekends. I reckon we'll be done by four at the latest.'

James grabbed something from the fridge. Smiling, he said, 'Your lunch, lots of protein, and three of your five a day in there.'

They hugged briefly before Gary smiled his thanks and headed out of the door.

James watched Gary drive off. He was looking forward to the weekend. Gary wasn't working, and they had invited some friends and neighbours round for a curry the following evening. But tonight, he was hoping to persuade Gary to come for a night out with him. A couple of his students were performing at a pub in town, and he was keen to hear their set.

Thinking about his students prompted him to make a move. Fridays were always busy as he liked to clear his desk for the weekend. And since he had been following his *Productivity in Life* guru, he made sure that he touched base with all of his students at least once a week. He made it clear to colleagues and students alike that he wouldn't email anyone over the weekend, and in return he didn't expect anyone to e mail him either.

'I'll be in work from 8.30am every day, so will respond to emails then,' he had explained. He smiled when he thought of the bitching that had gone on, but six months down the line, they were getting used to it and some of them were even adopting the idea for themselves. He had used his assertiveness training, explaining,

'I prefer not to work at home. I'm contracted to work thirty-seven and a half hours a week and I do that and more here at the university. So if you can't make the time to speak to me when I'm in work, or you need E- Mails answering promptly, then you must send them during working hours. If not, it'll have to wait until I'm back at my desk again.'

He was feeling quite anxious working up to making this announcement as he had been conditioned to be accommodating, and still felt slightly in awe of his colleagues. If he was honest, he was suffering a little from imposter syndrome. He still couldn't believe that he, James; perpetual student and backpacker, was actually working at the University.

He remembered with amusement the first time his resolve was tested. A student ran after him as he was going home.

'I need to talk to you about this essay, I can't seem to....'

'I'm leaving for the day now, but I can see you tomorrow morning at 8.30am, Dexter.'

He smiled as he recalled Dexter turning to him in disbelief and saying plaintively

'But I need to get this in by Thursday; it's 4000 words.'

'Yes, I do know that.' (He had set the essay, for goodness sake.) James kept walking, repeating that he could give Dexter half an hour the next morning.

He remembered he was tempted to give in but then he thought of what would happen. If he did it for one student, his time would never be his own. He also remembered that Dexter, bright as he was, always handed in his essays at the last minute and often missed tutorials.

As James headed for his car, he spotted Julia just locking her front door. She was attempting to carry a laptop, some fabric and paint samples as well as her handbag.

'Need a hand?' He smiled, and without waiting for a response, helped her carry everything to the car.

'Thanks James,' she smiled gratefully at him.

'An unusual set of tools this morning, Julia.' He was used to seeing her in her Clean & Easy uniform, complete with a trolley of cleaning materials.

Julia told him excitedly about her fledgling business and how she was seeing a client this morning. 'Wish me luck.'

'All the luck in the world; I always knew you were talented, Julia, just look at what you've done to your own house. You can tell us all about it tomorrow at the curry night.'

Julia smiled her agreement and drove off.

Chapter 16

Inside the court building, Gary looked yet again at his watch. He felt fidgety and slightly on edge. Being in court was the least favourite part of his job, but he and his team had spent many hours piecing together evidence and building a case against these two brothers.

Outwardly respectable, they had a landscape gardening business. It appeared to be a totally legitimate concern with twenty-two employees on the books, all paying tax and insurance. They were shocked at the allegations against their employers, and wouldn't hear a word against them. At first, Gary didn't think they would get anywhere. But he went with his gut feeling, and kept digging.

His persistence paid off, and once he had organised an interpreter to speak with Jakub, he found a seedy violent side to the business. Workers housed inadequately, passports being withheld. Jakub's accommodation, heated by an oil stove with no proper washing or cooking facilities, was shared by three other men. He and his fellow workers had never met either of the brothers. They kept their hands clean. They employed thugs to do their dirty work.

A breakthrough came when they got careless. A vehicle registered to them had regularly taken men to work at a local chicken factory. The factory employed the men through an employment agency. The factory paid the men the going rate through the agency, the men didn't speak to the other workers, but then they didn't speak much English. They did their shift, and that was all the foreman cared about. Gary had ground his teeth in frustration. Never anyone else's business, no wonder these bastards were so difficult to catch.

The agency was definitely a front for something, and no prizes for guessing who had a financial interest in it, The Merchant brothers, of course. The men had so many stoppages out of their wages. They paid for transport to and from work. Fines for lateness and the biggest insult of all was the money they were charged for their accommodation. Jakub said that he was in so much debt to them that he only ended up with £30.00 per week, which was why he had to steal food. Fortunately, Jakub's evidence allowed them to search several premises where they found twenty-three other vulnerable adults, all male, and in a similar state to Jakub.

Gary heard his name being called: 'Detective Sergeant Gary Hoskins.' He got up, gathered his notes and went to give his evidence. At the end of the afternoon, as he was heading back to his car, Gary reflected on the events of the day. He had given his evidence, and there was nothing more he could do. The judge would do his summing up on Monday. They would have to wait for the jury verdict. Gary didn't have to be in court for that, but someone would let him know the outcome. He had high hopes that they would get a conviction. But for now, he would follow James' advice and enjoy his weekend off. No e-mails, no phone calls.

He drove home in good time. Turning into Capulet Close, he parked on the drive, noting with satisfaction that it was before 5.30pm. Early for him; James would be pleased.

He turned off the engine, relishing the silence for a few minutes before letting himself into the homely bustle of number six. He loved living with James; they were friends as well as lovers. He was such good company, and they laughed a lot too.

James was always so positive, he always looked on the bright side and he could see humour in the darkest situation. He was definitely the outgoing one of the two of them. He couldn't bear silence, Gary could guarantee that if James was alone in the house, he would have music playing or the TV would be on in the background.

Gathering his things together, he began to get out of the car. He was looking forward to tomorrow's curry night, he enjoyed cooking and he made a really good curry.

That reminds me!

Reaching into the back seat, he carefully picked up the delicious smelling parcel. He had called into Gupta's and had bought a dozen freshly baked samosas for tomorrow evening. As he breathed in the delicious aroma of spice and cumin, he thought with satisfaction, *perfect, they're still warm.* James would be delighted when he was presented with a still warm samosa. He always bought a couple extra to eat as a snack.

Chapter 17

Later that evening, the two of them were getting ready for a night out in town. James had mentioned the pub, and Gary had readily agreed, especially when he found out that there would be music. They often went to open mic nights, and always enjoyed the performers and the eclectic mix of music, both covers and originals.

James was dressed in what Gary jokingly referred to as his beach bum outfit. He hated wearing trousers, and as soon as he returned home from work, he changed into shorts and T-shirt. This evening, he was wearing knee-length faded denim shorts and a soft white top. In deference to the chilly evening, he was also wearing a dark blue hoodie.

James wore his dark hair longer at the back and his fringe flopped over his face, he was always pushing it away. Gary was casually dressed too, although James had to smile to himself. Gary looked smarter in his faded Levi's and blue shirt than some of his university colleagues did in their shabby suits and shiny ties. James considered them a tad pretentious, cultivating the absent-minded professor persona.

Neither of them were big drinkers, but the music venue had some good craft beers. As they were both partial to a pint or two, they decided to walk in and bus back. It was a great start to the weekend, and a nice way to blow away the cobwebs.

On the way, Gary filled James in on the court case and his high hopes for a conviction. They discussed what would happen to Jakub and his fellow workers. They were all young and naïve; some had slight learning difficulties, and all were vulnerable. Luckily, since they had been rescued from the clutches of The Merchant Brothers, they had all been safely housed. And all but two were working. Those two were going back to Poland after the trial. The families just wanted them home.

Remembering his determination to enjoy his weekend, he linked arms with James and said, 'Now tell me a bit about this music, am I going to be impressed?'

As they approached the High Street, James told Gary a little about the lads who would be playing. 'They're both great guitarists, and one of them in particular has a lovely singing voice.' He went on to explain that Lary, an overseas student, was a huge Beatles fan. His musical partner, Luke, wrote his own songs. And Lary was a good lyricist, although he was happier performing covers.

'You can make up your own mind soon,' laughed James as he pushed open the door of The Kings Arms and ushered Gary inside. It was a cosy, old-fashioned pub with low ceilings and an aroma of hops in the air.

The music hadn't started yet, but the performers were all beginning to arrive. Lary and his friends were tuning up their guitars, and as they spotted James, they gave him an enthusiastic wave. James introduced them both to Gary. They noticed that according to the list on the wall, Lary and Luke were second to perform, so they went to the bar to order their drinks before settling down at a small table near the stage.

More people began to arrive, and the room began to fill up. Gary noticed an older lady over by the stage showing one of the organisers a piece of paper. He nudged James;

'Don't look now, you'll never believe who just showed up, it's only Freda.'

James grinned, 'Well, there's no law against her coming out on a Friday night to listen to music. There's no age limit, you know.'

Gary laughed, 'I know, I know, it's just that she can be a bit inappropriate at times. Remind me to tell you about the first time I met her some time.' James nodded in agreement.

The music was starting, so they turned their attention to the stage. The first singer up was a young girl who played guitar and sang folk songs. She had a sweet, melodic voice, and the audience clapped appreciatively. After three songs, she thanked the audience and left the stage.

Next up were Lary and Luke, they were an appealing pair, enthusiastic and keen to share the story of their musical partnership. They had been performing together since Fresher's Week nearly two years ago. Gary and James both loved the Beatles, and were impressed with the harmonies the boys were doing. Their guitar playing was very good too.

Luke shyly introduced the last song explaining that he had written the music and Lary the lyrics. It was a ballad style song all about lost love. It reminded Gary of Ed Sheeran, not his favourite style, but he could appreciate their talent. James was generous in his applause, and invited them over so that he could buy them a drink.

They sat together enjoying the next performer. He was a poet. He recited a couple of monologues that he had written himself. He was very funny. Lary explained that this chap was versatile, 'We saw him in Leicester recently doing a spot at a Comedy Club. He was brilliant, wasn't he, Luke?'

Luke nodded enthusiastically, 'Yeah, I think it's because his material is so topical, very clever.'

About 10pm, the compere for the evening announced a short break, saying that there were three more performers. Lary and Luke had drifted off. Being regulars, they were well known, and lots of people wanted to chat to them and show their appreciation for their music.

Gary watched them circling the room, greeting friends and strangers with an easy confidence that Gary knew he had never possessed. 'I suppose that's what travel and a university education does for you,' he commented enviously. 'You're like them; it just comes naturally to you. Look at them, I bet they're twenty-two at the most, and they can talk to anyone.'

He went on to explain that at their age he had only just joined the force.

'Basically, I was only really confident in the job with my work colleagues. Blimey,' his voice rose by an octave. 'They're even talking to Freda.'

James burst out laughing. 'So, you've been known to speak to Freda too. You're too hard on yourself, mate, everyone takes to you! You're one of the good guys.'

'Don't you think you might be a little biased?' Gary smiled. James was certainly good for his confidence.

When he looked up again, he saw Lary hurrying over to James. He bent down, said something and gestured over to Freda, who was at the bar with her friend. Gary's heart sank.

What had she just said?

He remembered with embarrassment their first meeting, and he just hoped she hadn't upset Lary. As he looked across, Freda caught his eye, her face lit up as she waved at him as though they were best friends. He acknowledged her greeting with a brief smile. He couldn't help noticing her friend sitting next to her patiently sipping a soft drink.

James gestured to Gary to include him in the conversation. Freda, it seemed, had big ambitions and a big voice. She wanted to sing two songs but didn't have anybody to accompany her, and she had asked Lary. Having heard him play, she thought he might be able to help. He hadn't been keen, but never backward in coming forward, she had told him that she was a friend of James and Gary. James had already told Gary about Freda singing along and surprising everyone at Dave's rehearsal, but he wasn't expecting that she would attempt to get someone to accompany her.

'She's got a nerve,' he muttered. But on the other hand, she hadn't been inappropriate towards these nice young lads....Yet.

James went with Lary to speak to Freda. Gary really didn't want anything to do with it, and he would hate for Lary to feel obliged just because she had exploited her connection to them. Anyway, it looked as though he was going to help.

James came back explaining that Lary was going to play 'Summertime' for her. The performer who was up next had promised to do a bit of percussion. Lary had discovered from the couple of bars Freda sung to him what key he needed to play in, but he also realised she had no idea when to come in. So he was hoping the percussion might help to keep time, and they could lead her in.

Everyone settled down to watch the next act, a trio playing heavy rock. James was in his element, lost in the music. Gary sat back sipping his drink, feeling a bit more relaxed, he really shouldn't allow himself to be intimidated by Freda. She was his mother's age, for goodness sake. He smiled as he thought of his mum. She would love it here. Mum and Dad enjoyed a good night out at the pub. When they next came for a visit, he would bring them along. James gave him a nudge.

'Hey, you're miles away, Freda's about to strut her stuff.'

They had often heard Freda singing along to the radio through the wall, and had never thought anything of it, but she could definitely sing. Lary was a sympathetic player. He understood that she was an inexperienced performer, and he led her expertly into the song, and even prompted her with the lyrics when she faltered. Altogether, it was a good effort, and the audience were generous with their applause.

To her delight, James and Gary had come over to congratulate her. Well, *James* had been the one with the pleasantries. He had even kissed her on both cheeks, continental style. Gary had just smiled and said that he had enjoyed the song. Lary persuaded Freda that one song was enough.

'Keep 'em wanting more;' he said giving her a cheeky wink.

She thanked Lary and gave him a grateful hug. As he walked off the stage and back over to Luke, he looked preoccupied. Glancing back at Freda innocently chatting to her friend, he thought.

Did she pinch my behind just then?

The organiser told Freda that in future, she should bring her own accompanist along, because most of the regulars had their own set to perform and normally wouldn't play for anybody else. He suggested that she come along on a Sunday teatime when they had a jam session. He explained that it was bit more informal, usually a couple of guitarists and a drummer. In fact, anyone that played an instrument could get up, and they would invite singers up too.

Freda was certainly up for that. She was fizzing with excitement, and was still buzzing from the attention and the applause.

After her triumph, she returned to Maisie, who to her annoyance was making a move to return home. She reminded Freda that she had work in the morning.

What a misery, she thought peevishly. *Selfish so-and-so knows I don't get out much.*

She wasn't inclined to be dragged away in the midst of all of this admiration. Unusually for Maisie, she had been quite sharp with Freda when her requests to leave had been repeatedly ignored.

'Stay if you like, Freda, but I did say it wouldn't be a late one when you asked me.'

With that, she actually stood up and put on her coat. Freda was in a quandary, should she tell Maisie that she would make her own way home? Or maybe cadge a lift with her handsome young neighbours. She was sure there had been a spark between her and Gary when they had first met.

He has hidden depths, that boy.

She remembered sitting with him in her garden, chatting away. He was a good listener. In fact he had hardly said anything about himself, just wanted to hear all about her. Even after all this time, she didn't know where he worked. Since James had moved in, they never really saw one another, apart from exchanging a greeting in passing. Of course, it never occurred to her that Gary did his utmost to avoid her.

Bringing her attention back to Maisie, who had turned towards the door, she made her decision.

'Alright, alright, I'm coming.' She looked back regretfully at James and Gary, who were sitting and chatting with Lary and Luke.

Oh well, just as well not to upset Maisie. I will probably need to talk her into one of these Sunday jam sessions; I don't want to be going on my own.

***

Later that evening Gary and James were running for the bus, and only just caught it by the skin of their teeth. They took their seats, out of breath but still laughing and chatting. The bus was almost empty, apart from a couple of teenagers taking selfies on the back seat and an older couple sitting at the front of the bus. They chatted with the older couple until they got off two stops later.

It was only when the giggly teenagers left the bus that they began talking about their evening. Gary said how much he liked Lary and Luke.

'They're such good players and it was good of Lary to go to so much trouble for Freda, wasn't it?'

James agreed, 'She's got a cheek, hasn't she? She doesn't care who she asks to do her a favour either.' He told Gary that Freda had burst into song last week at Dave's band practice.

'Valerie told her that her voice is too good to stay hidden and she should go to an open mic.'

Gary chuckled, 'So its Valerie's fault is it? We'll have to have words when she comes for her curry tomorrow night.'

James looked at him quizzically. 'I think it's about time you fessed up and told me exactly what happened to make you dislike Freda so much. You really don't like getting too close to her, do you?'

Gary nodded his agreement and once they were indoors with the coffee made and the fire lit, Gary began his story.

He recalled that he had only been living in the house for a few weeks.

'I'd just been transferred from London and I didn't know a soul apart from the people I worked with. We hadn't met and I was missing London and my friends and family, too.

When I was off duty, I was busy getting the house sorted, but it was a bit of a lonely time if I'm honest.'

James squeezed his shoulder sympathetically. 'Go on.'

Gary went on to explain that Freda had been having a new living room carpet fitted. 'She called round all of a fluster, saying the fitters wouldn't put the furniture back. She hadn't realised; her son had helped her move the furniture that morning in readiness for the fitters. He was still at work, so he couldn't help later on. Her friend helped with the small stuff, but would I bring the sofas in?

'I went round willingly enough. She was my neighbour after all, and my parents always encouraged me to be neighbourly. I remember she was very grateful, and offered me a cold drink which we had in the garden.

She started telling me her life story. It was interesting at first. She explained how she was the only original resident of the close. Six houses were built, and the builder went bust, so a housing association bought all six houses. All the other tenants bought under the right to buy scheme, and the houses have changed hands several times since.

'Then she got a bit too personal, said she hadn't had a relationship for more than ten years. The love of her life, he was fifteen years younger than her, did the dirty on her and she had trust issues. Here, it gets embarrassing.'

Gary shuddered as he recalled her saying archly that she preferred younger men and in her opinion, 'younger men benefit from an older woman's experience.'

He remembered he couldn't wait to get away. He stood up, thanked her for the drink and went to leave through the back gate. To his horror, she had made to kiss him, saying, 'You're a really good listener, I don't talk about my past to anybody, you know, but you're really easy to talk to.'

James looked at him, aghast. 'She's deluded, isn't she?'

Gary nodded vigorously. 'I hated lying, but I said I was already in a relationship and got the hell out of there.' He squeezed James' hand, 'I was only just coming to terms with being a gay man working in a notoriously homophobic environment. I couldn't bring myself to mention my sexuality to her.

James agreed. 'Knowing her, if you had, she'd have made it her mission to convert you.'

Gary grimaced at the thought, but catching James' eye, he roared with laughter and soon, they were both at it, tears streaming down their cheeks.

Once they had calmed down and were putting their phones on charge James noticed he had a text from Larry.

Did I imagine it, or did Freda pinch my bum?

He showed it to Gary, and it set them both off again, they were still laughing as they climbed the stairs.

Chapter 18

Julia was feeling decidedly optimistic. Since she had started designing her client's nursery, she had also been asked to help the children at the local school to create a mural.

One of her cleaning clients was the head teacher at the school, and she had asked Julia if she could be 'Artist in Residence' for a week, and she would work with all of the year groups. It wasn't a huge budget, but she worked out that she would probably earn more in that week than she would at Clean & Easy.

Over a glass of wine with Valerie on Thursday evening, she explained the quandary she was in, and it was Valerie who had suggested taking a week off. Then if more work came in, perhaps she could go part time.

Julia was grateful for her supportive friends. Ali and Angie were giving her business cards to friends and colleagues. Even Jake was caught up in the enthusiasm for getting Julia back into business, and he had offered to build her a website.

Her mum was delighted to see her buzzing with excitement over her new venture.

'It's funny, Mum, I didn't realise how much I missed bringing people's vision alive. I just love transforming people's living spaces.' Julia showed her pictures of the nursery she was working on, it was a small room, but she had created a space which would grow with the child.

Her mum admired the clever use of furniture and the storage for toys and books. The mural didn't take up the whole wall, and instead of nursery rhyme characters, it was a street scene depicting story book characters.

As they ate their lunch, Julia said that Callum, her client, had given her details to his grandparents. They were in the process of downsizing, and were moving into a house that had been empty for some time.

'Like that one next to Valerie?' said her mum, 'That looks like a sad old place it must have been empty for more than a year now.'

Julia smiled, explaining that it would look a lot worse if it wasn't for Valerie. 'She goes in and mows both lawns. She painted the gate last week. That woman has so much energy. I don't know how she does it.'

Julia took the coffee cups into the kitchen while her mum got her coat and handbag. The two of them were hitting the shops. Julia wanted to buy something to wear for the curry night that evening. She was looking forward to it. James and

Gary were great hosts, and she loved being with Roger and Valerie, they were such good company.

***

At number ten Valerie presided over the breakfast table in her sunny dining room. She was a statuesque lady given to wearing bright colours and chunky jewellery. She sat resplendent, wearing a red and gold kaftan with a red scarf tied around her hair.

She sat beaming at her husband and daughter as she poured coffee and served pancakes, fruit and yoghurt. Florence's weekend breakfast treat. Ever since she was a baby, she loved fruit. In fact, they called her their little fruit bat as wherever she had lived in the world, she had been more than willing to try all kinds of fruit.

Valerie laughed out loud and said, 'Roger, I was just remembering Thailand.' He looked up, grinned across at his wife and they both smiled at Florence.

Florence put down her spoon, and head in hands, groaned, 'No, no, no, this isn't another baby story is it?'

'Of course, it's our job as parents to embarrass you. Our parents did it, and their parents before them and you in turn will do it to your children,' Roger laughed heartily. At that, Florence smiled, she knew resistance was useless. Better to hear the story now than later at the curry night with an audience of neighbours, she thought indulgently.

Her parents launched into the much told tale of how the nanny they had employed in Thailand had to be warned that baby Florence must not be fed on demand. Thai people adore children, and Florence's nanny treated her like a little princess, feeding her all of her favourite treats all day long.

Valerie had a photo of her in pride of place on the piano at the age of eight months, dressed only in a nappy beaming into the camera, looking like a little Buddha.

Roger ended the story with a proud smile encompassing his wife and daughter saying. 'Luckily there was no harm done. Once you could walk, Florence, you took after your mother; A veritable whirlwind. She was never still, was she, darling?'

'No, she still isn't, I have to remind her to eat sometimes.'

Valerie smiled at her daughter as Florence cheekily whisked the last pancake and a dozen or so blueberries from under her father's nose, saying, 'I've never lost my taste for fruit, though, have I?'

Valerie looked from one to the other of her favourite people, feeling content. This was family, eating and laughing together, sharing the minutiae of everyday life with your loved ones.

She had been looking forward to this weekend for ages. Roger rarely made it home for a long weekend but he had been given a chance that was too good to miss, a meeting in Leicestershire on Thursday evening had made it possible for him to wangle the Friday off and he assured her he would not have to return to Scotland until first thing on Monday morning. For once, she thought she wouldn't feel like a single parent. When they went round to Gary and James for their curry, the Sunningdales would be going as a family.

Valerie didn't blame Roger at all, he had always worked away and it was only when Florence started full time school that Valerie had insisted they settle somewhere so that she could have a proper routine and an English education like her father. Before that, Valerie and Florence had always travelled with Roger.

They had been in Melbourne for a couple of years before moving back to England and buying the house here in Capulet Close. Valerie had a funny story that she liked to tell people. When they arrived back in the UK, she had visited several friends and relations with little Florence in France and back in the north of England too, where she had some distant cousins. She had been talking about Roger and one of her cousins said curiously,

'Roger? Who's Roger?

'My husband,' Valerie had claimed indignantly. Of course, she had seen the funny side of the situation. They were so used to Valerie turning up solo at family gatherings that they had completely forgotten who her husband was.

Valerie turned her attention to Roger, who was just leaving the table.

'Shall we have a bike ride today, ladies? The forecast's a bit blowy, but it looks bright enough out there and it's supposed to stay dry.'

Florence and Valerie nodded enthusiastically; they both enjoyed getting out and about in the countryside. But Florence felt much more confident when her father joined them. *Mum could be so unpredictable,* thought Florence with quiet amusement.

She remembered how upset she had been once when she was much younger. Dad had been working away and Mum had taken them to a country park, their bikes strapped onto the roof bars of the car. Everything had started calmly enough. Mum had taken the bikes down from the roof and checked that Florence had fastened her helmet correctly and was wearing her high visibility jacket.

She recalled that they had set off along one of the designated cycle paths. Valerie had seen something that had piqued her curiosity, maybe a bird hide or something. Florence never found out because suddenly she had changed direction and sallied forth, a reluctant Florence in her wake.

She remembered momentarily losing sight of her mother before hearing an almighty crash, a yell and silence. Florence had been beside herself, yelling, 'Mum!' hysterically; convinced her Mum must be dead. But no! Valerie arose laughing heartily from behind the shrubbery, having fallen from her bike bang slap into a dark, deep, sticky, black muddy puddle. Florence recalled bursting into tears and being enveloped in a sticky, smelly hug.

She remembered that they abandoned the bike ride. Valerie, pushing the filthy bike, had squelched her way back to the car and persuaded a bemused Park Ranger to wipe the worst of the mess off the wheels and saddle before they strapped it back on the roof bars. There wasn't much that could be done about Valerie though. Luckily she had some tarpaulin in the boot which she covered her seat with but Florence remembered with a smile that they had to drive home with the windows open wide as Valerie smelt so bad.

Chapter 19

Later that day, the Sunningdales were sitting in the lounge of their favourite country pub. It was the perfect place to be on a blowy Saturday lunchtime.

Roger gave a contented sigh as the three of them sat in front of a roaring fire sipping hot coffee. They had just finished lunch and were relaxing, letting their food digest before heading back home. They had followed the route, mainly along the cycle path which ran alongside the canal for two miles. It was lovely to observe wildlife.

They had even seen the heron, which had been magical. He had seen it before, but the three of them had been treated to the amazing sight of him swooping down into the water and emerging with a fish in his beak. All three of them had been transfixed as they gazed across the water enjoying the reflection of the sun sparkling through the water droplets like little jewels surrounding the fish.

They began to discuss it.

'Dad, let me look at that photo again?' asked Florence. Her father found the series of photos he had managed to snap. And the three of them looked through them, heads together, deciding between them which one was the best.

Since Florence was small, her mum had been very good at keeping photographic records of days out, holidays and special occasions. Since she had been old enough to manage a camera, her mum had encouraged her to do the same.

Florence thought with pleasure of her collection of scrapbooks. She had begun a wildlife one recently, and the heron picture would be a perfect addition. She handed back her dad's phone, and he agreed to WhatsApp the pictures to her later.

'Meanwhile,' he said, 'let's record this momentous occasion, it's not often I get to spend the whole weekend with my two favourite girls.' With that, he asked a passer-by to snap a picture of all three of them cuddled up together on the sofa.

As usual, the cycle home was a breeze. It was mostly downhill until you had to turn into the Close. As they turned into their road, Roger spotted Freda waving and smiling in their direction. Not a great fan of Freda's, she was one of life's complainers in his opinion, and he avoided her wherever possible.

Roger slowed down, gave a friendly wave but refused to stop. He was eager to spend as much time of this rare weekend home in his own house with his family. Gracefully, he manoeuvred the bike into the driveway and then into the front part of the garage where the bikes were stored, leaving space beside it for Valerie and Florence to leave theirs.

Looking back at Valerie listening attentively and nodding to Freda, he felt a pang of guilt. But to be fair, Valerie was much better at handling Freda than he was, she was such a joyous woman. Roger felt truly blessed to have met and married his lovely Valerie.

Florence too had escaped with just a polite greeting and had followed her father into the house, stowed her bike and was planning what she would do for the rest of the afternoon.

As it turned out, Freda had wanted to thank Valerie. She was pleased to report that she had gone to the Open-mic as Valerie had suggested. And not only that a nice young man, a friend of James' next door, had accompanied her on the guitar. She had sung 'Summertime' again and received loads of compliments.

Valerie was pleased for her. 'Well done you, it's not easy putting yourself out there and I'm impressed you got someone to play for you.'

Valerie was a bit shocked though when Freda confided in her that she thought Gary fancied her.

'I thought there may be a bit of a spark there;'
She whispered. Valerie looked at her and just couldn't help herself. She burst into peals of laughter.

'What's so funny?' snapped Freda, 'older woman, younger man? It's not unheard of, you know.'

'Maybe not,' responded Valerie tartly. 'As it happens, Gary's got a partner, and they're very happy.'

Freda looked at Valerie, raising her eyebrows disbelievingly.

'Well I've never seen her, and I'm there all day.'

Valerie couldn't believe what she was hearing. Did this woman never use her eyes?

'Freda, James is Gary's partner, don't say you hadn't realised?' hissed Valerie.

'Well of course, a good-looking bloke like that with no girlfriend.'

Valerie couldn't help giggling,

'Why did you keep hitting on him then?'

She nudged Freda who pulled a face. Seeing the funny side, she started to giggle too.

'Don't worry, Mum's the word,' Valerie whispered, and headed back to the garage with her bike.

Once back inside number ten, the three residents dispersed to various parts of the house. Florence was going to play her beloved piano. Roger took himself off to his garage, or 'Dad's Playroom' as Florence and Valerie cheekily referred to it.

It was a cosy space. He had a comfy chair in there, a small heater and an impressive music system. Roger had fiercely resisted digital and was the happiest man alive when a few years ago vinyl began to make a comeback. He sat in his chair, feet up on the stool in front of him and listened to his favourite punk music, The Ramones.

Listening to her husband yelling the lyrics to 'Beat on the Brat with a baseball Bat' it would appear incongruous to his work colleagues that this was a man who worked for a team responsible for overseeing the construction of our motorway network.

Roger was a serious and responsible man in his corporate life, but in his garage, he was thrust back in time to his carefree teenage years when he was a punk rocker.

Valerie, walking past the slightly open garage door with an armful of laundry, raised her eyebrows in exasperation as she heard him singing along to what she had always considered to be some very dodgy lyrics. She put the laundry into the washing machine, and smiling indulgently, she firmly but quietly closed the garage door.

***

At seven o'clock, Roger and Florence sat in the living room chatting as they waited for Valerie. They were due at number six in fifteen minutes, but knowing Valerie, they would be last to arrive.

Today she was having trouble with her hair; she had decided to wear it loose. It had been tied up all day, but she fancied going *au naturel* and just leaving her curly hair tumbling around her shoulders. Roger loved it like that but it did take some work to create the natural look. Bottles of conditioner, sprays and at least fifteen minutes with the hot brush to bring the curls under control were needed to achieve the look.

Florence was in the middle of telling her father about Mum's mistake on the evening of Dave's band practise which had led them to be sitting in The Seven Stars for half an hour instead of going to the Half Moon. 'We missed most of the first half.'

'Welcome to my world darling, I've got a million tales about Mum that could top that one. I call them, 'Valeryisms' because these things only seem to happen to your mum.'

Laughing heartily, they were interrupted as Valerie swept into the room looking as glamorous as ever.

'Come along you two, chop -chop. We don't want to be late now, do we?'

With that, she headed out of the door, leaving a bemused Roger to pick up the wine and lock the front door.

For once, the Sunningdales were not the last to arrive. As they walked up the path to number six, they were closely followed by Julia. Valerie couldn't help but whistle when she saw her. She was wearing a V-neck dress which swirled about her shapely legs. The autumnal colours suited her, and the amber earrings and pendant that she had accessorised her outfit with brought out the highlights in her hair.

Julia was still blushing when James opened the door and ushered them inside. She had forgotten what it was like to receive compliments and she was really enjoying her new look.

As Gary put the finishing touches to the starter, James offered them all cocktails. Valerie was touched that he offered a mocktail to Florence.

They really had thought of everything,

Smiling to herself she sipped her margarita appreciatively.

Just as Gary came to join them, the door went again.

'That'll be Dave.'

As James went to open the door, Roger caught Valerie's eye and made Julia giggle as he winked and whispered humorously, 'Down, girl.'

Remembering the night of the rehearsal, Julia said straight-faced,

'Dave never struck me as the nervous type before.'

She explained to a puzzled looking Gary about poor Dave's reaction to Valerie's effusive greeting. This amused Gary but also had the effect of setting both Valerie and Florence off at the very same moment Dave was being ushered into the room by James.

Valerie, heeding Roger's warning, contented herself with a brief continental style kiss on both cheeks. She didn't want to spoil Dave's evening or risk embarrassing their hosts.

Once everyone was settled with their cocktails and Gary had selected some music from their playlist, the talk turned to Julia's new career. James was eager to hear how she had got on with her client.

She told them about the bedroom and showed everyone pictures of the project. They were all very interested in the mural she was doing at the school.

Florence went over to show her the picture of the heron and the two of them sat for a few minutes heads together looking at the pictures. Florence agreed to send a selection to Julia, especially as the school wanted the children to look at and include pictures of local wildlife in the mural.

Chapter 20

Gary and James had been brilliant hosts and a lovely couple, thought Valerie as she sat after midnight with her feet up waiting for Roger to pour her a nightcap. Florence, bless her, had headed straight to bed after hugging her parents good night.

The two of them sat mulling over the evening as they sipped a brandy.

'It would be difficult to top that evening, delicious food, fantastic cocktails and great company.' Roger went on to say how much he had enjoyed the samosas.

'I'll get some for the freezer next time I am in Leicester getting my hair done,' offered Valerie. 'Gary told me where he buys them.'

They briefly talked about Julia's new image. Valerie was delighted that her friend was launching into a new venture; someone as creative and attractive as Julia should not be cleaning for others. She wasn't certain as Julia didn't talk much about the past but Valerie sensed that Julia had been badly hurt by her husband and had lost more than a marriage when they had divorced.

Roger put his arm around Valerie.

'Thanks for going easy on Dave, I know he's a bit of an odd bod and you like to take him out of his comfort zone, but at heart he's a genuine guy. It was a pleasure listening to him and Florence at that grotty old piano; he was impressed with her playing, wasn't he?'

Valerie smiled proudly. She had to admit it was the highlight of her evening.

It was Dave who noticed the old upright piano in the corner of the living room. It did look slightly out of place. The rest of Gary and James' furniture was modern, light wood and neutral. They had added splashes of colour here and there with cushions and photos of their travels. There was a large framed print over the fire place of the New York skyline. They explained that was a souvenir of their first ever holiday together.

'Who plays?' Dave had asked, gesturing towards the instrument. They both shook their heads and explained that Gary had inherited it from his gran. He had played as a child but hadn't the aptitude.

'I think Gran left it to me out of badness,' he said ruefully. Gary went on to explain that his gran paid for lessons but he hated it, the teacher was scary, she used to pinch him if he made a mistake. 'That made me so nervous I couldn't do anything. In the end the teacher told Gran it was a waste of her money. I can't get rid of it though, Mum would never forgive me.'

Rapidly changing the subject, he turned to Dave and asked him to play. 'James said that I missed a great night when your band played.'

Inspired, Dave immediately launched into 'Piano Man' by Billy Joel, to the delight of everyone who applauded enthusiastically. Dave had smiled modestly and turned to Florence asking if she would like to play something.

Florence replied thoughtfully, 'Well, I've been working on something, Scott Joplin's "The Entertainer".' She paused. 'You wouldn't like to help me, would you?'

Dave offered to take the bassline, and the two of them launched into a great rendition as Valerie and Roger looked on proudly and the guests all applauded. After that, it turned into a regular old singsong, Dave playing and everyone singing along.

'A real old fashioned get-together in fact,' thought Gary with a smile. 'Gran would be proud to see the old piano in use again.'

Valerie and Roger agreed it had been the perfect evening. Once they had eaten their fill of the delicious curry and James had made them all coffee, they sat around talking about anything and everything.

James was an interesting character. He told them that after university he had travelled, literally bumming around the world. America, Australia, Europe. He couldn't decide what to do with his life, to the despair of his parents. When he had eventually returned to the UK, he couldn't bear to work indoors. He was still restless, so he got a job delivering the post.

Gary took up the story, explaining that he had been here about eighteen months and felt lost and lonely. 'I didn't tell anyone what I did for a living. I had a bad experience with neighbours in London, so I just told people I worked in an office.' He threw James a fond smile, 'I met James one night in town, it was the middle of winter, I was bundled up in winter coat, scarf, hat and gloves and there he was with shorts, trainers and hoodie.'

James continued the story, 'Yes, we chatted for so long we had to call taxis because our last buses had gone.' They spent the following weekend together and it wasn't long after that that James moved in with him. 'It's thanks to Gary that I have the job at the university, he encouraged me to do my Masters. I couldn't have done it without him.'

Valerie recalled that James had gone off to make more coffee. And Julia, emboldened by the atmosphere and probably the amount of wine that she had drunk, had asked Gary what it was he did for a living. He only gave a slight pause before explaining that he was a Detective Sergeant with the Leicestershire Police Force.

'I hadn't realised,' said Julia. 'I knew what James did but I don't recall you ever mentioning your job.'

James returned with the coffee just in time to catch the gist of the conversation. When everyone was settled with a drink, James said, 'With Gary's permission, I want to share something with you all.'

He turned to Gary, who nodded his agreement. He obviously had a good idea of what was coming. James continued

'Folks, when I first got together with Gary, I found it so funny that he found it easier to tell people he was in a same sex relationship than to tell them he was in the police force. He told me he was in the civil service when I first met him. I was convinced he was a taxman.'

'Equally as disliked,' quipped Gary to everyone's amusement.

The conversation turned to the street in general. Valerie shared the news that number twelve had been sold to a very nice couple, Anne and Henry. From Monday there would be workmen in but hopefully the house would be lived in in the next month or two. Valerie went on to say that Anne had told her she was a keen gardener and Valerie said how relieved she was as the garden in particular was driving her mad.

'Houses deteriorate when they aren't lived in. I've been doing bits myself.

'Yes, she mowed both lawns and painted the gate; didn't you, Mum?' said Florence.

Julia wanted to laugh as Dave nodded sympathetically, oblivious to the neglected state of his own house and garden and the effect it had on her.

Dave had been the first to leave, he said his goodbyes and Valerie was amused to see that he shook hands with the men but approached the women gingerly giving them a farewell peck on the cheek. Valerie couldn't help but smile at the relief on his face when she refrained from hugging him back.

After he had gone, Julia was telling Roger about Freda singing at Dave's band practice. 'There she was, giving her friend a hard time. But once she was lost in that song, she sounded fabulous.'

'Valerie did mention it; I've never been a fan of Freda's. She's one of life's complainers.' Julia nodded her agreement as Gary chimed in.

'Hey Valerie, we've you to thank for that, then? Freda turned up at the open mic last night.'

Valerie roared with laughter, seeing the horrified look on his face.

'I know, she told me how helpful you both were, and the young lad who she persuaded to play for her. She was buzzing with it, thanked me for encouraging her too.'

Tempting though it was to tell them that Freda hadn't realised Gary and James were partners, she had made a promise to Freda and didn't want to make a fool of the woman, so she held her tongue.

James said, 'Gary never feels entirely comfortable with her.' Gary grimaced, just saying she could be a bit inappropriate at times. He exchanged a glance with Roger, who nodded and threw a warning look at Valerie. She smiled and skilfully changed the subject. She had been married to Roger for long enough to recognise that look.

Don't ask, I'll fill you in later; Florence doesn't have to hear this.

***

As Roger and Valerie were going about their nightly routine, loading the dishwasher and locking doors before heading up to bed, Valerie remembered to ask Roger about his conversation with Gary.

'Yes, I was glad you got the look, Gary wouldn't want to tell you himself and I certainly didn't want Florence hearing it, but it seems our Freda has a thing for younger men.'

As Roger launched into the tale of poor Gary's first ever encounter with Freda, Valerie couldn't contain herself.

'Your face, Roger, you look appalled. I did know something about it, as it happens. The silly woman told me today that she thinks there's a spark there between her and Gary! She honestly hadn't realised that those two were partners, although she had the good grace to laugh at herself when I spelt it out to her.'

Roger went on to explain that it was only after she turned up at the open mic and Gary worried that she would try it on with Larry that he told James why he felt so uncomfortable around her. Roger started to laugh, saying,

'He wasn't wrong either! Poor Lary sent James a text later that night. He was convinced Freda had pinched his bum.'

Sunday morning dawned bright and clear. Leaving Florence and Roger enjoying a lie-in, Valerie took herself out for a walk. She had written a card thanking Gary and James for a lovely evening and popped it through the door. She smiled as she took in the drawn curtains and the silent house, it did look as though they were still in bed.

She set off at a brisk pace, determined to get a decent walk in before she went home to prepare breakfast for her family.

As she passed Julia's gate, she heard her call, asking if she could join her. The two of them set off chatting and laughing, enjoying the quiet Sunday morning. Julia told her about her new clients.

'You'll never guess, remember the bedroom I showed you and the client said he'd mention me to his grandparents?'

Valerie was all ears she was really hoping that Julia would make a success of this new venture. She was fizzing with excitement and it was good to see.

'You won't believe it, but it's only your new neighbours.' She went on to explain that she had noticed a message on her phone when she got back.

'It was from Anne, I'll be meeting her at the house on Tuesday morning. They need some help decorating the living room as they have to fit furniture from two small living rooms into this much bigger room at number twelve.'

Valerie was delighted for her, she liked coincidences and she had a good feeling about her new neighbours. She was sure they would fit right in to life in Capulet Close.

The two of them walked along the canal and back through the park before parting company. Julia had some photos to look at. Anne had sent her pictures and measurements of the sofas that she ideally wanted to fit into the living room of number twelve, and she also wanted covers making so that they all matched.

She just had time to source some swatches of material and paint samples before Tuesday. The way things were going, she would have to give her notice in sooner rather than later.

Valerie wasn't quite as lucky; as she approached home, she spotted Freda setting off for a walk with her little dog. She could tell by her face that she wasn't happy.

Oh well only one thing for it thought Valerie mischievously, *here goes.* With that she launched into her charm offensive.

'Freda, it's lovely to see you and Freddie too.' She carried on talking as she bent down to pet the dog.

'I'm going to persuade Roger and Florence to come on a long walk to get some fresh air. It's such a lovely blowy day.'

Freda grimaced, 'I won't be walking anywhere else today. My back's killing me. It's agony some mornings, Freddie's lucky I could take him out at all today.'

She barely drew breath as she launched into a torrent of complaints, 'I was hoping to go to the teatime jam session, but that selfish so-and-so doesn't want to go out today, too tired apparently.'

Valerie presumed that comment was directed at the long suffering Maisie and lost patience.

'If your back's that bad, you wouldn't want to go anyway, would you? As for Maisie, you can't expect her to be at your beck and call every weekend I presume she's got a life of her own. And don't forget she works full time, too.'

Valerie found it hard to hide her smile at Freda's response. It was an apology of sorts but Valerie knew her game.

'Sorry to snap,' her eyes filled with tears, 'it's their fault.' Gesturing to her neighbours she said, 'They've really upset me. Playing music and singing they were, until gone midnight. I thought they'd have invited me along, I do live next door.'

Valerie had patted her arm gently, told her to go home and do some stretches to ease her back.

Always someone else's fault: Valerie had returned home shaking her head incredulously.

***

On Monday morning, the peace of the Close was interrupted by workmen depositing a large skip outside number twelve.

As Valerie waved Roger off on his journey back to Scotland and chivvied Florence to get ready for school, she was pleased to see that work on next door was already underway.

Chapter 21

The following week, Freda was feeling happier. Maisie had been persuaded to come along to the Sunday jam session, and she had been able to sing two songs. The players weren't quite as sympathetic as lovely Lary, but she had performed a passable rendition of Adele's 'Make You Feel My Love' and had received a lot of compliments when she sang 'Summertime'.

Since her chat with Valerie, she was doing her best to be considerate and to leave as soon as Maisie was ready. She knew that in order to enjoy the opportunity to perform, she needed to keep on Maisie's good side.

Looking out of the kitchen window, she spotted the plasterers at number twelve. The skip was full of mobility aids. Axminster carpets in shades of brown and orange, an old stair lift and a recliner chair. Freda felt a wave of grief as she was reminded of her mum, who had been reliant on all of those things in the last years of her life.

Freda wiped away a tear as she thought of her mum, short of money, seven children and a curmudgeonly husband. Freda's dad was strict, and he didn't hold with what he would call frivolities.

Freda, being the eldest, had to help her mum. She remembered entertaining her brothers and sisters when the radio was on; using a hairbrush as a microphone, she would pretend to be on *Top of the Pops*.

She smiled as she remembered introducing herself as 'Freda, the long-haired beauty from Leicestershire'. There she would be, the star performer belting out the latest number one. Her fantasy wouldn't last long. Her father's voice would cut across her reverie, saying sharply,

'Enough of that racket, our Freda, stop showing off. And get into the kitchen and help your mother!' There was no arguing either.

When Dad said, 'jump' you jumped. He was quick with a backhander, he believed in equality. The girls got a hiding just the same as the boys, she remembered bitterly.

I suppose times were different, she reflected as she thought of her youngest grandchild, no wonder she had so much confidence. Hannah was actively encouraged to perform.

A proper little diva, she smiled as she thought of little Hannah. When Blake brought the children round, Hannah would recite the latest song or nursery rhyme that she had been learning.

'Nanny, let me show you…' or, 'Nanny, listen to me.' Her little voice would command Freda's attention, and she took pleasure in her latest achievements. As far as she was aware, Hannah had never in the whole of her short life had anyone tell her she was showing off.

I suppose Mum and Dad were just too fraught and overworked.

She hurriedly tidied her kitchen, clearing the worktops and wiping everything down. Switching on her laptop, she was about to put her plan into action. This was probably the one and only time she wasn't going to ask for help with technology, she had to do this for herself.

She had been mulling it over for a while, and after her conversation with Valerie a couple of weeks ago, she had made up her mind. Her and her big mouth, why had she said anything about Gary?

Talk about show myself up, but how was I supposed to know the two of them were partners? They both seem so masculine.

She gave a sigh of regret.

Oh well, onwards and upwards, better get on.

Freda knew that if she wanted to meet someone, she would have to join a dating site. She had been considering it for a while now, but putting her foot in it so spectacularly with Valerie had given her the impetus she needed.

Later that day, she was feeling proud of herself. After signing up to a free trial on a dating website, she had even

121

managed to upload her favourite photo for her profile picture. It was taken only recently at a friend's wedding. Wearing a smart dress and jacket and a pair of high heels, her newly coloured hair a bit longer and in a flattering style, Freda was looking good.

Hearing Freddie bark bought her back to reality, and glancing at the clock, she couldn't believe she had been online for so long. It was twenty past five for goodness sake.

After taking the dog for a quick walk around the block, she was heading home at exactly the same moment as Gary drove into his driveway. He briefly raised his hand in greeting, but she barely looked at him as he gathered his things from the back of the car and hurried to his front door. Freda was itching to get back online to see if anyone had liked her profile.

Shaking some food into Freddie's bowl, she made sure he had plenty of water, gave him a quick pat and shut him in the kitchen. It was going to be a busy night. Freda scrolled through the profiles looking at dozens of men, but not one of them seemed to have that extra something that she was looking for. Eventually it came to her, they were all so bloody old. The truth of the matter was that she didn't fancy a single one of them.

All of a sudden, she had an idea. She spent some time writing down exactly what it was she was looking for in a man.

Treat it like a catalogue, girl. Describe what you want and don't settle for anything less. Be brave.

Having sorted things in her own head she edited her profile to say that she was looking for men aged thirty-five to fifty. Her previous partner had been fifteen years her junior and they had been together five years. She had really loved him, and she had thought he had loved her too, but she caught him out. He had been playing away. The unkindest cut of all was that the little Bimbo was ten years younger than him, and still a teenager.

Freda hadn't lied about her age in her profile. She had written that she was sixty, but was young at heart. She hadn't been so excited in a long time. 'Giddy', her mum would have said.

'Calm down, our Freda, you're the giddy limit.'

Freda smiled as she remembered her mum. Looking back, she believed that her mum should have made more effort to stick up for the children. Freda had been the rebellious one and her dad had tried to beat the spirit out of her.

Funnily enough she had just accepted it when she was young, but looking back, she felt that her mum preferred to turn a blind eye when Dad was in one of his rages.

Even after he had died, Mum refused to discuss the past, preferring to view their lives through rose coloured spectacles. This infuriated Freda, and she was ashamed to say that she had enjoyed provoking her mum by bringing up incidents from her childhood.

'Remember when Dad blacked my eye, Mum?'

Her mum would look at her sorrowfully, saying,

'Freda, he didn't, you always did exaggerate.'

Her brothers and sisters thought she should let it go. They didn't want to discuss their childhood, they believed in focusing on the good memories. She felt so hurt when Liz, the sister closest in age to her, had got very defensive, saying,

'For God's sake Freda, you're like a dog with a bone. You won't leave it, will you? Dad hit us, people did hit their kids then, you can't change the past. So what's the point? You're upsetting Mum. She's an old lady, and as soon as you bring it up, she gets upset.'

Liz had called her a bully.

'Bully? Who sorts Mum's shopping out and takes her to her appointments? Not you lot, that's for sure! You're too busy with your important jobs and your fancy holidays. Don't tell me how to deal with Mum.' She remembered slamming the phone down on Liz with grim satisfaction.

Sadly, since her mum had passed away, her siblings gave her the cold shoulder. And now they rarely got together. Lost in thought, she shed a few tears. Irritated, she blew her nose and wiped her eyes.

Pull yourself together girl, she admonished herself, turning back to her laptop.

Chapter 22

The following Friday at 8pm, Freda, face like thunder, was just stepping out of the taxi. Greg, the driver, knew Freda as she regularly used the services of Dial-a-Cab. She had been almost silent on the journey, which was most unusual. In fact when he came to think of it they usually enjoyed a bit of flirty banter.

'You OK, love?' he asked as she paid him.

'Why wouldn't I be?' She almost snatched the change from his hand.

'Keep your hair on, I was only asking. I was a bit worried about you as it goes.'

Hearing Freda's heels clicking along the pavement, he realised he was talking to thin air.

Ten minutes later, Freda, a glass of gin in her hand, was on the dating site looking at Lewis' profile page.

What the hell happened to you?

Her fingers flew over the keyboard as she typed. How dare he mess her about? She was livid, and felt such a deep sense of disappointment she wanted to weep. Everything had seemed perfect, too perfect perhaps.

When she had first been winked at by Lewis only hours after she had edited her profile, she couldn't believe her luck. He was forty-two years old, dark and good-looking. He said that he worked out and looked very fit. Freda hugged herself in delight as she imagined being enfolded in his passionate embrace and covered with hot hungry kisses.

He expressed a preference for older women, saying that they had life experience. He had mentioned being in a band, and said he was fed up of irritating young women who hung around after gigs wanting a date or photo with the band members. He went on to say that he preferred real women, those who have experienced life.

Freda was delighted, she wondered if he would let her sing if she came to one of his gigs. During the day, he was a builder working for his uncle's firm.

Just like Blake, we've got so much in common, it's uncanny.

She had told Maisie about him, explaining that like her, he was the eldest of a large family. And he also had a difficult relationship with his dad. Maisie had made some sarcastic comment about that being one too many coincidences, and had Freda not thought he might just be telling her what she wanted to hear. Irritably, Freda dismissed Maisie's response as jealousy.

In the following hours, poor Freddie got short shrift. She abandoned his walks and, ignoring his reproachful looks, just let him out into the garden.

Freda just couldn't keep away from the laptop, and by the Sunday, in spite of her friend's pleas to be careful, they had arranged a date for the following Friday. They were going to meet at 6pm at the Harvester. Lewis, bless him, was a real gentleman; He was going to book a room. Only so that he could have a drink he reassured her, no pressure for her to sleep with him.

Yes, he's responsible I do like that in a man.

She was completely besotted with him.

Their messages had quickly become flirty and then they had exchanged photos. Freda had sent a daring picture of herself in a red satin basque complete with stockings and suspenders. Lewis' response had been everything she could have wished for.

I can't wait for you to dress up for me.

She had to confess some of his messages had even made her blush, and she wasn't easily shocked. She hadn't dared tell Maisie half of the things they had said to each other. She'd be appalled.

Freda had printed off a copy of Lewis' photo and kept it in her purse. She had taken to flashing it about, saying she was in a relationship. Valerie was another one who hadn't been impressed. Freda recalled the usually smiling Valerie being quite sharp with her and ushering Florence into the car, saying that they were in a hurry.

She didn't even look at the photo, snotty cow and it was her that said I should get out there! You can't please some people.

Freda dismissed all thoughts of disapproving friends and neighbours and settled back to her fantasies. She got all hot and bothered just thinking about Lewis. The photo showed him stripped to the waist and drinking from a can of Coke, his chest gleaming with sweat. In the background was a row of half built houses. Maisie had muttered darkly,

'A bit staged don't you think? He looks like a model on the Diet Coke advert.'

Freda snatched the picture from Maisie, face like thunder. Maisie could believe what she liked, Lewis was lovely and he was all hers, she was only jealous. Freda recalled some of the compliments he had paid her, he said that she had beautiful eyes but what she most liked was when he listed in graphic detail all of the things he would love to do to her. She shivered in anticipation.

Roll on Friday.

***

Meanwhile, the much maligned Maisie was lost in thought, hard at work organising the stock rotation in the shop. She knew that in her effort to be a good friend, she was annoying Freda by pointing out holes in Lewis' story. She felt that he was telling Freda what she wanted to hear, making out they had more in common than they really did.

She was genuinely worried about how this was going to pan out. She had picked up the pieces of Freda's failed romances before, and she knew from bitter experience that an unhappy Freda was even harder work than a happy one.

She was startled out of her reverie by a lady with a beaming smile.

'Hello, you're Freda's friend we met at Dave's band practice. Do you remember? I'm Valerie, a neighbour of Freda's.'

Maisie did remember her.

'Not being rude, Valerie, but I'll have to carry on doing this while we chat.'

Valerie gave a hearty laugh, 'Well, women are good at multi- tasking.'

Valerie wasn't happy that Freda had been unable to resist telling her about Lewis. As far as Valerie was concerned, it was totally inappropriate. She continued.

'I was so cross, she came over just as I was taking Florence to her music lesson.'

Valerie explained that she only stopped because she remembered how down in the dumps Freda had been last time they had met.

'She had a few tears because Gary and James had a party and didn't invite her.'

Maisie nodded understandingly. Valerie continued,

'She came bounding over full of the joys and showed me a picture of a young chap, young enough to be her son and had the cheek to pass it to Florence! She's only fifteen, for goodness sake! She doesn't need all the gory details, telling us she's in a relationship indeed.'

Throughout the conversation, Maisie had continued pricing goods and arranging them in the chill cabinet. Once Valerie paused for breath, Maisie placed her hand on her sleeve in a calming gesture.

'I'm worried too, Valerie, but as soon as I say anything, voice any concerns at all, she snaps my head off. Freda can be hard work, but she's my friend so I don't feel as though I can criticise her to anyone else.'

Maisie went on to say that she had made Freda leave the open mic early.

'Her young neighbours were there and I think she really wanted to stay to the end.'

Valerie smiled sympathetically.

'I did tell her that she should be more considerate. Just a thought, Maisie, but maybe you shouldn't be quite so available.'

Valerie headed off to the vegetable aisle, giving Maisie a friendly wave as she hurried away.

***

Once Freda was indoors, she had quickly let Freddie outside. After a slug of gin, she was all fired up and ready to do battle. She felt so angry, she could spit. She felt she had wasted a week of her life on Lewis. Maisie would have plenty to say, no doubt, she had said he seemed too good to be true. And much as she hated to admit it, she was right. Who did this bloody Lewis think he was, treating her like that? Just wait until she reported him to Match Makers, she would get him blacklisted.

She had been so excited about the date, her first in nearly five years. She had dressed carefully in a smart knee length black and red dress. She hated the tops of her arms which she had always thought were a bit flabby and had pulled on a fluffy red shrug which concealed the bits that she was most self-conscious about. Along with her high heels, she had been dressed to impress and had admired herself in the mirror before leaving the house.

Maisie would be ringing her in a bit, the nine o'clock phone call, the only thing Maisie had insisted on.

'At least if you need an excuse to get away you can pretend it's a family emergency. If everything is OK, just say that you will call back tomorrow. '

Freda had agreed impatiently, she hadn't wanted a worried Maisie bursting in on a romantic moment between her and Lewis. *Hah, no chance of that now,* she thought bitterly reflecting on the events of the evening.

Chapter 23

She had arrived at the Harvester and ordered a drink at the bar. Time seemed to crawl by as she sat feeling very conspicuous, all alone, sipping a gin and tonic while all around her, couples and groups were drinking and chatting.

By ten past six, she was getting impatient when all of a sudden she espied a dark haired young man heading towards the bar. She was feeling sick with excitement. It was him, it had to be. She stood up, and as he turned from the bar, he caught her eye. It was definitely him.

'Thank you, Lord,' she muttered as she rushed over to him. Oh, he was gorgeous! He had clasped her in a warm embrace and had kissed her on both cheeks. She did feel a twinge of disappointment that his greeting hadn't included a kiss on the lips. He didn't carry on their flirty conversation either, in fact he seemed a little shy.

I suppose shyness is quite attractive in a man, she thought, feeling somewhat reassured.

Lewis had bought himself a drink and topped up her gin, and they had sat cosily in a little corner booth chatting. She told him about herself and how she had brought up her two boys as a single parent after her divorce. Lewis had a young son and he too was a divorcee.

Freda asked about his band, she had already told him that she loved to sing and recently she had been performing at open mics. She recalled that Lewis had changed the subject, saying that their band was having a change of line-up, so it would be a while before they were ready to play again. They were getting the new members up to speed first.

Freda thought back to their flirty exchanges and was impatient. She longed for Lewis to touch her but he seemed strangely reticent. In that instance, she decided to take charge. Stroking his strong muscular thigh, she whispered,

'Let's just finish this drink, then maybe we can go to your room and get to know one another a little better.'

'Mm, let me see if the room's ready, and I'll come and find you.'

He had put down his drink and hurried away to reception.

He is eager, she thought with amusement. *You still have it, girl, you could always get 'em going.*

Smiling, she relaxed into her seat, sipping the last of the gin and imagining how the rest of her evening would turn out. By the time she had finished her drink, Lewis hadn't reappeared. It was nearly 7.30pm, and he had been gone for nearly fifteen minutes. Puzzled, she wondered if he had meant that she should follow him to reception. Gathering her bag and coat, she made her way out of the bar, past the restaurant and into the hotel reception area.

'Can I help you, madam?' the receptionist smiled.

'Yes please, is there a room booked in the name of Lewis Gregory? It's just that he left me in the bar while he checked in, and he's been gone a while now.'

Looking at the computer, she shook her head.

'Sorry, there must be some mistake, no reservation in the name of Gregory.'

And that is precisely why Freda was back indoors by 8pm; her wonderful romance over before it had even begun.

***

Meanwhile, Maisie had been spending an uncomfortable evening at home, clock watching. Why the hell Freda couldn't go on a dating site like anyone else and be satisfied with chatting to men of her own age, she couldn't think.

Maisie had been single for some time now and she had built a nice little life for herself. Two holidays a year, a great job and good friends. She had been out with a few men, but it had never led to a long term relationship and that was enough for her.

Freda's problem is that she's still trying to attract the type of men she went out with when she was young.

She had tried to reason with Freda and pointed out that she had launched into sexting Lewis straight away.

'You don't even know if you're the only one he's messaging.'

Freda had not been happy, and had more or less told her to mind her own business.

The problem was that Freda had told her too much, and the information she was now privy to had worried the life out of her. This was why she was cleaning her already spotless living room at 8.30 pm on a Friday night. She was anxious to do the nine o'clock phone call, if only to put her own mind at rest.

You hear such terrible things about predators on dating sites.

Maisie knew that Freda was hard work, but she was one of her oldest friends, and they were close. When Freda was in the mood, she was good company, and they had enjoyed some great nights out together over the years. Maisie glanced at the clock. 8.40pm.

Blow it!

Picking up her mobile, she phoned Freda, who answered on the second ring.

'Hello.'

'Everything OK?' asked Maisie meekly.

'No, it's not, and I don't want to talk about it. I'm indoors sitting in my glad rags feeling so angry. Look Maisie, thanks for calling but can we talk about this another time?'

Maisie, feeling a little miffed, put the phone down. But not before saying that she was checking that she was OK. Two minutes later, Maisie's phone pinged.

Sorry, you're a good friend, thanks for looking out for me.

Maisie smiled. *Typical, speaks first, thinks later.*

Maisie thought back to Valerie's comment.

Mmm, maybe I should be less available and then she might appreciate me more.

Chapter 24

Julia was rushed off her feet, it was a good feeling; she was back doing what she loved. She had taken Valerie's advice and booked a couple of weeks off work, but she was seriously considering giving her notice in as work was snowballing.

On Tuesday, Anne had come to the house. Over coffee, she had explained her vision for the living room at number twelve. Although the plastering wasn't finished, the workmen had let Julia in once the room was completely empty. She had been able to measure up, and with her very clever computer programme, had produced a 3D scale model of the living room.

Anne had said admiringly, 'I wish Henry were here, he'd love that; he'd have drawn it out on squared paper the old-fashioned way.'

Henry had, however, measured the dimensions of all of the items of furniture that they wanted to put into the room. Julia was able to put all of these into the programme and show Anne various configurations of the room. Anne was delighted when Julia printed them out, and said she could take them back with her to show Henry.

'Now, this is my favourite part.' Julia reached over to grab a book of wallpaper samples, a paint chart and some swatches of material. Anne knew this was going to be an expensive job, but Henry had reasoned that it would be the last time they would need curtains and soft furnishings, so they may as well buy the best they could afford. Nonetheless, Anne could see the cost mounting, she knew that made-to-measure curtains don't come cheap, and Julia's services had to be counted in too.

She was fascinated by the way the computer programme bought the room alive. She had never had the vision when decorating, but having this facility was amazing. Anne said how delighted she was that Callum had recommended Julia to help with the decorating.

Anne knew they could never have organised all of this and coordinated the decorating, curtains and loose covers to all be ready at the same time. She left with several colour combinations of paint, wallpaper and soft furnishings.

The designs had been printed off in colour, and they agreed that Anne would talk to her husband and they would confirm with Julia in a few days exactly what they wanted. Julia had promised an itemised bill for her services; and those of the decorator that she used and the lady who made curtains and soft furnishings.

Saying goodbye at the front door, they both instinctively looked over at Dave's house.

'Does anyone live there?' Anne gestured to next door.

Julia grimaced and explained about Dave and his lack of pride in the garden.

'It looks worse than number twelve,' remarked Anne, 'and that's been empty for months.' Julia agreed, explaining that it was thanks to Valerie mowing the lawns front and back that it didn't look worse than it did. Anne was touched, saying that it was a really neighbourly thing to do and she would thank Valerie next time she saw her.

Talking of Valerie gave Julia an idea; next time she mowed her front garden, she would just do Dave's as well. She couldn't do much about the shrubbery, but mowing the lawn would make a big difference.

And I bet he won't even notice, she thought.

***

By Friday afternoon, Julia was looking forward to a few hours off. She had been working hard on the job at number twelve. Next week, she would be at the school working on the mural. So anything else that came in, she would have to fit in at the end of each day. She was going out with Ali and Angie later, only for a meal and drinks, but it was a good excuse to dress up and relax for a few hours. She headed off upstairs for a hot shower.

139

Meeting the girls on the corner, she spotted Freda, dressed up to the nines getting in a taxi. She gave her a wave as she headed towards her friends, an hour later they were sipping a welcome glass of wine and catching up on their news.

'I can't believe we only saw each other Monday. So much seems to be happening in your life, Julia! It's great, it really is.'

Julia certainly seemed more her old self. She was wearing smart wide legged trousers and a silk blouse. She had unearthed some of her nice jewellery, she hadn't wanted to wear it working for a cleaning company, but now she felt the need to look and feel stylish. After all, that was what she was trying to sell – style.

She had just started telling them about the work that she was doing for Anne and Henry and the coincidence about Anne being the grandmother of one of her other clients, when Angie's eyes widened.

'Don't look now but isn't that Freda?'

Of course, their eyes swivelled over to the booths near the bar. And sure enough, it was Freda.

'Oh my God, she's with a man, a *young* man.'

Ali reasoned that it could be her son.

'Really; I don't think you'd be running your hand up and down Jake's thigh like that would you?' giggled Angie, raising her eyebrows, which had the effect of sending them all into fits of giggles.

At that moment one of the waiting staff came over to say that their table was ready, they reluctantly left Freda to her romantic encounter and headed to the restaurant.

Chapter 25

The next afternoon, Gary and James were relaxing in the garden of number six, sipping a glass of wine and enjoying the sunshine.

'This is great, we don't often get to enjoy the garden without Freddie yapping away,' smiled James.

'I agree; you know I love dogs, and I'd make more of a fuss of Freddie. But...' Gary's voice faded away as he gestured towards the fence.

'I know, I completely get it, you don't want to encourage you-know-who?' With that, James slapped his knee, saying, 'Sorry, Gary, I should have told you before. I reckon you're off the hook as far as Freda is concerned.'

Gary looked at him sceptically. 'Oh yes, why's that then?'

James leaned towards him, and in a low voice, he said he had seen Julia that morning while he was shopping for vegetables. Julia had told him that last night she was having a meal with her friends, and Freda had been there with a man. They were all cosied up and she was stroking his thigh. James looked at Gary's stunned expression and said, 'Well?'

'Thank fuck for that.'

James roared with laughter; Gary so rarely swore. But when he did, he found it extremely amusing. Julia said that they went to the restaurant, so hadn't seen Freda or her young man again.

'Top up?' James gestured to the bottle.

'Please.' Gary held out his glass. He felt like celebrating. He was in line for a promotion after the successful conviction of the Merchant brothers. They had both received lengthy prison sentences, and there was another ongoing case to freeze their assets and to secure compensation for the victims.

This is why I joined the police, to get justice for vulnerable people who can't help themselves.

As James proposed a toast, they heard a commotion from next door. James put his finger to his lips, picked up the wine and gestured for Gary to grab the glasses and follow him into the house. The two of them slipped in their back door at the very same moment Freda came into her garden to take the washing off the line. Freddie had been driving her mad all day, yapping and being generally unsettled.

'For two pins I'd give you away' she muttered, throwing him a dirty look as he sat at her feet looking hopefully up at her, a ball on the ground next to him. Freda bundled the clean laundry into the basket, resolutely ignoring the ball. She stomped back into the house, laundry basket under her arm leaving a despondent Freddie to mooch around the garden.

***

After a long shift at work, Maisie was relaxing in her greenhouse. She found gardening therapeutic, and she couldn't resist making the most of the late afternoon sunshine as she watered her seedlings and gazed out over her small neat garden.

Her thoughts turned to her friend she had been summoned to join her for a drink. Maisie thought the invitation might be by way of a peace offering, she had been a bit snappy last night, even if she did apologise later. Maisie was considering refusing the invite.

I do have plenty to do at home after being at work all week.

She weighed up whether she could face Freda moaning about the dog, her kids, her bad back. The list could be endless once she got going, and of course, she still hadn't told her what had gone on last night. Maisie paused for a second. That was the decider. What had gone on last night? She grabbed a jacket and hurried off to visit Freda.

When Maisie arrived that evening, it was a sorry looking Freda who answered the door, her face was blotchy and tearstained and she was wearing her 'scruffs', as she always called her fluffy tracksuit. Freddie, affected by her mood, lay in his bed, head resting on his paws. He gazed mournfully up at Maisie as if to say,

'For God's sake cheer her up can't you?'

Maisie's soft heart melted at the sight of her tearstained face. She couldn't bear to see her friend so miserable and she gave her a big hug.

'Come on, nothing's that bad get the glasses, I've got a treat for Freddie in my bag. Let's pour the drinks and you can tell me what's been going on.'

***

The two of them were sitting on the sofa, a contented Freddie lying at their feet chewing his treat. Freda and Maisie were sipping sloe gin. Maisie's aunt made some every year, and it was delicious.

Freda had refused point blank to discuss her date with Lewis at first. But as she sipped her second drink, she began to relax, and slowly revealed some of the events of the disastrous evening.

Maisie smiled as she observed Freda's ability to rewrite the events to suit her. He wasn't all that fantastic in the flesh. Good looking, yes, but not as tall as he said. She went on to say that he was only about five foot eight; nowhere near the six foot that he had written on his profile.

Freda went on scathingly,

'Considering he had plenty to say when we were messaging, he hardly said a word when we were having our drink. He was slow on the uptake, even when I sat really close, he didn't make any attempt to kiss me.'

Freda admitted that she was back home by 8.00pm but couldn't bring herself to tell Maisie what really happened. She had intimated that it had been her decision to leave early.

Later that evening as Maisie walked home, she couldn't help but marvel at the cheek of the woman. Freda had been really down. It had taken a lot of effort on her part and almost half a bottle of Aunt Sal's sloe gin to lift her spirits. It would appear that her experience with Lewis hadn't deterred her from looking at younger men; in fact, the two she had her eye on were younger than Lewis.

'That reminds me; while you're here, look at the laptop. It'll only take you five minutes. I just want rid of Lewis on Match Makers.'

Maisie had quickly done as she asked.

'Just block him. In fact, anyone that you don't want contact with, just block them.'

Maisie leaned across and showed Freda how to use the dropdown menu to block or hide someone.

'Thanks, but I'll probably have to ask you again, you know I'm useless with technology.'

Maisie felt a surge of irritation.

She's not useless, though, is she? She set that profile up and even uploaded her photo.

Chapter 26

By the following Friday afternoon, Freda was feeling happier. Maisie had taken her to the Sunday jam session, and she had been in her element singing. It had been a bit quieter, so she was asked to sing another song, which threw her a bit.

She was beginning to realise that being a regular performer might actually involve some work. Anyway, she got away with it by joining up with another performer. They impressed the audience with a rendition of 'I Got You Babe.'

Luckily, Jeff - the chap who had asked her up - had the lyrics written down. Both parts, since then, she had written some lyrics down to Amy Winehouse's 'Back to Black' and had been singing it all week. She had just about nailed it, and she just hoped that Maisie would be persuaded to come out next Sunday too. She didn't quite have the confidence to turn up on her own yet.

Another thing that had boosted her mood was that Blake had called.

'Can I bring Hannah over later, Mum?'

She was delighted. She checked that she had some treats for Hannah in the cupboard, and settled herself with a cup of coffee and a magazine as she waited for them to arrive.

As soon as she saw the two of them on the doorstep, she guessed that he had an ulterior motive. That boy always looked furtive! Ignoring Blake, Freda bent down and swept Hannah into her arms.

'Come along, gorgeous, let's see what we can find for you in my cupboard.'

Hannah clapped in delight she knew Nanny would have a tin of her favourite chocolate biscuits.

'Are you stopping for a drink, Blake?'

Freda settled Hannah at the table with her biscuits and a drink of milk, and turned to her son. He was a good-looking lad, very like his dad had been at that age, but he had such a surly expression. In fact, the only time she saw him smile was when he was talking to Hannah. She was a little darling, no doubt about it.

Her heart filled to overflowing as she watched her little granddaughter chat away to herself, pretending to give her dolly bits of biscuit. She exchanged a smile with her son

They didn't agree on much, but they were united in their adoration of little Hannah.

'Nah, I won't stop. I need to get off, Mum. Can I leave Hannah here for an hour? Mandy will be back from work at 4pm, she can send Archie over for her when he gets back from school.'

'OK. Make sure she does, though. I've got things to do this evening and I need to get ready.'

Once Blake had what he had come for, he was away. Hugging his mum and kissing Hannah, he dashed off, saying, 'Thanks Mum. Love you.'

Freda and Hannah spent the next hour having a dolly's tea party, Hannah's favourite game. Freda had an old stainless steel tea set and some tiny plastic cups. She gave Hannah some weak squash to pour out for them and the dollies had biscuit crumb cake. The floor got soaking wet and sticky, but Freda didn't mind. When Hannah was tired of the game, Freda encouraged her to sing some nursery rhymes.

She smiled as she mopped the sticky floor, listening to Hannah's rendition of 'Wheels on the Bus.' By the time the front doorbell rang at 4.15pm, Freda was exhausted. She always forgot how tiring looking after a toddler could be.

Hannah was excited to see her big brother. She adored him and wouldn't leave him alone. Freda smiled to herself when she looked at Archie he was getting to that gangly stage and tended to grunt instead of talk. But he always had a kiss for his Nan and he was a lovely big brother to Hannah.

There was no love lost between her and Mandy but give the girl her due; she was a good mum. The kids were always polite and well turned out too.

'Come on then, trouble.' Archie took Hannah by the hand, kiss Nanny good bye.'

Freda held out her arms, and Hannah ran into them, giving her a smacking kiss on the cheek. She stood at the door waving to the pair of them until they disappeared out of sight.

As she went to close the door, Freda noticed a small card stuck in the letter box. She looked at Freddie, who had spent a subdued afternoon in his bed.

'You didn't let me know about this, did you, you little sod?'

She bent down to stroke him, she knew he was sulking. He always kept out of Hannah's way. She was much too boisterous for him, he remembered with horror the last time she came, she tried to include him in her doll's tea party. He wasn't having that.

Unfortunately, Freda hadn't liked it when he had growled at her beloved Hannah, and had shut him in his cage. To his disgust, he had to stay in there for the entire afternoon. How he had sulked when Freda finally let him out. She smiled; sometimes it was just like having a child.

Looking at the card, Freda felt a rush of excitement, her parcel from Honey Luv had arrived, and she had missed it with Hannah being here. Oh no, it had been left at Dave's.

Deciding she couldn't wait until Dave dropped it round, Freda flung on a jacket, put the door on the catch and ran over to number six. She walked up the path.

How on earth does he stand all that shrubbery over the front window? It must be so dark.

She knocked on the door, paused, and then - after a few minutes - knocked again. She was sure Dave was there, his van was in the garage; the roof of the van was just visible through the window in the garage door. She was just turning away when she thought she saw movement. Craning her neck to look over the shrubbery, Freda saw a glimpse of a slight woman with long brown hair and a green cardigan leaving the table and heading into the kitchen.

I knew he had a woman in there, I saw her before but I wonder why he hasn't answered the door just because she's there.

She waited a couple more seconds and headed off back home. As soon as she walked back in the door, the phone rang; it was Blake.

'Hi Mum, thanks for looking after Hannah, was she good for you?'

'Yes, good as gold, we had a tea party for the dollies. She loved it.'

For once, Blake wanted to talk but Freda had things to do. She had a hot date tonight, and she wasn't about to let Blake put her behind. She was already wrong-footed. She could do with getting hold of that parcel.

151

As she put the phone down on Blake, the bell rang. She saw Dave's silhouette complete with floppy hat through the glass door. She flung open the door and almost snatched the parcel from him in her eagerness to get her hands on it. Freda thanked him and apologised explaining that she had to get ready as she had company later. She went to shut the door and paused for a second.

'I meant to ask, who was the woman in your dining room tonight? I called round for the parcel but nobody answered the door.'

Dave turned away saying,

'Probably my sister, she was sorting through some photos for my dad's ninetieth birthday.'

Freda nodded and smiled.

Bloody rude, though, it wouldn't have hurt her to open the door. Oh well.

Looking at Dave, she said, 'Better go. Thanks for bringing the parcel round.' She gave a little wave before shutting the door.

As Dave walked down Freda's path, he felt a sense of relief that his secret was safe for the time being. Freda had swallowed his explanation, although the bit about sorting photos for his dad's birthday was true. He felt a pang of guilt when he thought of his dad; they had always been close, but his dad would never tolerate Kandy. He was of the generation where men were men. He still used expressions like 'Pansy' and 'Nancy boy'. Dave winced; he couldn't bear to disappoint his dad. Kandy would have to stay at home for now.

He remembered the first time he put on women's clothes, it was shortly after Diane had left. He had discovered a silk dressing gown at the back of the wardrobe. It felt lovely and still smelt faintly of Diane's perfume. Instinctively, he had slipped it on, revelling in the feel of the silky material against his skin. He had found being enveloped in the familiar fragrance strangely comforting, it reminded him of his wife's presence, and the house hadn't felt quite so empty. After that, if he was feeling a bit low, he would slip the dressing gown on for a while. It had seemed to help.

Chapter 27

Back at number eight, Freda was lying in a foamy bubble bath sipping a gin and tonic, as she luxuriated in the hot water. She was so excited that she could barely contain herself, in just over an hour, he would be here.

After the debacle with Lewis, she had felt so down, but recently she had been exchanging messages with a handsome young soldier.

His name was Bryn, and he was on leave staying with family in Coventry. Freda knew she was taking a risk, but she couldn't face another meeting in a pub.

I'm not doing that again, sitting there waiting feeling like Billy no mates.

This time, after much consideration, Freda had decided that Bryn could come to the house. She hadn't told a soul; she was worried that Maisie would only try to talk her out of it. Or worse, turn up to check on her. No, this was her decision, and she couldn't wait.

When he had first winked at her online, she wasn't sure at all. He was only twenty-six, a bit young even for her. He had admitted straight away that he didn't want a steady girlfriend, being a soldier wasn't conducive to a long term relationship, and no girls of his own age wanted to get involved with someone who might be away for long periods of time.

Freda was bowled over, their messages quickly became flirty. And once she realised he was only in Coventry, she had invited him to the house.

They had been playing a game where they would share their fantasies. Bryn confessed that he had always fantasised about making love to a woman who was blindfold.

'Really,' responded Freda, more curious than concerned. 'And then...?'

He went on to explain how he would like her to be dressed, and once he had had his wicked way he would just leave! Slip away without being seen.

'You mean I'd have to be blindfold before you even arrived?' she demanded. 'I wouldn't even see you. Like the Scarlet Pimpernel.' She had laughed out loud.

'Well, yes, I suppose so.'
He had been complimentary about her willingness to even consider indulging in his fantasy.

'You're sure, aren't you? I wouldn't want you to do anything you weren't comfortable with' he had said earnestly.

As Freda dried herself, she shivered in anticipation. One thing she knew for sure was that as soon as Bryn had had his way with her, that blindfold was coming off whether he liked it or not.

Maisie would be horrified if she had even a hint of her plans. She was a good friend, but so set in her ways. When they were younger, they had enjoyed clubbing together. Maisie was newly divorced at the time and hadn't wanted to get involved with anybody new. Unlike Freda, who was always on the prowl; In fact, that is how she met John, at a club. It had taken her a long time to get over him and none of the men she had met since had measured up.

Maisie suggesting she gave men of her own age a chance was a joke. What her friend didn't know was that she had met up with an old school friend a few years back through Facebook.

He was a nice enough bloke; Stuart, his name was. In fact, they had met up as a group, a school reunion. It had been a good night, she remembered; having a laugh and a few drinks. One thing had led to another, and they had ended up in bed together.

She shuddered as she remembered the disappointment. Sex with him had been like trying to shove a slug into a slot machine. No thank you, she had no intention of repeating the experience and trying to raise the dead.

Life is for living, she told herself firmly as she went off to get ready.

Freda had carefully opened the parcel and hung the skimpy outfit over the back of the chair in her room. She smiled wickedly, Bryn was in for a treat, all of his fantasies were about to come true.

Before dressing, she had carefully applied her makeup and styled her hair. She had already dusted the room, put the soft velvet throw on the bed and turned the lamps down low. She took a last look around the room. Satisfied, she headed downstairs, unlocked the back door and switched on the lamp. She scattered rose petals along the hallway, up the stairs continuing the trail along the landing and right up to the bedroom door.

Freda sent Bryn a message reminding him to let himself in and to turn the key in the lock. She then instructed him to follow the trail of petals up the stairs. She quickly sent another text.

There is a present for you behind the door.

With just five minutes to go, Freda slipped the outfit over her head, added the accessories, tied the blindfold firmly and lay down exactly as Bryn had instructed face down on the bed.

She could feel her heart pounding in her chest; her mouth was dry with excitement. The velvet throw was soft against her cheek and she breathed in the scent of the perfume that she had dabbed on to her wrists and throat making her almost giddy with longing. She couldn't wait to feel his strong arms around her.

Wait, she could hear a light tread on the stairs. It took all of her willpower to keep still. For two pins, she would rip the blindfold off and be facing the door when he came in. But no, she had promised to indulge his fantasy, so she would keep her promise. She kept absolutely still, hardly daring to breathe as she heard the handle turn and the door slowly opening.

Suddenly, her heart was in her mouth as she felt herself being shaken roughly by the shoulder.

This wasn't meant to happen she thought, more angry than frightened as she struggled. The blindfold was ripped from her eyes, leaving her blinking furiously, getting used to the light. To her horror, she found herself face to face with................ Blake.

For once, neither of them could think of a thing to say. Staring at his mother, open -mouthed, Blake was first to break the silence.

'Mum,' he asked curiously, 'why were you lying face down on the bed wearing a blindfold and dressed in a nurse's outfit?'

Freda, grabbing her dressing gown, snapped;

'Mind your own business.'

With that, she stomped downstairs and into the kitchen.

Chapter 28

Dave had a few things on his mind. Dad would be ninety next week, and Dave thought he really should organise some sort of celebration. He was wondering if it would be a good idea to hold it at the pub at the next rehearsal.

He and his brother John had already taken Dad out for lunch. John's wife had suggested inviting Diane. She had always been close to his family, and Dave knew that she popped in to see his dad from time to time.

In fact, when he had texted Diane to suggest it she seemed really pleased, and said that she would arrange for their daughter Heather to give her granddad a quick FaceTime call from Spain where she was working at the minute.

Such a simple thing and his dad had loved it. Heather was close to his parents when she was small and she had grieved terribly for her grandmother when she had passed away.

I ought to make more effort with Heather.

He had really enjoyed chatting to his daughter, and was fully intending to organise a call with her himself. Diane was

159

in regular contact with their daughter, judging by the shared jokes and easy interaction at Dad's birthday lunch. He wondered if Kandy was encouraging him to be more in tune with other people's feelings.

Or maybe I'm just getting in touch with my feminine side. He smiled at the very idea.

***

Sharon at The Half Moon was very happy with the success of the rehearsal evenings. They'd had three now, and next week would be the fourth. Jed from work thoroughly enjoyed the music, and he usually bought a couple of mates along. Dad's friend Jim was still coming along and getting everyone up dancing. Even Freda had been to two out of the three, saying coyly last time that she wouldn't be there because she had a date.

Dave couldn't help wondering why she didn't bring her date along, but he supposed she'd had a better offer. This time, Roger would be home. So if he came along, at least he might have more success in avoiding one of Valerie's rib-crushing embraces.

Roger had been chatting to Dave at the weekend. Florence had some important music exams, and one of them included a recital. Roger was explaining that he missed quite a lot of Florence's school performances, but always tried to make it to the music ones. He had taken a week's holiday, and said how much he was enjoying doing the school run and being there when Florence got home.

Dave tentatively asked Roger what he thought about them having a celebration for his dad's birthday during the rehearsal. The rest of the band had been all for it, Roger said he thought it was a great idea.

'Being ninety is an achievement, Dave, your dad's amazing! I hope I'm half as active if I'm lucky enough to get to his age, and the Capulet Close lot would enjoy it too.'

'Okay, we'll go for it.' Dave knew that he was not great socially, and in the normal run of things, he wouldn't have thought of involving other people in his dad's birthday. He knew he would hate it if anybody did anything so public for him, but seeing how much his dad had enjoyed the birthday lunch he thought it would be worth the effort.

***

Once he was back indoors, Dave decided to measure up for some blinds for his front windows. Since Kandy had become part of his life, the ivy over the top of the house and the shrubbery in front of the living room window no longer offered him the privacy he needed.

The irony was that he had succeeded for such a long time in keeping himself to himself, and now when he could really do with the privacy thanks to the band and their regular rehearsals, his social life had really taken off. What with work, evenings with his neighbours and keeping an eye on his dad, he was struggling to find time to just be Kandy.

He no longer had the parcels delivered to the house, it was too problematic. Freda was becoming curious, and she would never believe he was buying that many clothes. Thanks to online shopping, Kandy had a decent wardrobe, better than his own in fact. Dave grinned as he thought of his latest purchase, a mid-calf floaty skirt with a cashmere long-sleeved jumper. It was all about the material, the softer and finer the texture the better.

Once he had told Sharon that the following Tuesday they would be celebrating his Dad's birthday as a surprise at the end of rehearsal, she asked him if he was thinking of doing food.

'I could do you some simple finger food, and I can even put a banner up and organise a cake if you like.'

He agreed quickly to all of her suggestions. It wasn't that he was mean, he was happy to pay Sharon. But food, cake and decorations hadn't even occurred to him. His dad's friend Jim suggested that Dave bring along a playlist so that the rehearsal just took place the first half of the evening. And his dad could then enjoy the rest of the evening, chatting and socialising with his guests.

When he had told Julia his plan for Tuesday, she had mentioned the ivy again. He took the wind out from under her when he told her that he was going to have the ivy completely removed.

'You're paying somebody?'

Dave explained that he was doing some work indoors and wanted to tidy the outside up at the same time.

'Funny really, have you noticed that the grass isn't growing as quickly as normal? I can't remember the last time I mowed my front lawn.'

Julia smiled,

'I wasn't going to say anything, Dave. But the last couple of times I mowed my lawn, I did yours too.'

His face was a picture; she wasn't sure whether he was annoyed or embarrassed. But she smiled and reassured him,

'It's no trouble, I had the mower out anyway, only took ten minutes.'

In truth, Dave had only just decided to cut the ivy down completely. Once he had the blinds, it would no longer be necessary. Julia wasn't someone to be ignored. And when she said she had been cutting his lawn, he did feel a bit of a twit, and realised how caught up he had become in his own desire for privacy.

It also occurred to him that once the ivy grew back, it would continue to annoy her. Julia, he was sure was perfectly capable of getting her own ladder and cutting the ivy down herself.

Julia had promised Dave that she would let everyone know about his dad's birthday, and was going to take a card round to everyone in Capulet Close for them to sign. As she set off for Freda's, she had a thought.

What on earth is his dad's name? We can hardly write, 'To Dave's dad'.

Smiling to herself, she walked up Dave's path and knocked on the door. Tapping her foot, she waited before knocking again. She knew he was at home she had only left five minutes ago in order to fetch the card. Irritated, she turned away.

'Julia.'

Turning back, she saw Dave wrapped in a voluminous dressing gown, peering around the door. Indicating the card, Julia laughed and explained that she didn't know his dad's name.

'Jack, his name's Jack,' he said, closing the door as quickly as he could.

Bloody hell, that was close.

Dave returned to his spare room and removed the dressing gown. He ran his hands over the arms of the heather-coloured cashmere sweater: it felt as soft as silk. He brushed back his short grey hair, and carefully put on his new chestnut brown wig. It was cut in a stylish bob, and suited Kandy better than the long-haired wig that he had first used.

He had started to shave his legs, having learnt his lesson after ruining several pairs of ten denier tights. He had never thought about his legs before, but admiring his reflection in the mirror, he didn't think they were bad! Especially now he had mastered the art of walking in his heels.

Julia had managed to get the card signed by all of her neighbours except Freda, she would catch her later. There was something puzzling her about Dave, she couldn't put her finger on it, but it was something to do with him coming to the door in his dressing gown. If he was showering, she wondered why he didn't just wait until he was dressed again and catch her another time. It was almost as if he was worried she would keep coming back.

The curtains were all tightly drawn, he's hiding something.

Eventually, she spotted Freda coming back with Freddie. She was just telling her about Dave coming to the door in his dressing gown when Freda said;

'He might have a woman in there. You might have interrupted something, Julia.' She added that she was surprised he had answered the door if he had someone in there, and she told Julia about the time she had seen a woman whom he later said was his sister.

'She didn't answer the door, just walked off into the kitchen when I knocked.'

That reminded Julia of when she had asked him about the lady she had seen when she had dropped the note round. He had been evasive then.

Freddie was getting restless, so Freda signed the card and hurried back indoors. She hadn't been to the last rehearsal as she had at last had a successful date with Bryn; after what had happened with Blake, she hadn't thought it would ever happen.

She remembered putting the kettle on and locking herself in the bathroom, with Blake saying,

'But Mum......' She was hoping he would have left by the time she came out. She had found a text from Bryn saying he was running late; by now, she was so upset that she sent a message cancelling him. He wasn't happy, and had called her a timewaster. She felt sick at the thought that if he had been there on time, he might have come face to face with Blake.

She remembered splashing her face with cold water and returning to the kitchen. Blake was sitting at the breakfast bar.

'Still here; I don't see you for weeks and now you're here twice in one day! What do you want? I'm really not in the mood.'

Blake looked at her uncertainly;

'Mum you text me. I came for my present.'

Oh, the humiliation! Scrabbling for her phone, she looked back at the texts she had sent. And sure enough, she had sent that last text to Blake by mistake.

Refusing to discuss it further and unwilling to admit that the text came from her, she hustled him out of the door and took herself off to bed, feeling very sorry for herself indeed.

Things were still a bit frosty with Blake, he could be a bit dim but she was in no doubt that gradually it must have dawned on him what she had been up to that night. It had never been mentioned again, and thankfully, he still bought Hannah to visit. Her presence was a welcome distraction. They didn't have much opportunity to talk when she was there.

Blake's unexpected arrival that night had nearly ruined everything. Bryn was furious, and for a while she was too embarrassed to respond to his messages.

Meanwhile she was talking to another young man. He was flirty, told her he had a sports car and offered to take her for a spin. He too liked his women to dress up, and they had spent a pleasurable night together with both front and back doors firmly locked indulging in both of their fantasies. Freda dressed in her red satin basque and fishnet stockings, and Jan. (pronounced Yan) wearing his tightest trousers leaving little to the imagination.

She remembered the feeling of his smooth, muscular chest as she rubbed him all over with baby oil and still felt a shiver of desire when she thought of him. Although she had talked to Maisie about the men she was messaging, she no longer told her when a date was happening.

Even so she couldn't resist telling her about Jan and their night of passion. She was pleasantly surprised to find that he was happy to spend the night, and the next morning he was up and dressed quite early. He had taken her hands in his, gazed into her eyes and had crooned; 'Lovely Freda.' Oh, he had such a sexy accent! 'I to leave but we play again.'

He was Latvian, which did make him quite exotic in Freda's eyes, but the language barrier made conversation quite difficult.

Not that we had much conversation last night.

Freda had a smile on her face all that day.

They had never quite made another date, and Freda hadn't had her promised trip in the sports car.

Meanwhile, Bryn had been back in touch. And she had explained what had happened, and how upset she had been. She hadn't admitted that it was her fault that Blake had turned up; she felt enough of a fool as it was.

The following month, he had a twenty-four hour pass. He had persuaded her to try again. This time when they made the arrangements they made doubly sure they were not interrupted, she asked Bryn to text her once he had arrived. He was to give her five minutes to get ready, and on no account was he to forget to turn the key in the door.

The only problem was putting Maisie off without saying why. It was rehearsal night, and in spite of Freda's complaints about the music and not being allowed to sing, she hated to miss out on any social event. Reluctantly, she came clean with Maisie, but she made out her date was with Jan so that her friend wouldn't worry.

Although the secrecy and subterfuge was exciting, in reality, Freda had found the encounter deeply disappointing. She hadn't particularly enjoyed the physical experience either. Bryn, true to his word, had turned up bang on time. Freda had enjoyed the preparation and the anticipation.

Her heart had been in her mouth as the door handle turned. Bryn had not said a word through the whole episode. She couldn't have said they had sex; it was more her lying there, accepting what he was doing to her. He didn't even kiss her. Not that he hurt her or was particularly rough, but it was all very mechanical. And once he was finished, just as he described in his fantasy, he made to leave.

Freda, who was beginning to feel short-changed, ripped off the blindfold and caught a glimpse of him. Bryn had grinned wickedly at her and had whispered,

'Naughty girl' before blowing a kiss and running lightly down the stairs. She heard the back door slam behind him and made her way down the stairs, checking that the doors were bolted.

Looking at the time, she realised it had taken her longer to get ready for Bryn than it had for him to act out his fantasy. The Stompers would only just be starting their second set. She could have kicked herself; she had done herself out of a good night out.

Chapter 30

Maisie and Freda were the first to arrive at The Half Moon the following Tuesday. Sharon had put up a banner and a few decorations, and she had prepared a finger buffet which she would bring out after the first set. They were impressed. She had done well at such short notice.

The band arrived and Freda caught Jack's eye as he spotted the banner. She was feeling a bit sentimental, remembering her mum's eightieth birthday and the tea party she and her sisters had organised. She rushed over and made a fuss of him, telling him that he was amazing for his age, and finding a picture of her mum on her phone surrounded by her children.

'Were you pleased with the album your daughter put together for you? My mum would've loved something like that I wish we'd thought of it.'

Oblivious to Jack's puzzled look, Freda headed back to Maisie.

Dave was delighted to see his neighbours and work colleagues out in force, and Dad's friends were already having a good time dancing to the music.

Dave and his dad weren't given to physical displays of affection. However, his dad had come over to Dave with a beaming smile, saying, 'I can't believe that you organised this when you'd already taken me out to lunch!' And then he shook him by the hand. Dave smiled at his dad, and just as he was turning away, Jack said,

'That neighbour of yours, the one that talks a lot. She was asking about my daughter, is she all there?'

Dave shrugged. Bloody hell, Kandy was going to cause some trouble if he wasn't careful!

Thinking on his feet, he just told his dad that Freda must be thinking of Diane, and meant daughter-in-law.

When Roger and Valerie arrived, Dave and his dad greeted them together. To his relief, Valerie contented herself with a brief peck on his cheek, and instead treated Jack to her warm greeting. He was swept up in a hug and pressed enthusiastically to Valerie's ample bosom as she wished him a happy birthday. Unlike Dave, Jack quite enjoyed it. Indeed, he looked quite flushed with pleasure as he took up his guitar.

Julia was sitting with her friends. She had organised a small gift for Jack to go with the card and it was safely in her bag under the seat. As they sipped their drinks, Julia gave them an update on her latest job Henry and Anne would be moving into number twelve the following week.

Julia had a successful week doing the mural, and had enjoyed working with the children. She showed them both the school website with a photo, her hands covered in paint, working with a group of Reception children who were daubing the lower half of the mural in green paint with splotches of red.

Laughing at Angie's quizzical look, Julia shrugged, saying, 'They painted grass and poppies. It's all they could manage really, the smaller children worked low down.'

She showed them the finished mural and they agreed that it was pretty spectacular.

'How much of it did you have to redo?' Ali knew what a perfectionist Julia was.

'Not a lot, to be honest.'

She admitted that she was surprised at how well the children worked as a team. She went on to say that she found out those who were good at drawing and got the best artists from each class to sketch out an animal, bird or insects. The not-so-confident pupils painted in block colours, and the rest added detail.

'Anyway, girls, I must tell you. I've actually given my notice in.' Smiling as they both cheered, she told them that she had had a bit of luck which meant that she could leave sooner rather than later, but she would tell them how it had happened at their next girls' get-together.

'Let's enjoy Jack's birthday, it's a long story, and I've got things to show you too.'

The whole evening was a great success. After the rehearsal was finished, Dave had set up a playlist of quiet music, and the food had been served. Everyone mingled and chatted.

Gary and James arrived late, but James went straight over to Jack, wished him a happy birthday and bought him a drink. To Gary's relief, Freda was chatting away to Maisie, and they were both laughing uproariously. He was beginning to think that James was right, it did seem as though Freda had lost interest in him, thank goodness.

Sharon brought out the birthday cake, which to everyone's admiration was in the shape of a guitar. Julia presented him with the gift and card from the Capulet Close residents. She had found a silver tie pin in the shape of a guitar, which he promptly fastened on. Unlike his son, Jack was old-school, and always dressed formally in a shirt and tie when he went out. He was visibly touched, especially when they all sang 'Happy Birthday'

Afterwards, James, who was great at tech, put some songs on a laptop complete with lyrics, and asked if anyone wanted to entertain the birthday boy with a song. Needless to say, Freda was first up. She sang her party piece, 'Summertime.' It was a hard act to follow, and nobody else was keen. But Sharon, who it turned out had a good voice, sang 'Country Roads'.

After that, they all danced the night away to James' impromptu disco. Dave did have another moment of disquiet when James and Gary exchanged a hug as they sat together towards the end of the evening. His dad's face was a picture.

Please, Dad, don't say anything.

Thankfully, Valerie came to the rescue; Dave could have kissed her, He wasn't sure whether she anticipated his dad's disapproval, or she was just sensitive to atmosphere. But before his dad could say anything at all, Valerie had swept Jack away to dance. Gary and James by this time had moved on to Julia's table, and were asking about the new neighbours. Dave felt able to breathe again.

At the end of the evening, he got up with the microphone and thanked everyone for coming and making his dad's birthday a night to remember. He thanked Sharon personally. The food, decorations and the cake were all much appreciated, and everyone had enjoyed themselves.

***

The following Sunday, Dave and his dad were having their post mortem. His dad got the first round in, and they were talking about a new song that they were thinking of doing. Dave said he would work out the arrangement as the other guys weren't familiar with it.

They chatted briefly about Sharon's fundraiser. It was definitely going ahead, and she really wanted the band to play. She had come up with a date, the last weekend in July;

and was going to do a barbecue and a raffle as well. 'What's it in aid of?' asked Jack. 'I forgot to even ask.'

Dave explained that Sharon had lost her niece at the age of four to a terminal illness. She saw how the loss had devastated their whole family but in particular her two nephews. They were adults now, but remembered living in a house overshadowed by sadness.

Sharon did her best, taking them out on trips and making sure they had some normality in their lives. In memory of her niece, she had set up a charity to support siblings of terminally ill children. It funded a support group, family holidays and respite care. But it relied entirely on donations.

Jack agreed it was a good cause, and he reckoned they could put on a good show. Dave was a bit taken aback when his dad, who was still on a high over his surprise party, said,

'I like your neighbours, Son, but I didn't have them down as a pair of pansies.'

Dave tried to make light of it, but his heart sank. Unusually, he decided to challenge his dad.

'What do you find so offensive about them?'

Seeing the look on Jack's face, he said, 'I'm not being funny, Dad, I'm curious. It was only at the rehearsal that you realised that they were a couple. You liked them well enough before that.'

Jack shuddered, 'All that hugging and kissing. It wouldn't have done in my day.'

Dave took a deep breath and said,

'Well, Valerie's always hugging Roger; you actually loved it when she hugged you! I saw you grin from ear to ear.' He nudged his dad, trying to get him to smile. But he remained stony-faced, insisting that in his day, men were men. In the end, they agreed to disagree, but Dave did say to his dad that he would be upset if he said anything negative about his neighbours.

'We all like Gary and James, Dad. They're good neighbours, and I don't want to upset them. You might not approve, but you have to move with the times.'

Diane would be impressed, I'm challenging the patriarchy.

Having stood up to his dad for once, Dave stood up a little straighter. However; he left with a heavy heart, feeling unable to reconcile a life with Kandy. He knew that if it wasn't for his dad, he wouldn't need to be as secretive. His neighbours, he was sure, would be accepting. He wouldn't even mind the ribbing he knew he would get from his colleagues at work. He smiled as he imagined Jed.

'Bloody hell, Dave, no self-respecting woman would put make up on like that! You look like a pig in lipstick.'

Jed would then give him a list of local make-up artists, or put him on to one of his many women friends to help him improve his technique. Smiling sadly, he headed for home.

Chapter 31

Julia was waiting at number twelve for Eva and Patrice to arrive. They were going to bring the sofas and hang the curtains. Anne and Henry would arrive with the rest of the furniture later. The decorators had finished work, and the house was clear of the previous owner's possessions.

Julia had organised for the rooms to be professionally cleaned from top to bottom. New hardwood floors had been installed downstairs. And the bedrooms, stairs and landing were all carpeted in a flat, closely woven cream carpet.

A blank canvass essentially.

This was the favourite part of her job. She felt like an artist arranging the rooms and choosing fabrics and colours, creating a picture that her clients were happy with.

She couldn't believe how much work was coming in, and it was all thanks to the bedroom that she had designed for Callum and Alicia. Ali and Angie had been too impatient to wait until their next Monday get-together to find out how she had managed to give her notice in so quickly, so she had explained everything on the way home.

It had turned out that Alicia was what you call a 'social influencer.' Julia went on to explain that Alicia was very successful. Basically, she filmed the things she did; services she used; clothes she bought; holidays she went on, and posted to her social media account. She had hundreds of thousands of followers. Ali and Angie still didn't get it.

'She's not famous, though?'

Julia laughed. 'Well, she earns a living from it! And thanks to her sharing the pictures of my work and hash tagging me, I'm getting more enquiries than I can manage which is why I decided to hand my notice in.

She had quickly shown the girls one of Alicia's posts. They shook their heads, bemused at the number of followers she had. Ali squealed with excitement when she spotted Julia's name and pictures of the nursery she had designed.

Julia was really pleased that Jake had been true to his word and had got her website up and running. It had been a great help as she didn't have to have her work interrupted by phone calls, all enquiries could go through the website. He had even offered to update it regularly for her, which was fabulous. She fully intended to pay him and to employ an office manager eventually, but she had to get some capital behind her first.

In some ways it felt as though she had come full circle, starting off a fledgling business which is what she had done with Steve all those years ago. Working alone she could pick and choose the type of work she took on. Steve chased the bigger jobs whereas Julia had always preferred the intimacy of designing living spaces and working closely with her clients.

Just at that moment, her reverie was interrupted as the van emblazoned with **Curtains by Design** drew up, and Eva and Patrice greeted her at the door.

'Anne and Henry will be here later, let's get on.' Patrice and Eva had worked with Julia before, and they were excellent at what they did. Eva was going to hang both sets of curtains. They had taken the sofas to their workshop, and had made the fitted the covers there.

Once inside, the three of them worked swiftly; hanging curtains, putting covers on the three sofas, putting them in place and arranging the new cushions just so. Julia was very happy with the results, and couldn't wait to see Anne's face when she saw her new living room.

Just at that moment, the bell rang. And there was Valerie; holding a beautiful vase of roses, a card and a bottle of wine. She held them out to Julia, saying that the card was signed by everyone in the Close, and asking Julia to add her own name before leaving it for Anne and Henry.

Julia thanked her, thinking that they were lucky to have Valerie as a neighbour, she was so thoughtful. They chatted for a few minutes, with Julia amusing her friend with the tale of Dave not realising that she had been mowing his lawn.

'The good thing is, though, that the ivy's all gone. Had you noticed?'

Valerie smiled and admitted that yes, she had noticed, and pointed out the new blinds at the front of the house.

'They look so much better than those grotty old curtains; they didn't even meet properly in the middle.'

At that moment, they were interrupted by the removal van, followed closely by a small saloon car. Valerie headed back next door with a friendly wave to the occupants of the car, and a reminder to Julia that she would see her Thursday evening for a glass of wine and a catch up.

Julia had never met Henry, but she warmed to him immediately. He shook her by the hand and thanked her for the work she had done, saying how impressed he had been with the 3D images of the room.

Anne was tugging his arm enthusiastically, drawing him into the living room, where Patrice and Eva were waiting proudly to show them the sofas. Julia was going to help arrange the living room furniture when it came off the lorry, according to the design that had been chosen.

She followed them indoors. There was plenty of work still to be done. Once the furniture was in place, with Anne's permission, she would take photographs for her website.

Chapter 32

Anne lay awake, luxuriating in the silence of their new house. Henry, bless him, was still sleeping soundly.

That man could sleep on a clothes line.

She smiled fondly at him as she leaned over and gently stroked his cheek. She reasoned that it must be the long years of shift work. Henry had been a train driver for most of his working life, every little boy's dream. He had endured the unsociable hours and long shifts without complaint. He had really loved his job. And although he had embraced retirement with enthusiasm, she knew that he still missed 'playing at trains'; a term for 'going to work', coined when the boys were small.

Anne had been a stay-at-home mum when Adam and Ben were young. She remembered that Henry's comings and goings at odd times had been confusing for the boys. Sometimes Daddy was there at bedtime and other times he was sleeping during the day and they would have to creep around and not make a noise. At other times, they would wonder why he was leaving the house on a Sunday when their friends' dads would be taking them out on day trips or to the park.

'Where you going, Daddy?' asked three-year-old Adam one Monday evening as Henry set off for his night shift.

'Be a good boy, I'll be back at breakfast time. Daddy's just going to play at trains.'

Adam had kissed Henry goodbye, satisfied with his explanation. It wasn't until later that week when Anne was picking him up from playgroup that Katherine, the playgroup supervisor, had asked if Adam had a train set.

'It's just that today he was drawing Daddy, and I asked what Daddy was doing.' She smiled as she passed Anne Adam's annotated drawing of Daddy.

This is Daddy playing at trains.

Anne had chuckled, explaining that was what Henry always said when he left for work. From then on the whole family referred to Henry's work as playing at trains. Even their grandson Callum, who was about to make them great grandparents any day now, had always asked when enquiring of Henry's whereabouts, 'Where's Granddad? Playing at trains?'

Henry reached across and gently took hold of Anne's hand.

'I forgot where I was for a minute,' he yawned contentedly. 'Capulet Close is a whole lot quieter in the mornings than Fenton High Street.'

They both smiled; in truth, the noise had never bothered them. They had lived in the three- storey house crammed in between a hotel and a bakery for more than forty years. They had both loved the bustle of the High Street. Even the racket caused by the early start at the bakery and early morning deliveries to the hotel had ceased to bother them after the first few weeks.

They had loved that house. Anne felt a pang of nostalgia as she thought of the happy times they had spent there. The location was perfect, and living in the middle of town meant that they could both walk to work. As soon as the boys were old enough, they enjoyed a level of independence denied to most of their peer group simply because everything was on their doorstep. Not for her the tedium of chauffeuring children everywhere. Once they were teenagers, they could get to most places by themselves.

Anne silently chided herself. Selling up hadn't been an easy decision, but the old house was like the Forth Bridge - a continuous round of jobs. Once they had both retired, they had come to realise that it was a bit of a money pit. A big four-bedroomed house for two people meant that they were rattling around like peas in a drum. Half of the rooms never got used unless the family stayed over, or friends visited.

Even though they hadn't seriously considered moving late last summer, they had been out for a drive and had seen this house on the market. The property ticked all of the boxes. It had a spare double room for when they had guests, a smaller single room for office space and a garage for Henry's music room. He was of the opinion that it was criminal to waste a garage on housing a car. The dining area, Anne had observed with satisfaction, was plenty long enough to accommodate her eight place dining table. Best of all, there was a utility room leading off the kitchen. In their old house, Henry had made a utility room in the back of the garage.

'Gruel, Annie?'

Henry's voice interrupted her thoughts.

'If I must;' she pulled a face.

'I know it's not your favourite, but it's good for you,' he said with mock severity as he grabbed his fluffy dressing gown and headed downstairs to the kitchen. Anne smiled to herself; it was hard to believe that the former chip-eating, beer-drinking Henry had transformed into a svelte, salad-loving exercise junkie.

Downstairs the kettle was on, the table was set for breakfast and Henry was already well into his exercise regime. He had already completed his sit-ups, and was now skipping. They were also taking daily walks, and he was doing plenty of stretching exercises to strengthen his back. Forty-odd years of folding his tall frame into a tiny train cab had played havoc with his back. Retirement had been good for him, he had shed two stone and he felt much better for it too.

Henry began mixing the oats that they would be eating for breakfast, and methodically chopped the fruit and poured the tea. He called Anne, he knew she didn't enjoy the porridge, but she tolerated it for his sake. She knew it was good for his new healthy eating regime.

Anne came into the kitchen just as Henry had served up the porridge. 'Breakfast is served, madam,' he said comically, the tea towel over his arm and a plate of porridge in his hand.

'Gruel, fruit, tea,' he intoned as he put each item down in front of her. 'Is there anything else I can get for you, madam?'

Anne began to giggle, 'Oh Hen, do sit down! I can't take you seriously! You look like a giant teddy bear in that dressing gown.'

He smiled as she tried the porridge. She put the spoon down. 'It's a bit hot,' she said, completely deadpan. 'Shall we go for a walk in the woods while it cools?'

Spoon halfway to his lips, he caught her eye and they both dissolved into giggles. Anne recovered before Henry; if something tickled him, he had been known to cry with laughter. For some reason he couldn't control himself, and every time he looked at his wife, it started him off again. He often thought that one of the reasons they had enjoyed a successful marriage was their shared sense of humour.

During the morning, the two of them made good progress, unpacking the boxes and making the living room more homely. Henry acknowledged that it had been a great idea to use Julia's services to decorate the living room. It was thanks to her that they were able to move in and just unpack. Not only had she supervised the decorating, but she had coordinated the cleaners, workmen and the laying of the flooring too. The downside was that they had to put the furniture in storage and stay with Adam and Helen for a while. Henry had found that quite difficult.

Helen wasn't the warmest of people, and he and his daughter-in-law didn't always see eye to eye. Anne was unusually quite stern with him and said,

'It's not for long; let's just go with the flow. It's very nice of Helen to have us. Adam won't be there half of the time, he works away all week.'

What she was trying to say, he supposed, was that it was Helen who would be making the compromises, letting someone else use the kitchen and coming back from work every day to find her in laws in residence.

As he was hanging up some pictures, he looked around the room. Julia had done a marvellous job. The lined striped curtains and matching cushions looked good, the autumn colours contrasting nicely with the copper tones of the new sofa covers. He did wince slightly at the enormous cost of the move. The extravagance of paying somebody to do what they had always done for themselves in the past did go against his principles, but he had seen the sense in it. As he said to Anne,

'We may as well pay what we can afford now it's an extravagance that'll never be repeated in our lifetime.'

His daughter in law had asked, 'Why ever not? If you want nice things, have them. You can afford it.'

Grinning cheekily, he had responded, 'Lovely as they are, these curtains should be gold plated. They cost over a thousand pounds for both windows, but they do have a thirty year guarantee. I don't think I'll be worried about new curtains when I'm nearly a hundred, do you, Helen?'

She had given him a frosty smile; she really didn't understand her father-in-law, even after all these years.

Chapter 33

That afternoon, the two of them had decided to give themselves a break from unpacking, and take a walk.

'Come on, Anne, get some decent shoes on. Let's go exploring.'

It wasn't the most pleasant day, chilly, overcast and quite windy. But Anne and Henry tried to walk most days and rarely, if ever, let the weather stop them.

Anne came down the stairs, her light brown hair twisted into a knot at the top of her head. Henry watched her as she stood at the mirror applying her make-up. He was always surprised at how little she had changed. She had retained her trim figure and still looked good in a pair of jeans. 'Cute butt,' he whispered, patting her bottom.

'Oh, Hen; love really is blind, isn't it? You still think of me as a twenty-something, I love you for it.' She laughed up at him, kissing him on the lips. Looking at him curiously, she asked, honestly, don't you see the grey in my hair or the lines around my eyes?'

She went on to say laughingly that as she was doing her make-up in the mornings, 'It looks like a road map spread out before me.'

Henry smiled; 'you haven't changed a bit, Annie. I'm the envy of my friends. They all wonder how I managed to nab a hot bird like you.'

She laughed, giving him a playful nudge in the ribs,

'Flatterer; Come along, let's go and explore our new neighbourhood.'

One of the reasons she had been persuaded to move to Capulet Close was the location. Yes, they would still need a car for visiting family and friends, or for long journeys. But the railway station was only a twenty minute walk away. And there was a nice pub, the Half Moon, within walking distance. There were a variety of shops at the retail park, and a bus service that left every twenty minutes. Everywhere was so green, Anne thought with pleasure of the walks they would enjoy. There was a canal nearby, and a nature reserve only a couple of miles away.

Another selling point was the garden. At the old house, they had a yard. She had kept it well stocked with flowers in pots and it was full of colour all year round. They whitewashed the walls every year. During the summer months when they sat outside, it gave the yard a distinctly Mediterranean feel, a nod to their happy holidays in Spain. However, she was looking forward to bringing this garden to life and filling it full of colour.

She thought fondly of the gardening club she started at school. Many of her pupils hadn't had much access to green space, so there was always a waiting list of children keen to join. They planted bulbs and seeds, and she taught them how to thin the plants before planting them out. Eventually, they had enough plants to have pots of colourful flowers planted up at the front entrance of the school. By the time she had retired, Gardening Club had created a vegetable plot for each year group.

As they walked, they discussed their new neighbours.

'Valerie's lovely, it was so good of her to pop round.'

Anne agreed, she thought that Valerie was a breath of fresh air. Calling in last night, she had left them a delicious fruit cake, told them about bin day and given them the number of her window cleaner. She had also given them a potted history of the other residents in the Close.

Henry was planning to introduce himself to Dave, especially now that he knew he played piano. Henry was a talented musician himself, and since retirement, he had a few projects on the go.

The two of them headed out of the Close and along the path towards the canal. They had a lovely walk, enjoying signs of spring. Daffodils waving their yellow heads and an enormous bank of purple and white crocuses greeted them as they rounded the corner.

As they walked hand in hand along the canal path, a watery late afternoon sun began to peep through the clouds, at the very same moment, the wind dropped, making everything about five degrees warmer.

Chapter 34

Later that week, Henry was outside mowing the front lawn when he spotted Dave parking his van in the drive. Henry gave him a wave and went over to introduce himself. Anne, who at that moment was talking on the phone to Helen, spotted Henry striding down the road and smiled to herself. He had been dying to catch Dave. She could tell he was getting withdrawal symptoms from not having anyone to chat to about music.

'Sorry Helen, yes. I was listening, and yes, please let us know as soon as Alicia's had the baby.'

She reminded Helen that it didn't seem five minutes ago when they had all been on tenterhooks waiting for Callum's arrival. Helen agreed with her, and they spent a few more minutes reminiscing before Anne put the phone down. It was funny really; she was excited about the new baby, but didn't feel the same way as she had about Callum's birth. That was Adam and Helen's prerogative now.

Callum was an only child, and her and Henry's much adored only grandchild. Callum and Alicia spent a lot of time with both sets of parents, just as Adam and Helen had spent a lot of time with them when Callum was growing up. It would be lovely to have a baby in the family again, and she was sure that Helen and Adam would be doting grandparents, just as she and Henry had been to Callum.

Later, when they were eating their meal, Anne asked Henry about his chat with Dave.

'Well, I won't be jamming with him he's not that kind of musician.' Henry went on to explain that Dave had invited them along to his band practice the following Tuesday at the Half Moon. Seeing Anne's face, he said, 'I know what you're thinking. But it'll be an opportunity to meet the neighbours.'

Dave had told him that a few people from Capulet Close usually came along, and it was a good night.

'Oh, in that case, I'm in. I could do with some female company. I hope Valerie will be there, I'd like to get to know her better.'

After dinner, Henry tidied the kitchen, while Anne sat in the living room reading. She was just looking at the back wall which so far was completely bare.

'Henry, we need to get a picture or something for this wall, any ideas?'

Henry couldn't stop laughing. Anne had insisted on decluttering the old house, knowing that there wouldn't be as much room here. Indeed, this room was the most minimalist they had ever had. Henry had a Spotify collection, so his CDs were stowed away in his garage until he could bear to part with them. Anne had her many books upstairs in the small office-cum-library. As well as that, she had parted with most of their ornaments, only keeping the ones with most sentimental value.

She had kept all of Ben's paintings, the first one presented to them when he was only seven years old. It had been done at school and put in a homemade frame. She smiled as she thought of it. *My Family*, he had called it, and she still kept it on her dressing table. She had kept some of the thoughtful gifts that Adam and Helen had given them over the years, and she treasured Callum's first gift for them bought with his own money, which was a key hook with a garish picture of the Eiffel Tower on it. They had been touched when he proudly presented it to them when he returned from his first school trip away, and it was now on the wall in the utility room housing their collection of house keys.

Henry came in, drying his hands.

'Anne, we had that huge frame with photos of the boys when they were little. You took the photos out, put them in an album and got rid of the frame. You said, 'I'd like at least one bare wall in the new house.'

Anne went over and gave him a hug. 'So, a girl can change her mind, can't she?'

Incredulously, Henry shook his head. He was pretty certain that by next week, he would be hanging something on that wall.

As it happened, Henry's prediction was absolutely correct. Ben called. He was keen to hear how the move had gone. They chatted for a few minutes before Ben told them the real reason he was ringing. To Anne's delight, he said he was coming up for the weekend.

'I want to see Adam and Helen. I've got a gift for Callum's baby and one for you. I think you'll be pleased.'

Their younger son was a talented landscape artist and ran an art gallery in Cornwall. Henry surmised that their gift would be a painting, so suggested to Anne that she waited and wasn't to think about the back wall until after Ben's visit.

Anne couldn't wait to see him. They didn't see as much of him as they would like, but they did have some lovely holidays in his cottage, he was a good host and always made sure they had a good time while they were there. Ben shared his dad's love of music, and performed at open mics, but wasn't as keen getting his own gigs. She hoped he would bring his guitar with him, whenever he and Henry performed together, it was always good fun.

Henry was an experienced musician. Since he was a teenager, he had always been in a band and was a good bass player. Even with the restrictions of shift work, he had always been involved in some kind of music. When the boys were young, Anne had rarely been able to come to the gigs. But as they grew up, she had been a force to be reckoned with, encouraging friends and work colleagues to come along and be part of the appreciative audience.

Henry smiled as he thought of the many times lately that Anne's posse of friends had been the audience. Henry knew that times had changed. When he was first in a band, pubs and clubs would be rammed at weekends. But nowadays, with a smoking ban and the worries about drink driving, trade just wasn't what it was.

In recent years, he had concentrated more on playing the guitar and was in demand as a pub singer. Since retirement, he had been getting more solo gigs, which at first had made him nervous. But now he loved it. He still had work in the book, but he really needed to get to know what was going on locally so that he could get work here in Leicestershire. That was another reason he was keen to see Dave's band. He wanted to introduce himself to Sharon at the Half Moon. Dave had said she was going to do the fund raiser in the summer and he was wondering if he could offer to play as well.

***

Later that week, Anne was enjoying a quiet afternoon baking in her sunny kitchen. She loved being in here, she had a lovely view over her back garden and had been encouraging the birds with a variety of feeding stations.

Already this afternoon, she had been amused by a bunch of blue tits squabbling over the suet logs. Just as she was taking a tray of scones out of the oven, she heard Henry come back with the shopping.

'Good timing, I've just put the kettle on.'

While Henry put the shopping away, Anne made tea and buttered scones. Taking the tray into the living room, they settled themselves down and soon the conversation turned to their night out at the pub. Henry had been impressed with Dave's set up.

Anne smiled as Henry animatedly told her about their skill as musicians and their top quality instruments.

'Dave's piano must have set him back a bit, that's concert level equipment.'

Anne agreed that they were a good band, but pointed out that they didn't have a lot of go in them.

'They're supposed to be a swing band. As a newcomer, I wouldn't dream of saying anything. But when they introduced themselves as the Soar Valley Stompers, I caught Valerie's eye and we both had to stifle a giggle. The poor old drummer couldn't stomp to save his life, bless him, he can barely get on the stool.'

Anne looked across at Henry. Music was no laughing matter to him. He was respectful to all musicians, and Anne knew there was a bit of him that worried that he might be judged on his age rather than his ability.

'That's not very nice, Annie, you wouldn't like it if anybody said that about me.'

Anne reiterated that it was just her opinion, and of course no one would say that about Henry.

'You've got an amazing set, you sing as well as play. And unlike Dave's band, you've got something in there for everyone. No, of course they wouldn't.'

Taking one look at her indignant expression, he laughed. 'Quite right; they wouldn't dare.'

Chapter 35

The residents of Capulet Close were looking forward to the weekend. Valerie and Roger were hosting a meal on Friday evening to welcome Anne and Henry to the Close. Julia was really looking forward to it; her social life was picking up along with her business, and she couldn't be happier.

Valerie had included Freda in the invitation. She had politely refused, explaining that she and Maisie had found 'A karaoke place that we want to try out.'

Valerie smiled at the (we) she could imagine that the enjoyment that night would be all Freda's. When Valerie told Roger last night over their FaceTime chat, he laughed loudly.

'I think maybe Freda still feels a bit awkward after what she told you about Gary.'

Valerie tittered; 'Yes; and so she should.'

Dave regretfully declined saying that he was away for the weekend and wouldn't be back until Sunday. Valerie felt pleased with the arrangements, eight including themselves, perfect.

Dave was busy working out what to take with him. His suitcase was open on the bed, and he looked at the list of suggested items that he was going to need. He was nervous but excited. When he had seen a leaflet on the floor of the paper shop, he had picked it up and taken it with his Sunday paper. It wasn't until he got home that he realised with a thrill that it was advertising a weekend in Brighton for cross dressers.

He read some of the reviews, and went online to look at the hotel and the itinerary. He had no idea that these places existed. Should he go? It was expensive, but he would like to just go somewhere he could enjoy wearing Kandy's beautiful clothes and not have to rush to get changed. Going out would be scary, though; he wasn't sure if he was ready for the challenge.

The decision was made for him. When he rang, they said there was a vacancy this weekend due to a cancellation, but then they were fully booked until September. He was worried that if he didn't book now he might never do it.

The recommendation was that guests brought a daytime outfit and an evening outfit. Two pairs of shoes, one medium or high heeled and one flat or low heeled. They recommended including a wig which should be short or medium length because, 'The Lanes can be windy, and clients have been known to lose long wigs.'

The thought of Kandy chasing the long chestnut bob in heels gave Dave a good laugh but recently he had purchased a shorter better quality wig which suited Kandy perfectly.

Included in the cost of the holiday was a guide who would also do a full make-up, and spend the day taking the client out and about, it all looked very reassuring, with the guides - Alison and Daisy May - ready with a live chat if the guests had any questions or worries.

Dave had lost count of the number of times he had checked the contents of his suitcase. He loaded everything in the van and headed back indoors. He checked the itinerary for what must have been the hundredth time.

Honestly, it's worse than a first date, I'm so nervous.

It didn't help that he would miss his Sunday lunchtime pint with his dad, it had become a tradition since his mum had died, and his dad wasn't happy. John, his brother, had just told him to go.

'Dad can come to us on Sunday. You're entitled to a weekend to yourself, you know.'

He smiled as he thought of his dad, who he knew would make him feel guilty as hell when he next saw him. But if he could spend a weekend just doing as he pleased, it would be such a relief. He had always been a private person, but he hated the way he was being driven to secrecy.

It's not that I'm ashamed of Kandy I just know that Dad won't be able to accept her.

Just as Dave was satisfied that he had everything, he had a thought; he hadn't packed anything for Dave.

You idiot, you've got no clothes for travelling home in, no shaving gear! You're leaving and coming home as Dave, remember.

He was whistling to himself as he hurriedly went back inside, and packed a change of clothes and some shaving gear.

The journey to Brighton would take him three and a half hours along the M1 and M25. He had come straight from work, so he stopped off for some food on the way. By eight o'clock, he had found his way to the boutique hotel tucked into a side street. He managed to park in the guest car park. His van looked completely out of place squashed in between a soft top sports car and a neat little Mazda. He couldn't help wondering what sort of car Kandy would drive.

Definitely a sporty number, smiling, Dave gathered his luggage and headed to reception.

By nine o' clock, he was unpacked. Tomorrow's daytime outfit, the flowery skirt and cashmere sweater, hung on the hanger. The wig was on a wig stand on the dressing table, his silk underwear and sheer tights stowed safely in the chest of drawers. Kandy's low-heeled court shoes were polished and stored with their shoe trees in the bottom of the wardrobe. Dave took a lot more care of Kandy's clothes than he ever did of his own.

He was in a bit of a quandary about tomorrow evening. According to the itinerary, they were going to be taken to a club and they were advised to 'dress to impress'. Going to a club was outside his comfort zone and he really didn't think the outfit that he had bought for the evening would do at all.

It was smart but not glitzy. When he had voiced his concerns to Daisy May during their live chat, she had dismissed his worries, saying soothingly;

'We like to give our ladies the best experience. That means you need to feel like a million dollars, so if by Saturday evening you fancy something more glamorous, you can hire one of our evening gowns.'

She named a price that made his eyes water, but he did feel better knowing that he had a choice.

Chapter 36

Just as Dave was deciding whether to venture downstairs to the bar Valerie had seated her guests around her large dining table. Anne looked appreciatively around the room.

'What beautiful furniture.'

Her hand stroked the smooth wood of dining chair, which was so heavy that Roger had to move it to enable her to sit down. He told her that it was Cherrywood, and they had bought it when they had lived abroad. He smiled across at his wife, saying, 'Our furniture is as well travelled as we are. Isn't that right, darling?'

Valerie agreed, explaining that it had gone from Thailand to Australia before finally coming back to Capulet Close. With Florence's help, she bustled about, bringing in a tureen of steaming soup and soup bowls. Once everyone had been served, Roger proposed a toast.

'Welcome, Anne and Henry. We wish you many years of happiness in Capulet Close.'

There was a unanimous cheer as everyone raised their glasses. Soon, they were all enjoying the delicious food and chatting to their new neighbours.

Anne thought that Florence was such a lovely girl. She joined the company, helping her mother in the kitchen and clearing the soup plates without being asked. She couldn't help thinking how different her sons had been at that age. They were helpful, certainly. But if they had friends round, the boys would opt to eat earlier and stay out of the way.

Maybe it's just the difference between boys and girls.

Gary and James were telling the company about their next holiday. James explained that they were going to Thailand, Vietnam and Cambodia. Gary said that since he had been with James, he had been taken out of his comfort zone.

'I'd been on quite a few foreign holidays with my parents, and later with groups of friends. But we always played safe, booked through a travel agent and stayed in resorts.' He smiled as he told them about their first holiday together.

'Air B&B in New York, can you imagine it? I was sure we'd get mugged on our doorstep, but honestly, it was fine. It turned out to be one of my favourite holidays where we actually got to talk to local people.'

James laughed out loud. 'I had to organise holidays on a shoestring as a student, so that's what got me used to travelling light. I backpacked all over the world.'

But, as he said, tongue in cheek: 'I'm middle-class now, working at the university and being with Gary. So I've gone a bit more upmarket, our holidays are more of a compromise, I try to incorporate a bit more luxury.'

They all laughed as they saw Gary's relieved expression, he really needed everything planned out. Roger and Valerie had visited all three of those countries, and unearthed some holiday photos showing must-see places for their trip.

As they sat with their coffee, everyone complimented Valerie on the meal. She was an excellent host, and the food had been delicious.

The room was very cosy, lots of rich fabrics and thick carpets; very different to Anne and Henry's minimalist look. Looking around, there were cabinets full of the blue china that their meal had been served on, even the serving dishes had matched.

Anne noticed the weight of the cutlery and the elegant Lazy Susan that held the cheese and biscuits which were served after the main course. Valerie and Roger had a beautiful home, and they were such lovely people. Her and Henry had been made thoroughly welcome since they moved in and Anne in particular felt as though she had known Valerie and Julia for years instead of a mere month or two.

Julia put forward her plan for a fundraising committee she was thinking that it could be quite a big event, which would mean that Sharon would raise a lot more money for her charity.

'It's a shame Dave isn't here, I wanted to ask him what he thought about getting other musicians involved, where is he? I was hoping he'd play for us again.'

Valerie explained that he was away for the weekend, which prompted Julia to wonder if he was with his lady friend. Gary shook his head firmly.

'There's no way Dave has a lady friend, he told me that since his wife left, he's just not interested.' Quoting Dave, he said;

'Women, they're complicated, mate. I'm better on my own.'

Seeing Julia's disbelieving look. He reiterated, 'Honestly, Julia. He really did say that.'

Julia said that she had seen a woman quite late one evening in the living room. Another time, when Freda had knocked the door, there was a woman at the table. She had left the room, but hadn't answered the door, which Freda had thought odd.

'He told her it was his sister.'

'Dave hasn't got a sister; just a brother, John.'
Roger explained that he had met Dave and his brother out with their dad one Sunday, and he remembered Dave saying there were just the two of them.

Anne smiled as the men quickly lost interest in the conversation and started talking football, but the three of them continued to speculate about why Dave was being so secretive. If Florence hadn't returned to the room at that moment, they may have voiced the thought that had occurred to all of them that maybe Dave was using an escort service. It would explain his comment about women being complicated.

Valerie spotted Florence, and quickly changed the subject, asking her daughter to play something on the piano for them. Florence kept them entertained for the next half hour with some classical pieces. She asked if she could play them a song she had written herself, she had written some beautiful lyrics too and had a lovely singing voice. Henry thought she was very talented. They all clapped and cheered as she smiled and bowed modestly.

'This is where we need Dave; sighed Florence, 'we could do our duet.'

Anne looked at Valerie. 'Henry could get his guitar.'

That was it! 'We want Henry, we want Henry,' chanted Valerie, laughing as everyone joined in. Shrugging and smiling, Henry popped next door to get the guitar. James, under Valerie's instruction, mixed a jug of Margaritas. They all settled down with their drinks as Henry played, and everyone sang along.

After an hour or so, Henry put the guitar down and said firmly, 'Someone else's turn now.'

Valerie suggested that maybe they have another coffee and Roger could get Alexa to play some music. Soon they were sipping their coffee and chatting, the mellow sounds of a jazz band playing in the background. Anne was just telling everyone that they were going to be great-grandparents any day now when her phone rang. Needless to say, by the time she got to it, the phone had stopped ringing.

'I'd better ring back, it's Ben.'

Henry explained that their son Ben was visiting for the weekend, he would be arriving tomorrow and would be staying for a few days. Anne moved into the hallway just as the phone rang again.

'Mum, where are you? I'm outside, the house is in darkness.'

Anne finished talking to Ben, and went back to the party. 'Sorry everyone, we'll have to go.' Turning to Henry, she said, 'Ben's outside. He was with Adam and Helen, guess what?' Smiling tremulously at Henry, she said, 'They've gone to the hospital with Alicia's parents. Alicia's having the baby.'

Thanking their hosts and hugging everyone goodbye, they hurried out to Ben. Anne was delighted to see him and he was hardly out of the car before she had given him the biggest hug. Henry was pleased to see his son. But his greeting was much cooler, contenting himself with a handshake and an affectionate pat on the back. Henry didn't feel comfortable with these man hugs, and felt utterly confused by fancy handshakes that seemed so popular among the younger generation.

Just as they were helping Ben to unload the car, Valerie opened the front door of number ten. Julia stepped out hugging her host goodbye, and walked towards them. Naturally, Valerie stopped her and said, 'Ben, this is Julia. Remember she did the bedroom for Callum's new baby? And she created order from the chaos that was number twelve.'

Julia looked up at the same time as Ben removed a large package from the back seat of the car;

'Great timing Mum; lovely to meet you '

Julia caught his eye and laughed out loud. He was in a bit of a predicament he really had nowhere to go with that huge parcel apart from into the house. Turning away, hoping she didn't look too flustered, she said;

'Lovely to meet you too Ben; Enjoy your weekend.'

Once they got inside, Anne put the kettle on, and Ben filled them in on the events of the day. Adam and Helen had made dinner. Afterwards, they had been invited over to Callum and Alicia's. Ben had always been close to his nephew. Helen and Adam had taken Callum to Cornwall every summer to see his uncle when he was a child.

Ben had painted a picture for his new great-nephew. Luckily, his picture was a seaside landscape, which he thought would be restful for a child's bedroom and certainly didn't look out of place on the opposite wall to Julia's amazing mural. Thank goodness he hadn't painted story-book characters. Anyway, they had thought Alicia looked tired. She said her back was aching, so they said their goodbyes and went back to Adam's.

At ten o'clock, they had a phone call from Alicia's parents. Alicia was in the second stage of labour, and they would let them know when the baby arrived. Ben said he would have stayed to keep them company, but then Callum had phoned and asked if they wanted to wait at the hospital. He didn't think it would be long now.

'I thought then that I may as well come to you tonight, sorry to be a party pooper.'

Anne and Henry laughed. Ben was always such good company; as far as they were concerned, he could visit any time. They were just drinking their tea when Anne's phone rang. It was Helen. Anne could hear the tremble in her voice as she said;

'We're grandparents, Alicia's a bit tired, but the baby's beautiful. We're all over the moon.'

'Congratulations, give them all our love. By the way, Helen…'

'Yes?'

Anne burst out laughing, 'Have we got a great-grandson or granddaughter?'

Even Helen chuckled, 'a beautiful little boy, four kilos.'

Anne had a quick word with Adam. Imagine her son being a granddad. By the time she got off the phone, Ben was pouring them a glass of wine and they were raising a glass to the new baby. Later, as she headed off to bed,

Anne was thinking, *four kilos? What's that in English?*

Chapter 37

Dave was awake bright and early on Saturday morning; he hadn't gone downstairs the night before, he had been far too nervous. Instead, he had showered and shaved. He had even remembered to shave his legs and under his arms, and to moisturise.

He felt a flutter of excitement at the thought of being 'dressed', which was the service that he had paid for. The other thing that he was looking forward to was being made up; he had never had the confidence to try make up himself, but he was hoping being made up professionally would give him the skills to try it himself.

He rang down for a continental breakfast, which was bought to his room by a glamorous blonde. She was nearly six foot tall, and had a cascade of curls falling to her shoulders. She set the food out and poured the coffee. Then, to his surprise, she said,

'Welcome to Ladies' Day at the Grande, Kandy. I'll be back in half an hour to get you dressed.'

When he realised that it was Daisy-May, his dresser he blurted out, 'Blimey, it's going to be a long day! I had to get up at seven.'

Daisy-May gave a throaty laugh. Pointing to her hair and makeup, she announced;

'Early? Have a heart, darling, I start at six. It takes a lot of work to look this good.'

Dave felt relieved, he was in good hands. He was waiting at the dressing table when she returned. He hadn't been able to bring himself to pack a nightdress. Instead, he had worn a pair of pyjamas and had brought along his old voluminous dressing gown. Daisy-May, however, was not ready to begin.

'Come along let's check your legs and face.' To his utter embarrassment, she scrutinised him closely.

'No sorry Kandy. You'll have to have a much closer shave.'

Kindly, she explained that to get the best look, it must be on a closely shaven face. Obediently, he went to the bathroom and carefully shaved and moisturised again.

Sitting in front of the mirror, he felt a tiny bit apprehensive as Daisy-May explained each step of his makeover. First, she brushed his hair back and held it in place with a wide headband. Lately, he had paid more attention to his hair simply because it was easier to put a wig on over short hair.

First, she plucked his eyebrows. Looking at him critically, she asked permission to trim his nose hair. He had never done this in his life, and he let out a howl of anguish at the first pluck. His eyes were watering, but the look Daisy-May gave him rendered him compliant.

He muttered, 'I wasn't expecting that, the eyebrows were bad enough.'

Daisy-May chuckled. 'No pain, no gain, my darling.'

Once she had applied a moisturiser to his face and neck, she explained that she was going to dab on some foundation to even out his skin tone. Dave paid close attention to each step; he had already decided to experiment with makeup. Kandy needed to look more feminine.

After this, Dave could really see the transformation because Daisy-May did something called 'contouring.' It really slimmed down and shaped his face, softening his jaw line and giving him a more feminine appearance.

Bloody hell, it's like looking at my mother.

When he was a child, everyone said he favoured his mum; slight, fair-haired and blue-eyed. Whereas John was more like their dad; stocky, slightly darker blue eyes, darker haired and much more robust looking.

By the time Daisy-May had added a spot of blusher and a dusting of face powder, Dave hardly recognised himself.

'Now, let's look at your outfit. Yes, that's fabulous; I've got the perfect eyeshadow palette to go with that heather-coloured sweater.'

She completed the look by coating his lashes with two coats of mascara, and outlined his lips with a dark pink lip liner before filling in with a pink lipstick called 'Diva'.

Handing him his clothes, she said that Dave should dress and then she would help him with his wig.

In the bathroom was a huge mirror that took up one complete wall. Dave was able to see Kandy from every angle and he absolutely loved how she looked.

Who would have thought that makeup would make such a difference hey Kandy?

Opening the door, he couldn't stop laughing as Daisy-May let out a piercing wolf whistle.

'Wow, you look a million dollars. Now, let's get that wig on.'

The shorter wig had been expensive, even more expensive than the cashmere sweater. But as soon as he was wearing it, he realised that it was worth every penny. It elevated the look, and Daisy-May showed him how to adjust it. The lacing in the scalp part could be tightened; great for someone like him who did have quite a small head.

Even though Kandy had an extensive wardrobe, it had never occurred to Dave to make sure she had a handbag and purse. Luckily, Daisy-May came to the rescue. They had a range of clothes and accessories that could be hired. By the time they were ready to go out, Kandy was wearing a string of pearls, some clip-on earrings and a dainty marcasite watch. Over her shoulder hung a small leather bag containing the Diva lipstick, ('for touching up, darling'), a small purse containing cards and cash and a packet of tissues.

'Ooh, before we go, photo opportunity,' trilled Daisy-May. She took his phone and snapped some photos. There was one of Kandy sitting at the dressing table, and another full-length, smiling into the camera.

Taking a quick glance, Dave was surprised how glamorous she looked. The best he had ever managed at home was a pleasant-looking middle-aged woman, a bit frumpy if anything. But now, with expensive clothes, accessories and some decent make-up; why, Kandy looked like a smart businesswoman.

'OK, let's hit the Lanes, I get the impression that Kandy needs to stock up on make-up and possibly accessories.'

Smiling, Daisy-May helped Kandy into her leather jacket and opened the door.

Chapter 38

Julia and her mum were enjoying afternoon tea in Farmers, the local garden centre. Julia was filling her mum in on the news from Capulet Close and telling her about the lovely evening that they had spent at Valerie's house.

She mentioned the delicious meal and how Florence had played the piano for them. Julia continued, 'They've got a lovely home; lots of things from their travels and beautiful Cherrywood furniture and lots of matching china too.

Just as they were deciding whether they could eat the last two cakes or ask if they could take them home, Julia spotted Anne and Henry, closely followed by Ben. Julia waved Anne over to introduce her, while Henry and Ben headed to the counter.

Anne was bubbling with excitement as she hugged Julia and said hello to Maria. She told them about the new baby, and by the time Ben and Henry had joined them with their drinks, Julia and her mum were chatting to Anne, eating their last cake and finishing off their tea.

Henry was telling Maria what a marvellous job Julia had done with the house

'Honestly, we literally just had to unpack and put things where they belonged. I'd recommend your daughter's service to anyone who was moving into a place that needed such a lot of work, moving in was seamless.'

Maria tried to catch Julia's eye, smiling proudly, only to see that she was deeply engrossed in conversation with Ben. He was showing her some pictures on his phone, and she was laughing up at him.

Maria smiled to herself as she carried on chatting to Anne and Henry. Julia was obviously attracted to Ben, and it looked as though the feeling was mutual. She just hoped that he was free; in her opinion, it was high time her daughter found someone she could be happy with.

They all got up to leave at the same time. Anne and Henry were taking Ben, Helen and Adam out for a celebratory meal later that evening. Then tomorrow afternoon, they were going to drive over to see Callum, Alicia and the new baby.

'Call in before you go, Anne, I've got a card and a gift for them.'

Anne agreed, and walking out to the car park, she couldn't help smiling to herself as Julia and Ben hung slightly back from the group. Henry and Anne had walked

Maria to Julia's car and were chatting away as they waited. Henry looked back, calling humorously, 'Hurry up, children! Don't keep the oldies waiting.'

Julia looked at Maria and felt a stab of guilt. Her poor mum couldn't stand for too long with her arthritis, and there was she enjoying herself chatting to Ben, instead of settling her Mum in the car.

She said a hurried goodbye and rushed over to her mum, apologised for keeping her waiting, solicitously helped her into her seat and made sure she was comfortable. By the time she was in her seat and buckled up, Ben and his parents were waving goodbye from their own car.

As they drove away, Maria commented on what a lovely couple Anne and Henry were.

'He was full of praise for you and the work you did for them.'

Julia gave her Mum a sideways glance. 'Yes, he did thank me and seemed relieved that I'd co-ordinated everything. But to be honest, it was Anne that I dealt with. She reminds me of you, Mum, probably why I took to her so quickly.'

Casually Maria remarked;

'You seem equally taken with Ben, what was he saying to make you laugh?'

Julia frowned. 'I don't know, was I laughing? He was just telling me about the art gallery that he runs, and he was complimenting me on the work I'd done for his parents.'

Julia went on to explain that Ben had seen the mural, admired it and had shown her the picture that he had painted for the baby.

'I remember now, he'd contemplated story book characters but did a seaside scene instead.' We both said that, 'Great minds think alike.'

Maria kept a straight face and said,

'Yes, everything they say is funny when you're falling for someone.'

'Mum, that's enough I've only just met him. And he lives in Cornwall.'

Julia hid a smile as she changed the subject. She did like Ben, she liked him a lot and she could tell that he liked her too. She had discovered that they had a lot in common and they had both been on their own for a long time. Maria held up her hands in mock surrender.

'Sorry, only saying.'

Julia shook her head. Her mum was incorrigible, she had to laugh. She felt like a teenager again.

Back at her mum's, she sorted out some soup and a couple of bread rolls that Maria could heat up later if she was peckish.

'That's lovely, but I can't see me eating anything else tonight, that afternoon tea was gorgeous. I'm absolutely stuffed.'

Julia made sure her mum was settled and had everything she needed before heading for home she had some work to do tonight. She was determined to keep Sunday free. She was hoping Ben would join her for a walk in the morning.

***

Later that evening, Anne was sitting in the living room dressed and ready to go out. Ben and Henry had been playing guitar together and had reluctantly gone to get ready once she had reminded them of the time. Anne was enjoying a quiet five minutes looking at the back wall.

The large parcel that Julia had seen Ben struggling with was in fact, as Henry had predicted a picture that their son had painted especially for them. With all of the excitement last night Ben had put the painting to one side, saying that he would show them properly in the morning when there would be plenty of natural light to do it justice.

The next morning, even before breakfast, Ben - after a drumroll - dramatically unveiled the painting. He was delighted at their reaction. Anne had gasped when she had seen it. He had created a detailed picture of Fenton High Street, complete with the bakery and the hotel, and crammed in between was their house.

'Ben, it's amazing, look Hen! There's next door's cat, remember he used to lie across our porch because it got the afternoon sun?'

Henry smiled as he spotted that Ben had included his old bike that he would chain to the downpipe by the front door, ready for cycling to the station.

In fact, Anne saw something different in the picture every time she looked at it. Even now she had spotted two figures walking hand in hand along the street. As she got up to take a closer look she could see that it was her and Henry, her Radley bag slung over her shoulder and she was wearing her old red coat that had always been her favourite. Anne laughed out loud as she noticed that Ben had added his dad's ginger hair.

More than bit of artistic license Ben.

She smiled to herself because Henry's hair had been completely silver for at least ten years now. Taking another look, she marvelled at Ben's attention to detail, she could see that Henry was wearing his railway uniform.

Ben returned to the living room and joined his mum in front of the picture. He hugged her, saying, 'Glad you're enjoying it. You're not too sad, are you? I know how much you and Dad loved the old house.'

Anne told Ben that the picture was a perfect gift.

'The house was a family home, Ben. Dad and I are much better off here now we're on our own and retired.'

Ben agreed, saying how surprised he was that they had been invited out for a meal.

'Only been here a month, and here you are organising fundraisers and having meals with the neighbours,' Ben smiled affectionately, 'Adam and me, we call you a one-woman social events organiser.'

Henry arrived at that moment, all dressed up in his best blue shirt and a fancy waistcoat. He looked at Ben and grinned. 'I think maybe Valerie's got something in common with your mother there, Ben. She recognises a fellow organiser, they're best friends already.'

Ten minutes later, they were in the car and heading for the restaurant. Henry was looking forward to spending time with his sons. He loved it when they were all together, a rare occurrence with Ben working and living so far away.

Adam was a family man devoted to Helen and Callum, he was sure Adam would be a much better grandfather to the new baby than he had been to Callum. He had loved him and made a fuss of him, but again, the shift work played havoc with family time. Often, it was Anne who spent time with their grandson when he was small. However, he had bought Callum a train set, and it was something that they had enjoyed doing together.

Chapter 39

Daisy-May had taken Dave shopping, and far from it being the stressful experience he was imagining, it had been an education. It soon became obvious to Dave why Brighton was such a popular venue for the LGBTQ community.

Dave knew that if he had been alone he would have been embarrassed and would have scurried by the loud colourful groups eyes down and praying not to be spoken to. Daisy-May and Kandy, however, fitted right in. Obviously having someone with you who belonged to the community ensured there were no embarrassments.

The shop assistants were welcoming and most people that they met were in Brighton for the same reason as they were. So conversation, when it happened, was fun and light-hearted.

Laden with bags, footsore and weary, Daisy-May suggested lunch. Dave had worried that he might have to go back to the hotel to use the facilities in his room, but no. Very discreetly, Daisy-May explained that Molly Brown's Restaurant catered for the Grande Hotel's clients. The facilities were single cubicles with hand-washing facilities and a very helpful cloakroom attendant called Esme, whom Daisy-May assured Kandy; would be more than willing to touch up one's make-up for a small tip.

Dave looked around the restaurant appreciatively. He would never visit anywhere this classy as Dave, but he could see other men dressed up a lot more flamboyantly than Kandy, looking perfectly at home.

Daisy-May whispered that some of these 'ladies' did live as women. Dave was fascinated, but he could never imagine doing that himself. He confided to Daisy-May that he just wanted to spend a whole day dressed in fabulous clothes and experience it.

'I do dress up at home, but I've found the preparation for this exhausting. So I think this will be an occasional treat, not something I'll be doing every day.'

Back in his room, Dave removed his wig, hung up Kandy's clothes and put on his old dressing gown. He had enjoyed his day so far. Lying on the bed, he took a quick look at the time. 3.30pm. Daisy-May had said she would return at 5pm to refresh Kandy's make-up and get her ready for the evening.

In the literature, one of the suggestions was to go to a nightclub, Dave had never fancied the club scene, and he didn't think Kandy would either. Instead, Daisy-May offered to book dinner and a cabaret, which he readily agreed to.

He must have dozed off, because he was woken by a sharp rapping on the door. Daisy-May, sporting full evening make-up and false eyelashes, bustled in with two evening dresses over her arm. Seeing his face, she said,

'Just in case, you did say your outfit for this evening wasn't very glitzy.'

Dave's eyes lit up when he saw the midnight blue midi dress. It had a modest round neck and very plain long sleeves. But the neck and the cuffs of the sleeves were trimmed with sequins. He had bought some jewellery in the Lanes, a long string of blue beads and some matching clip-on earrings, a perfect outfit for dinner and a show.

Blimey, I'm even thinking like Kandy!

'Would it be ok to try the midnight blue?'

Daisy-May agreed with a smile, and Dave went over to the dressing table,

'Sorry, darling, I'm going to have to ask you to shave again. A teensy bit of five o' clock shadow is peeking through.'

Dave sighed.

I definitely couldn't keep this up, I've shaved more today than I normally do in a week.

Shaved and moisturised, he returned to the dressing table. Slowly, before his eyes, Daisy-May transformed his face with foundation, contouring and shaping until Kandy reappeared ready for a night on the town.

'Blue is definitely your colour, darling, you look FAB,' declared Daisy-May as she took more photos.

At the cabaret, they were shown to a table. They had paid for a two course meal and were offered the wine menu. Forgetting for a minute that Kandy should probably have a cocktail or a dry white wine, Dave made Daisy-May wince by saying,

'Do you have a pint of bitter?'

'Nooo,' wailed Daisy-May. 'Have some finesse; this is a club, not your local pub.'

Turning to the young waiter, Daisy-May whispered something.

'He's going to bring you a beer in a half-pint ladies' glass.' She grinned and nudged Dave, and soon they were both laughing. Daisy-May was very feminine, drinking prosecco and even sitting with her knees together, legs crossed demurely at the ankle.

There are just so many things to think of, I'll never remember it all.

The meal was nothing special, but Dave was too wound up to worry about the food. He enjoyed another pint of bitter served in half-pint glasses. However, he only really felt comfortable when the lights went down and the show began.

There was a drag act which involved some impressive singing and dancing. Next up was a very funny comedian and then there was a handsome young man with a very good voice, who to Dave's embarrassment came off the stage and sang romantic songs to the ladies.

This was the first time that he questioned the wisdom of coming here. The fear of being serenaded at the table was almost as bad as being embraced by Valerie. He started to gather up his bag, whispering to Daisy-May that he needed the bathroom. Luckily, she guessed what was happening.

'Don't worry, they know me here. It'll be me he sings to, not you.'

She patted the seat. Sure enough, Enrico the singer slunk seductively over to Daisy-May and sung 'Sex Bomb' to her, writhing up and down her chair and finishing by plonking himself onto her lap.

Back at the Grande, Dave thanked Daisy-May, telling her that it was an experience he would never forget. Making his weary way back to his room, he started the long and complicated task of deconstructing Kandy. Taking off the make-up, hanging up clothes and putting the jewellery away was a job in itself and Dave was asleep almost before his head hit the pillow.

Chapter 40

On Sunday morning, Julia was up early, she felt restless.

What's got into me, I'm like a teenager with a crush.

Busying herself with housework her thoughts were with Ben. Considering that two days ago she didn't even know of his existence, it did seem strange and a little bit wonderful that since yesterday afternoon he was never out of her thoughts.

It must have been his voice.

When she had left Valerie's, he had been struggling with that huge parcel, so she had only seen his eyes. But when he had spoken, she could hear the laughter in his voice. He had a very slight accent which she couldn't quite place, but now realised it was Cornish.

Once she had met him properly when he was with his parents, she had looked into his blue eyes, and his warm smile had enveloped her. She had felt her stomach do somersaults. He was easy to talk to as well. She had pretended she couldn't remember what they had talked about, but she did, she remembered every word.

She had told Ben that she always went for a walk on a Sunday morning, and he had said that he would love to join her. Glancing at the clock, she popped upstairs to put on her trainers. She looked the part; a few weeks previously, she had bought some running gear. She never ran, but wearing the proper footwear did make her take the early morning walks more seriously, and she always walked briskly.

Just as she was about to leave, she saw his shadow through the glass of the front door and her heart started to beat a little faster. Opening the door she was met with his warm smile, and instinctively she moved towards him,

He held out his arms and they hugged. She didn't want to be the first to let go, it was lovely just to be held. Ben's voice whispered,

'I don't want to be the first to let go, but a small dog with a cross-looking owner is over there looking daggers at us.'

Looking up into his smiling face, Julia burst out laughing.

'That's Freda and Freddie, she's not cross. She always looks like that!' she whispered. After locking the front door, she and Ben began to walk briskly towards the canal.

After a while, Ben slowed down and led Julia to sit on one of the benches. The clouds were beginning to clear, but it was still very damp. She was touched when he whipped his scarf out of his pocket and spread it on the bench for them to sit on. They sat in silence for a few minutes and then he took her cold hand in his warm one.

'Julia, I know with me living in Cornwall and you being here, it might be difficult for us to have a relationship. But I'm not imagining things, am I? I feel as though I've been waiting so long to meet you.'

Julia laughed, 'It's true. Earlier when you said,

"I don't want to be the first to let go" I was thinking exactly the same thing. It just felt so right.'

Looking at him anxiously, Julia said,

'Ben, do you think we could make this work? I've got to be honest, I couldn't think of moving to Cornwall. My home, my business is all here. And you've seen my mum, she really needs my help.'

'Of course we can, all good things are worth working for.'

He kissed her gently and then drew her into a warm embrace, and there they sat, looking across the water, Ben's arm circling her protectively; her head on his shoulder.

Making their way back to Capulet Close, they bumped into Valerie and Roger. Julia introduced them to Ben. Valerie made them laugh as she said with mock severity,

'Oh! It was you who cut short our dinner party, was it?' They spoke for a few minutes before Valerie hugged Julia goodbye and whispered, 'quick work girl, well done.'

Back at number two, Julia asked Ben to take the gift that she had bought for the new baby with him.

'Has he got a name yet?'

Ben smiled down at her. 'Callum said they're going to call him Henry, after Dad. He doesn't know, though. They're going to tell us that when we get there later.'

Julia made a drink. They sat side by side on the squashy sofa, sipping their coffee and chatting. Ben was so tactile and as they were talking, he touched her hand or brushed the hair away from her face.

He was complimentary about the living room and was really impressed when she showed him what the house looked like when she first moved in.

'Wow, you've totally transformed it.' He was telling her about his cottage, which was very comfortable, but much plainer than number two.

'It's quite small. The walls are whitewashed, the floors are stripped pine and the only colour on the walls comes from my pictures. And of course, there's the sea view.'

'Sounds perfect;' Julia leaned in closer. Her heart beating a little faster she couldn't believe what she was about to do but she couldn't stop herself. She breathed him in, he smelled of fresh air and lemons, she kissed him gently on the lips. His eyes opened a fraction wider and for a second, he hesitated before he leaned in towards her. Not taking his eyes from hers, he touched her lips with his own, gently at first and then more urgently. His hand cupped the back of her neck and he teased her lips with his tongue. Warmth suffused her whole body; she drew away briefly.

Holding his gaze, she slowly and deliberately undid the first two buttons of his shirt.

Ben swallowed hard. 'Are you sure about this?' In return, she removed her top. Their eyes locked as they continued to slowly undress one another, until eventually they were a naked tangle of limbs and lips enjoying the feel of skin on skin.

Eventually, they had made their way to the bedroom where they made love again and now they lay spooned together with Ben stroking Julia's hair, feeling the most relaxed and happy he had been in a long while.

She had shed a few tears, which had alarmed him at first until she whispered that they were happy tears. Afterwards, she had dozed off in his arms and now he was just enjoying holding her as she slept. He couldn't believe that she had become so important to him in such a short time.

He didn't remember ever having such intense feelings for anyone before. He had loved Karina and had been devastated when she had gone back to Poland. But looking down at Julia's sleeping face, he felt consumed with happiness.

I love her.

Reluctantly, he looked at his watch. He would have to make a move or else his parents would be sending out a search party, they were due at Callum's in a couple of hours and he would need to get showered and changed first.

He gently traced her jaw line with his thumb and enjoyed watching the slow smile spread over her face as she opened her eyes and saw him gazing down at her.

'I've really got to go. I'll come back this evening.'

They enjoyed another lingering kiss before Ben went downstairs to find his clothes. He briefly returned to the bedroom, he had dressed and he had gathered up Julia's clothes.

'Sorry, I've found everything except your bra.'

Laughing, he left her clothes on the bed and kissed her goodbye, saying that he would be back later.

Julia lay in that delightful state between sleeping and waking hardly believing what she had done. Almost instinctively in the living room she had reached for Ben, her longing and her desire for him had taken over her normal caution, thank goodness he had felt the same way, her instincts hadn't let her down Ben felt exactly the same way she did.

Grabbing her dressing gown she was unable to stop smiling as she made her way downstairs thinking;

I wonder what did happen to my bra.

Returning to the living room she burst out laughing as she spotted it draped over the coffee pot on the side table.

***

Just as Ben walked up the path, Anne opened the door.

'There you are we were worried that you wouldn't be back in time. Did you have a lovely walk with Julia?'

Ben picked up Anne and swung her around.

'Mum, I love this little Close. You and Dad have fallen on your feet here, everyone's so welcoming.'

He gave her a smacking kiss on the cheek, passed her the gift that Julia had sent over and ran upstairs to the bathroom.

Anne exchanged a bemused look with Henry, who had just put his guitar away and was changing his shoes.

'I think Ben's fallen for a certain young lady,' laughed Anne indulgently.

Henry looked thoughtful.

'He's smitten right enough, just hope it's reciprocated, it's taken him a while to get over Karina. He doesn't need his heart being broken all over again.'

Anne gave Henry a hug, called him an old softie and told him that Ben could look after himself. She reminded Henry that the writing was on the wall for him and Karina when she said she didn't want to buy the cottage with him. He agreed that it was all very odd.

When they stopped to think about it, they had gradually started to see less and less of Karina. In fact, the last time they saw her was at Callum's wedding to Alicia. After that, whenever they went to Cornwall, Karina would be on holiday with a friend or at an artist's retreat somewhere. Ben usually visited his parents on his own and occasionally they would chat to Karina via FaceTime if she was at home when they called Ben.

Eventually Ben had come to see them and had said that Karina had gone back to Poland. Her grandmother had left her some property and she had decided to stay. Ben was clearly upset. Anne remembered that he didn't really want to talk about it. But one night over a drink, he had told them that Karina never quite committed to their relationship.

She even baulked at getting a cat, saying that it was too much responsibility, and she had made it perfectly clear that she did not under any circumstances want children. Ben had gone along with this, he said, partly because he loved her free-spiritedness and at that time he hadn't even thought about children. Then, when she wouldn't even commit to buying the cottage with him, he realised that he was losing her.

Henry gave Anne a warning glance as he heard Ben's tread on the stairs. He was dressed in a blue linen shirt, faded blue jeans and a pair of Sketchers trainers. Anne reached up and straightened his collar.

'Very handsome; let's go and meet the newest member of the family.'

Chapter 41

Just as they were leaving number twelve, Dave drove into the Close. As they passed him, they gave him a wave, prompting Henry to tell Ben about Dave's band. Anne amused their son with the story of them having the unlikely name of the Soar Valley Stompers.

'Annie,' warned Henry.

'Sorry, I shouldn't laugh, but it tickles me every time they say the name.'

She looked across at Henry, and sure enough, his lips were twitching. He would never admit it, but she could tell he was amused too.

Unlike me, Henry, you're far too nice to show it.

Smiling to herself, Anne changed the subject just as they arrived at Callum and Alicia's house.

***

Back at Capulet Close, Dave was busy unpacking and putting everything away. He had really enjoyed himself in Brighton. He had bought make-up and a few accessories, and he intended to look at a few YouTube tutorials before practising.

One thing that he had realised over this weekend was that he wouldn't want to live as a woman. He enjoyed dressing up as Kandy a couple of evenings a week. At home, he found it relaxing just dressing in women's clothes and doing something as simple as sitting reading the paper or eating a meal.

The personal grooming side of things was quite labour intensive, and he was surprised at how tiring it was shaving, plucking and moisturising. And he could not endure that nose plucking every day. No, Kandy would remain ordinary and dowdy. But now and again, he would go all out. In Daisy-May's words, she would be 'FAB, darling.'

He had just made himself a drink when someone knocked on the door. It was Julia, he ran through the reasons she could be calling.

Can't be the ivy, it's all cut back. Not the grass, because I've taken my turn and cut hers as well as my own.

He had a quick look round to make sure nothing of Kandy's remained on show, and opened the door.

He needn't have worried, Julia just wanted to ask him what he thought about including other musicians in the fund raiser. She was pleased to hear that he had thought of it himself and they talked about her idea of a committee.

'I'll promote it if you like, we could even sell tickets, what do you think?'

Dave was enthusiastic, telling her that Henry had already offered to play, and he was intending to ask Florence. Julia suggested that Dave should ask them, and once he had some idea of who could commit to playing and for how long, he could let her know. Then she could put a programme of events together.

He said goodbye, and just as he was about to shut the door, she turned back and said, 'Did you have a nice weekend? We missed you on Friday night. Florence wanted you to help her out with the duet.'

Dave smiled and said that yes, it had been nice, but didn't elaborate further.

***

Back at number two, Julia was looking at herself in the mirror, she couldn't stop smiling. She was wondering if people could tell just by looking at her that she had spent the morning in bed making love with a man she had only known for two days. She never wanted to forget the feeling of waking up in Ben's arms, his smile being the first thing she had seen.

She really hoped that they could make this work, and when she had visited her mum earlier on, she had blurted it all out. Her mum had as usual listened, and it was only when Julia paused for breath she said wryly,

'Well, I thought you liked him yesterday but looks like that's an understatement!' They had both laughed.

One thing her mum had said that put things into perspective was,

'Julia, whatever you decide to do, I can't be part of your decision.'

She pointed out how much Julia did for her, and how thankful she felt.

'I have friends and my sister, and I'm not hard up. I can do what other people do, and buy in help. I'm a lucky woman to have a daughter like you, but you need a life of your own. You put your life on hold for Steve, and look how that turned out. I could see straight away the way you and Ben feel about one another.'

Julia had felt so grateful to her mum, tearfully they had hugged but she had gone home walking on air. She spent the next couple of hours checking her work schedule for the week ahead. She finished a few admin jobs that could be done immediately. She rescheduled a couple of Monday's appointments and closed her laptop.

Ben would be leaving tomorrow after lunch, and they had agreed to spend as much of that time together as possible. She did feel a bit guilty that she was taking him away from his parents, she knew how much Anne had been looking forward to his visit, but she was hoping they would understand. Wait until tomorrow night she would have plenty to tell the girls. She felt her cheeks grow hot as she thought of seeing Ben later on.

Later that afternoon, Gary and James were just coming back from enjoying a pub lunch. They had met some friends and were feeling quite merry, having consumed a couple of pints each. Just as they walked into the Close, they saw Freda with Freddie. Gary, feeling emboldened by the fact that he was with James, called over and made a fuss of the dog, who was beside himself with excitement at the prospect of having a fuss made of him by two extra people.

Freda looked a bit subdued, so James asked her if she was OK, and if she had enjoyed the karaoke. She brightened up, saying that she had sung quite a few songs and that she and Maisie would probably go back again.

'I'm a bit fed up as it happens, Maisie won't go to the teatime jam session, miserable so-and-so said she thought we were doing the karaoke instead.'

James looked at her, thinking he must have missed something.

'Freda, if you want to go that badly go on your own. You must know some other regulars there by now.'

Gary couldn't help but grin to himself as Freda looked at James and said, 'Do you fancy coming along?'

James laughed out loud and said,

'No, it's a school night. I've got to wash my smalls.'

At that moment, Henry and Anne's car slid into the drive. Gary and James called them over. But before they could be introduced, Freda blurted out,

241

'I saw you hugging Julia this morning. I didn't know she had a boyfriend.'

Ben smiled at her, saying;

'Pleased to meet you; Freda, isn't it?

And this must be Freddie.' He bent down to fuss the dog, smiling to himself. Mum had always taught him to disarm people with a smile, even if they are rude and irritating.

Anne couldn't resist showing them all pictures of their new great-grandson, telling everyone they had just returned from meeting him for the very first time. Henry smiled as the neighbours made all the right noises.

Freda reciprocated, showing them photos of Hannah when she was a few days old and a more recent one of her looking adorable, standing on the bottom stair and singing a nursery rhyme.

To Henry's amazement, it was James who asked how much the baby had weighed and what his name was. He was impressed.

Even I didn't ask how much he weighed, it wouldn't have occurred to me.

He couldn't resist telling them, however, that the baby had been named Henry after his great-granddad. He felt quite touched, although he would never mention it. Anne had insisted on taking a photo of the four generations, which was now her screen saver, and he had to admit to feeling quite emotional looking at the picture of all of them sitting on Callum's sofa with him cradling little Henry in his arms.

Throughout this exchange, Ben had been throwing the odd glance over to Julia's house. As they headed home to number twelve Anne said, 'Not you, Ben. You've been dying to get over to see Julia since we got out of the car, go on, you can tell her how pleased Alicia and Callum were with the teddy that she bought for little Henry.'

Ben smiled at his mum gratefully. 'Don't wait up. I've got the spare key.'

Chapter 42

Once Freda was back indoors, she settled Freddie with a bowl of water and a few biscuits. Thinking about what she had said to Ben, she did feel a twinge of guilt. She had wanted to put him on the spot, and that was mean.

When she had seen Julia's blissful expression as Ben hugged her this morning, she had felt a surge of pure jealousy. What was wrong with her? She felt like such a bitch. She felt a prickle of shame as she remembered that Ben had spotted her looking at them. When she had heard Julia's peal of laughter, she had wondered if they were laughing at her.

These last few months, impervious to Maisie's pleas to stop, she had continued having liaisons with young men from Match Makers. Some she had seen more than once and she had enjoyed the heady excitement of texting and exchanging photos. But the physical aspect, apart from the few encounters with her handsome young Chippendale, Jan - had been deeply disappointing.

She was striving for something, what exactly it was, she didn't know. Until this morning, that is, when she had seen Julia and Ben together.

Just the way they looked at one another, how he held her for the longest time, neither one of them wanting to let go, made her realise that they were in love.

She didn't have that with any of the men that visited her. There was absolutely no emotional connection. And if she was being honest, she knew there never would be. They were looking to her to fulfil their fantasies. She allowed them to do the things that their wives and girlfriends would never countenance.

She had a moment of clarity after seeing Anne and Henry with Ben. They were a close family and enjoyed an easy relationship. Anne got on well with her daughter-in-law, the whole family had got together to visit the new baby and they had accepted without being upset that Ben wanted to spend the rest of this precious weekend with Julia.

Thinking about the awkwardness between her and Blake, she had to admit that it wasn't all down to that awful night when he had blundered in and found her waiting for Bryn. No, it was awkward because she didn't get on with Mandy, and then there was the relationship with her siblings.

Things had gone badly wrong there after their mum had died. Taking stock, Freda realised that she should be building bridges with the people she loved before trying to start new relationships. She had a lot of thinking to do.

Upstairs at number two, Julia was taking a long soak in the bath; Ben had used the shower and was wrapped in a towel. He was trying to find his way around Julia's kitchen. Eventually, he prepared a simple pasta dish, having made a tomato sauce out of some large overripe vine tomatoes and some garlic and chopped basil. He lit a candle, found half a bottle of white wine in the fridge and set the table.

Ben smiled as he remembered Julia's delight at seeing him appear a lot earlier than she had expected him. She drew him into the house and greeted him with a long lingering kiss.

His lips tingled and his skin felt sensitive to her touch. He showered her face and neck with the lightest of kisses, and by mutual consent, they went upstairs. Their lovemaking lasted a long time, and only when it was over and they lay contentedly in the cocoon of the duvet did Ben tell her about the afternoon.

He told her how his dad had been delighted that the new baby had been named after him.

'He'd never admit it, but I thought I saw a tear in his eye.'

She smiled when he said that, Henry was an old softie. Callum and Alicia had loved the teddy, and had sent their thanks. Ben showed her a picture of little Henry, and Julia found herself oohing over him, he really was gorgeous. Ben made her laugh when he told her about Freda.

'I just ignored what she said and petted the dog. I don't know if she thought Mum didn't know about us and she was trying to cause trouble, or if she just speaks without thinking.'

Julia nodded;' I think she just speaks without thinking, she isn't malicious just a bit thoughtless.'

He went on to say that his mum had sent him packing when she realised he was looking longingly over at number two.

Taking a large bath sheet out of the airing cupboard, Ben went into the bathroom. Holding the towel up, he said, 'Dinner's about to be served. Come on, let's get you dried and dressed for dinner.'

She stood up, and he wrapped her up and carried her to the bedroom.

'It's very tempting to just take you back to bed,' he whispered, 'but I think we need to eat something to keep our strength up.'

In the end, they sat in the kitchen wrapped in large bath towels, eating pasta, drinking wine and talking nineteen to the dozen. Julia was impressed with his cooking skills.

'I can't believe you produced something as delicious as this with the inferior ingredients from my fridge, you didn't even ask me where anything was.'

She leaned across and kissed him gently on the lips savouring the intimacy and the taste of wine and tomatoes.

Steve never would have done anything like this; he would have taken me out to dinner, but would never think of cooking for me.

'I don't know how I'll manage without seeing you for the next couple of weeks.'

Ben was lying next to Julia, stroking her hair as he tried to work out when he could next fit in a visit. She had been telling him about the fundraiser, and how Dave was hoping that Henry and some other musicians would be playing.

'I've promised to do the publicity for it, I'll check with the landlady first. But it's for such a great cause, and if we make it a big event, it'll make more money.'

Taking her iPad away, closing it firmly and putting it on the bedside table, Ben started kissing her.

'I need to leave by twelve tomorrow.'

Returning his kisses enthusiastically, Julia drew away slightly and said cheekily, 'That's twelve hours away! How many times do you think we can make love between now and then?'

Ben gave her his lazy smile before covering her lips with his own, and drawing her into his arms. 'One...' he whispered.

After breakfast the next morning, they were trying to work out the logistics of a long distance relationship. Looking at her intently, Ben brushed the hair gently away from her eyes and said, 'Julia, whatever happens, I promise I'll be back for the fundraiser. I've still got   holiday due.'

In turn, she promised to try to get a few days off and finish off any outstanding jobs. They agreed that they should get away for a few days. It was difficult starting a new relationship any time, but with Ben's parents only over the road and the neighbours interested in their romance, it was a bit like being on a stage; albeit one with a sympathetic audience.

It was Julia who drew away first, saying gently, 'I hate goodbyes, but you'd better go back to number twelve, your parents have hardly seen you.'

Reluctantly, Ben made a move. He was going to have lunch with Anne and Henry, and then drive back to Cornwall. He was back at work first thing in the morning. In the end, they agreed to FaceTime at 10.30pm so that they could say goodnight.

'Roger and Valerie make it work, so I hope we can.'

Julia's heart sank a little at the thought of not seeing Ben for five weeks.

Chapter 43

Henry was practising his set for the fundraiser, and his singing could be heard from the garage. Valerie was very complimentary.

'Is that really Henry? I know he sang at my house, but I hadn't realised what a good range he had. That's a Dusty song, isn't it?'

Anne smiled, and explained that Henry was a great fan of Dusty.

'That's our song,' she whispered as he launched into "The Look of Love". 'It's a bit embarrassing at gigs because he sings it to me.'

'Aah, that's lovely! Roger and I call you the lovebirds, you know. You're so cute, the way you go off on your walks hand in hand.' Valerie laughed heartily as she saw Anne begin to blush. 'Sorry, Anne, only teasing I just hope Roger and I are still as happy as you two when we've put the time in you have.'

Valerie had been admiring the painting and had let out a shriek when she had spotted Anne and Henry on the picture.

'There, hand in hand, he's captured you two perfectly.'

She gave Anne a nudge and they both laughed. Anne said that Ben meeting Julia had turned into a bit of a whirlwind for all of them, but the whole family were delighted for them.

Anne confided in Valerie that Ben had been on his own far too long.

'His last girlfriend was very independent, very reserved too, they never seemed like a proper couple to me. She rarely came to stay with us, and when we went to Cornwall, she was often away.'

They swiftly changed the subject as they were joined by Julia. Anne went off to get more tea, and the three of them settled down to their meeting.

True to his word, Dave had asked the others to play. Henry had smiled to himself as he remembered Dave waxing lyrical about the talent in Capulet Close alone. He had said, 'Florence is only young but she plays and sings and reads music! She even writes her own songs.' He went on to say, 'I've heard you in that garage, Henry, I reckon you could do a full day on your own.'

Henry had laughed, and joked, 'Steady on, Dave! I think people might get a bit fed up if I performed for the whole day.'

'Exactly,' agreed Dave, 'that's why we need to do a short set each.'

Henry looked at him, and realised that there was no irony there. Dave was a nice bloke, but didn't do jokes. Henry was only just getting to know him, and realised that he took everything literally.

'OK, we've got me, your band, Florence; Who else?'

Dave said, 'What about Freda? She really wanted to sing with the band, but our lot couldn't jam along for her. They only read music, but you could, Henry, you're good at improvising.'

***

Julia updated the others on what would be happening on the day. Sharon was organising a raffle, and she had managed to secure some high value prizes such as a weekend break and theatre tickets. Casually, Julia mentioned that Ben had offered to donate one of his seascape paintings. Scrolling through her phone, she showed them the photo of the picture he had gifted them. He would bring it with him the Friday before the fundraiser.

Valerie said, tongue in cheek, 'Are you getting the spare room ready for him then, Anne?'

Anne smiled at Julia, saying, 'Where do you think he'd rather be staying, Valerie; with the love of his life or with his aged parents?'

They both laughed affectionately as they saw Julia's face light up, just hearing his name bought a smile to her lips and Anne had noticed that she mentioned his name at every opportunity.

I remember what that was like.

Anne had offered to go over and ask Freda if she would be willing to sing some songs, Freda had been flattered, especially when Anne had told her it was Dave's idea to ask her.

'Really, he wouldn't let me sing with the band, I had to go to an open mic to get the chance to sing.'

Patiently, Anne had explained that Dave's band couldn't just jam along, but Henry was willing and able to accompany her on the guitar. She asked Freda to call in later in the week to talk to Henry, but meanwhile, think of three songs that she knew well enough to sing.

As soon as Anne had left, Freda was straight on the phone to Maisie. 'You'll come, won't you? It's in a good cause, and the tickets are only a fiver each.'

Maisie was pleased for her friend. She thought Freda had a lovely voice, and had supported her by taking her to karaoke and to the Sunday Jam session.

Phew! That lets me off the hook for a couple of weeks then.

Maisie thought that if Freda was busy rehearsing, she wouldn't want to be out and about so much.

It simply never occurred to Freda that she got a lot more out of their nights out than Maisie did. Sometimes, especially if Freda was having a crisis of confidence, Maisie felt as though she spent most of the night massaging her friend's ego. On a good night, she ended up sitting on her own as Freda enjoyed a tipple and lapped up the admiration and the applause of the audience. Freda had also taken a while to realise that when Maisie had had enough and she said she was going, she meant it. Maisie had taken Valerie's advice and had put some boundaries in place.

***

James offered to sell tickets once they were printed, and he thought that Lary and Luke might be interested in doing a set too. He promised to mention it to them, and let Dave know as soon as possible. Henry and Dave were thinking that they might use the next Stompers rehearsal to have a run through with everyone who would be playing. That gave everyone two weeks to practise their songs.

Florence was really happy to be performing at such a big event. So far, she had only been involved in recitals or concerts that the school put on. It would be great to be involved in a proper fundraiser. She smiled as she recalled her mother's reaction to Dave's request.

He had stood on the doorstep, refusing Valerie's invitation to come in. He always seemed a bit nervous around her mother, and she couldn't help noticing that he stood a respectable distance away from the door. Valerie had called Florence straight away, and he had visibly relaxed as he explained the plan of the day and how long she would be expected to play.

Florence jotted down notes, and promised to drop her set list round to Julia so that it could be added to the programme. Once they had finished talking about the event,

Florence could see that Dave wasn't sure whether to talk to Valerie again or just go. So she thanked him and said, 'Dave's off now, Mum.'

Poor Dave looked like a rabbit in the headlights as Valerie launched herself at him, giving him an enthusiastic hug and saying,

'Thank you for thinking of Florence. It'll be such a good experience playing with all of you.'

With that, she stood on the doorstep smiling broadly, and waving to him as he staggered back to the safety of his house.

Chapter 44

Julia was cuddled up on her sofa with the fleece blanket over her knee, waiting for Ben's FaceTime call. Ali and Angie had teased her mercilessly when she kept looking at her watch this evening. Angie had been hosting their Monday night, and they knew that Julia and Ben's FaceTime had become sacrosanct. So although they enjoyed winding her up, they made sure that the evening finished in good time for her to get back home for Ben's call.

In fact, the Monday that Ben had left to go back to Cornwall, Julia had been hosting the evening. She had asked them if they wanted to hang about and say hello to him, but they could tell that she was anxious to see him again, so took pity on her and declined.

'No, we'll leave you love birds to it. You can introduce us at the fund raiser.'

Julia smiled as she remembered their excitement when they had heard her happy news.

'Do I look different?' she had greeted Angie as she opened the door to her that evening.

'You look very happy and excited. Is it more work? Have you won the lottery?'

Ali joined them a few minutes later, and Julia poured them all a glass of prosecco and declared,

'I'm in love, girls! Can you tell? I can't believe it, I met him as I was leaving Valerie's on Friday night, but just said hello. I could only see his eyes; he was carrying an enormous parcel. Then I met him again Saturday afternoon, in a garden centre of all places.'

They both hugged her, absolutely delighted for her. She whispered that they had spent most of the weekend in bed. She blushed as they whooped, cheered and raised their glasses.

'About time, here's to girl power.'

They were joking, but it was obvious to her friends that she was besotted with him. By the end of the evening, they knew almost as much about Ben as Julia did, and they were very much looking forward to meeting him.

Julia answered the call, and as Ben's lazy smile came into focus, they caught up on their news. They were still Face timing every night, and never seemed to run out of things to talk about.

Julia couldn't help comparing Ben to Steve, she realised it was a very different situation because her and Steve had met when they were so young, and had worked together. But even in the early days of their relationship, Steve had never really been interested in her friends, or what she had been doing.

Ben, on the other hand, loved to hear about her Monday nights with Angie and Ali. He always asked about her work and how the fundraiser was coming along. And he was always telling her how much he loved and admired her. Steve had loved her, but he wasn't a very affectionate man, even before their marriage was coming to an end. She recalled that he rarely kissed her in passing, or even held her hand if they were out together.

'Guess what, I've got a surprise for you.'

Ben couldn't guess what it could be.

'A weekend away? Have you painted me a picture?

With every guess, Julia's smile widened.

'Don't keep me in suspense,' he wailed.

'OK, I'm driving over to see you tomorrow night, staying until Thursday morning.'

His face lit up. 'Julia, that's just the best news! Thank you, I love you for this, what a great surprise. We'll go on beach walks, and you can come to the gallery with me and meet everyone.'

Looking back to his relationship with Karina, he realised that everything was on her terms. He had loved her independence, but Karina would never compromise. The fact that Julia was willing to drive for five hours midweek in order for them to spend a day together made him realise that she felt exactly the same as he did.

As Julia lay in bed that night, she hugged herself with excitement. Tomorrow, she would be spending a whole day and two nights with Ben. She couldn't wait. She could kick herself that she hadn't thought of it before. It was only when she was at her mum's on Sunday and she was saying that it would be another four weeks before she saw Ben that her mum said,

'Why? It's a five hour drive, Julia, not another country.'

Her mum had pointed out that there had to be some benefits to being self-employed.

'You can set your own hours, can't you?'

Julia remembered Ben saying that all good things are worth working for, and that prompted her to have a rethink. She worked the rest of Sunday in order to get ahead with a couple of projects she was working on. She knew that Ben's day off from the gallery was a Wednesday, so she had arranged to travel to Cornwall after she had finished work on Tuesday afternoon, then she could spend all of Wednesday with him. And she could travel back on Thursday morning. Julia fell asleep with a smile on her face, dreaming of walking barefoot in the sand, hand in hand with Ben.

She was up bright and early Tuesday morning she packed enough clothes for two days. The forecast for Cornwall was bright, breezy and about 18 degrees. Just right for beach walks. Ben had told her to pack something nice for

Wednesday evening as he wanted to take her out to dinner. She realised when he said that that they had never been out together, apart from walks, that is.

A jolt of pleasure hit her as she remembered why that was. They had spent more time in bed together than anywhere else.

Flicking through her wardrobe, she chose a floaty dress that came to just below the knee. It had a V-neck with embroidery around the neck and the hem; it was one of the dresses she had bought just after she started the business. She had worn it once before when she had been out with her friends, and she had felt like a million dollars in it. Teamed with her amber jewellery, it complimented her colouring and bought out the highlights in her hair. Slipping in a pair of low-heeled shoes and her denim jacket, she thought that she had chosen well.

She had a couple of clients to see this morning but she aimed to leave by 2.30pm at the latest. She was hoping to be with Ben by 8pm. She left her bags by the front door and headed out to the car. She waved to Dave, who was leaving for work, and then she saw Anne hurrying towards her.

'Julia, before you go, can I have a quick word?'

Anne told her that she had a brilliant idea for the fundraiser. She had spoken to Sharon about it, she was going to have her head shaved, and people could sponsor her. Julia wasn't sure she would be able to bring herself to do such a thing herself, but she admired Anne, and agreed that it would bring in a lot more money. She gave her a hug, and told her that she would be seeing Ben that evening. Anne laughed,

'I know he was on the phone last night as soon as you'd told him! Bubbling with excitement, he was. I was thinking last night that he was with Karina for more than twelve years, and I don't remember her ever doing anything that thoughtful for him.' She paused.

'Julia; do me a favour; don't tell Ben about the head shave. I'd prefer to tell the boys myself, I don't think they'll like the idea. I know Henry didn't, but I've talked him round.'

Julia agreed, and they parted company.

***

The idea had only occurred to her as she was brushing her hair last week. Just two weeks after having her hair professionally coloured, those grey streaks were already reappearing. Henry had suggested leaving it and letting it grow out gradually. He had hugged her and told her, 'The grey will just look like highlights.'

Anne looked at him incredulously. 'Henry, it won't, I'll look like a badger with light patches all over.'

She smiled at him, he genuinely didn't think it mattered whether her hair was grey or not. And actually, neither did she; it was just that she couldn't bear looking at it while it was growing out.

It was then that the idea came to her. She could have her head shaved on the day of the fundraiser. She could get sponsors, and that way, her hair would grow back naturally. She would save a fortune at the hairdresser's. When she told Henry, he had hated the idea.

'But I love your hair Anne. I never liked it when you had it really short. It's looks lovely now you wear it a bit longer. Let me do it; I wear mine short anyway.'

Anne couldn't stop laughing;

'Bless you Hen. You're such a lovely man but nobody's going to pay to see someone with hardly any hair shaving their head. It'll raise more money if it's someone like me.'

Eventually, Anne persuaded Henry to at least let her suggest it to Sharon. After all, it was her fundraiser.

Chapter 45

Later that morning, Anne was busy in the kitchen. Henry was in the garage with Freda, patiently coaching her through one of her songs. Anne could hear that Freda was repeatedly making the same mistake, and although Henry was being very calm, she could sense that Freda was getting frustrated. So she took in a tray of tea and suggested they took a break. Anne complimented Freda on her singing.

'You've got a lovely voice, and I love the songs you've chosen.'

Henry asked Freda if she thought it would help if he made her a backing track of all of her songs; that way, she could practise at home. He reminded her that it was going to be a lot different to a jam session or karaoke.

'This is a professional gig; you can't just sing the songs a couple of times and say that'll do.'

Freda left Henry later that day with a CD and instructions to sing them all several times a day.

'Next time we meet, Freda, you need to know those songs and the lyrics inside out.'

Freda confided in Maisie when they spoke later that day that she was getting bored with them already.

'Henry says I've got to sing them until I'm sick of them, or else I'll never get them right. But I reckon when this is over, I'll never sing them again.'

Freda was finding singing with Henry quite difficult; he stopped her for every little mistake, even making her start again if she got the slightest thing wrong. He was a hard taskmaster, and Freda felt as though she was being made to work very hard indeed.

Freda had at last decided to build some bridges with her family. Instead of moaning that Blake only brought Hannah over when he wanted something, she spoke to Mandy. She had always presumed that Mandy didn't like her, but when she answered the phone, she seemed genuinely pleased to hear from her. They had a short conversation, and then Freda told Mandy about the fundraiser and that she would be singing. She offered to get Mandy, Blake and the children tickets. Mandy had been chuffed to bits,

'Thanks, Freda, that's a lovely idea. Blake will love it, especially when he knows you're singing. He's always telling the kids what a great voice Nanny's got.'

Really?

Freda was taken aback to hear this, she was usually lucky to get two words out of her son, and it was hard to know exactly how he felt about anything. Before she could stop herself, she asked Mandy if she would like her to pick Hannah up from nursery one day a week.

In a fit of generosity, she suggested that she could stay for tea and Archie could pick her up later. At first, she didn't think Mandy was keen, as she hesitated before replying. But she thanked Freda and asked if a Wednesday would be OK, because that was the one day she couldn't guarantee getting back in time.

Freda felt so happy when she came off the phone that she decided to strike while the iron was hot and phone Phil. He was the youngest of her siblings and she somehow thought he would be more receptive to her suggestion than the others. When he answered the phone, she could hear from his voice that he was pleased that she had called.

'Yes, I'm in, sis. I remember you making us listen to you when we were kids, the Long-Haired Beauty from Leicester, I seem to remember.'

They laughed together and reminisced some more. It was an emotional phone -call, Freda was the last person to back down over a row. But she missed them badly and she wanted them to be there to hear her sing and share in her success. Phil said that their brother John was working away, but he would speak to the girls, he was sure they would love to come along.

James popped round to see Dave after work. Luckily, he had seen him drive into the garage, and he knocked the door straight away

Good job too. Glad he didn't knock later, he'd have interrupted my make- up tutorial.

Relief made Dave more affable than usual, and he invited James to step inside. James was too polite to show it, but he couldn't help being shocked at the state of the hallway. Piles of post littered the floor, and there were a couple of unopened parcels on the bottom stair. The carpet was covered in fluff, and the downstairs doors were all shut. He could only guess at the state of the rooms beyond.

Realising that Dave wondered what he was there for he quickly got to the point. . James confirmed that Lary and Luke were happy to play at the fundraiser and quickly showed Dave a recording of them singing, and playing "Hey Jude" and "Here Comes the Sun".

Dave was impressed, especially with their harmonies.

'Thank them and let them know that they'll need to come along for the run through at The Half Moon.'

James agreed and went back home. As he opened the front door, he couldn't help contrasting the light bright hallway with the coats and shoes neatly put away in the hall cupboard with the dusty, dark cluttered hallway of number four.

Chapter 46

Dave made himself a quick meal, and once he had put the dishes in soak, he went upstairs. He had found a tutorial on YouTube, and decided to follow it step by step. He felt a small tremor of excitement as he shaved and moisturised, before getting his make-up out and setting it out on the dressing table.

Before starting with the make-up, he had got himself changed. Kandy was quite casual today - jeans, white trainers and a blue and white striped long-sleeved T-shirt. Putting on the headband as instructed, Dave used foundation and blended it with a sponge to even out the skin tone. Blusher was used to highlight cheekbones, and a dusting of powder completed the look.

He wasn't seeking to contour and shape or to use the layers of makeup that Daisy-May had applied. He was just hoping that using a small amount correctly would make him look more feminine. He outlined his lips, and instead of using Diva as he had in Brighton, he contented himself with a pale pink lip gloss. Critically, he looked at himself, it didn't look quite right.

Oh yes, those eyebrows.

Grimacing, Dave got the tweezers and tugged the offending hairs from under his brows. Once he had used an eyebrow pencil for definition and had coated his eyelashes with mascara, he felt better, more like Kandy. He carefully put on his wig, made some last minute adjustments and with one last look in the mirror, he headed downstairs. Not giving the state of the hallway a thought, Dave headed back to the living room to spend the evening watching TV.

He was so caught up in the film that it was a few seconds before he became aware that the phone was ringing. Muting the television, he reached over, and his heart sank. It was his dad.

'Hi Dad, you OK?'

'I didn't see you last Sunday, I ended up at John's for dinner, and you know those two don't drink. I missed out on my pint.'

Dave grinned to himself. 'Yes, thanks, Dad. I had a great weekend away, nice of you to ask.'

Grumpily, his Dad said, 'Well, good for you. Let me know in good time next time you go away, and then I'll get out of going to John's. I'd have been better off taking myself out for a pub lunch.'

Dave was just about to jolly his dad along when he caught a glimpse of Kandy in the mirror.

'Are you still there, Son?'

Dave felt such a crushing sense of guilt come over him that he couldn't get any words out for a few seconds. When he did finally answer, he said croakily,

'Dad, I'll call you back tomorrow. There's someone at the door.'

The evening was spoilt, the pleasure in relaxing in Kandy's clothes just watching a film had gone, he could feel his dad's disapproval through the phone. He knew that was ridiculous, but he felt just by talking to his dad while he was dressed as Kandy, he was being deceitful. And his dad never tolerated lying from either of his sons. Dave was honest by nature, and he was finding his deception very difficult to live with.

In the end, he decided to call his daughter. Since his dad's birthday, Dave had made a lot more effort to contact Heather regularly, and they had got into the habit of chatting one evening a week. He had to smile, because she was always so busy, often she would be on her way to a bar or club or maybe on her way home from work. Unlike him, she wouldn't stop to take the call she would just carry on walking. So the conversation was peppered with traffic sounds and the occasional babble of Spanish voices. She always seemed glad to hear from him, and he was pleased that he had instigated it.

Dave took off the make-up, hung up Kandy's clothes and pulled on his tatty old dressing gown before making the call. To his surprise, Heather was actually at home for once.

'Glad you called, Dad, I'm catching up on a bit of cleaning. Mum's coming out for a few days, and you know what a clean freak she is.'

Dave looked around his living room and smiled; from what Heather had told him, her housekeeping was more to his standards than her mother's. So it was going to take her more than a few hours to get her apartment straight before Diane arrived. She asked him about the fundraiser and then they talked about holidays. When he mentioned Brighton, she burst out laughing.

'You didn't tell Granddad, did you? I can imagine him, he'd be saying...', and in a scarily accurate imitation of his dad, she said;

'Don't know why you'd bother going there, Son, wall to wall poofs and pansies, wasn't like that in my day.'

Dave laughed heartily at that, but he just said,

'You know your granddad. He was more irritated at missing out on our Sunday pint he didn't even ask where I'd been.'

'Well, he won't change now, will he?'
There was a second's pause in the conversation, and Heather, catching Dave off guard, said,

'Dad, what were you doing in Brighton?'

Before he could stop himself, it all came pouring out. The occasional wearing of her mother's dressing gown when he was feeling low and how he had been dressing as Kandy at home. He apologised for keeping his distance since she had moved away. When she did come home, not only did he presume she would rather stay with her mother, but he felt awkward inviting her to the house because he had Kandy's wardrobe upstairs.

Dave finally paused to draw breath. Heather hadn't hung up. In fact, the line was so quiet, he wondered if she was still there. Hardly daring to breathe, he waited. Heather sounded a little subdued when she spoke.

'Dad, it's a lot for me to take in. I can't say I'm not shocked, but it does explain a lot.'

Just sharing his secret, Dave felt as though an enormous weight had been lifted from his shoulders. Later that evening, he had a text message from Heather, telling him,

Love you Dad, let's Face Time tomorrow night.

***

The next day in his lunch break, Dave gave his dad a quick call. They arranged to go for their usual Sunday pint, and his dad was delighted when he suggested that they stay for a pub lunch. They chatted for a minute, and Dave was amazed when his dad said, '

'I look forward to our Sunday pint all week; it's not the same going to John's.'

Blimey, that's not like Dad to climb down. He must have missed me.

Later that evening, Heather made the FaceTime call. He smiled to himself. In many ways, she was like her mum. Good with people, sociable and friendly. But in other ways,

271

she was like him. Messy and she didn't care how she looked. Her apartment, in spite of her blitzing it the day before, still definitely wouldn't meet Diane's exacting standards. Clothes didn't bother her either; with Heather, it was about comfort over style.

As her face came into view, she came straight to the point.

'Dad, I'm OK with it. Honestly, I am, but I do have a lot of questions.'

Dave felt a lump in his throat, when she was a little girl, she drove Diane mad. She always questioned everything. Dave remembered it was something that he had loved about her; she was so curious. And he was endlessly patient, doing his best to answer her, but in a way that satisfied her childish curiosity.

'Fire away, I'm just glad you're taking it so well.'

Her first question was whether he was going out all dressed up. Dave explained more fully his feelings around dressing up. He said that he was fearful of her grandfather finding out.

'He'd presume I wanted to be a woman. He wouldn't understand that there are people like me who just enjoy dressing in women's clothes.'

He went on to explain that after going to Brighton, which he had thoroughly enjoyed, he wouldn't really consider going out alone dressed up.

272

'It was great there, I had someone with me, the places we went to catered for cross dressers, and it was good fun.'

He pointed out what hard work it was just to get dressed and made up.

'I had to shave three times in one day, I usually only shave three times a week.'

Heather teased him, saying, 'Yes, that was always Mum's gripe, wasn't it?

'*Your personal grooming, David, leaves a lot to be desired.* That always irritated her.'

He grimaced, 'I do feel bad about the way I was with your mum. I should have made more effort.'

Heather said something quite insightful at that point.

'Dad, don't beat yourself up, I think you and Mum were just too different. You stayed together for long enough to launch me into the world, and that was enough, I can tell you're both much happier living apart.'

He made Heather laugh, telling her about the club and the young man singing to Daisy-May. He finished the call feeling closer to his daughter than he had in a long while.

Chapter 47

Julia drove into Capulet Close on Thursday afternoon. She felt blissfully happy after spending time with Ben. As she unpacked the car and ferried everything back into the house, her thoughts were still in Cornwall.

It had been a good journey, and she had arrived by 7.30pm, earlier than either of them had expected. She had parked the car just in front of the cottage, and before she could get out, Ben was tugging the door open. They were so happy to be together that they stood on the pavement, arms around one another, talking and laughing. Julia breathed him in, just enjoying the feeling of being in his arms..

Reluctantly, Ben had let her go. He opened the door to the cottage and ushered her inside. She was surprised to see how light and airy it was. It was an old fisherman's cottage, only two streets away from the beach. The smell of the sea hung in the air, and the sea breeze was gentle in the chill of the evening. As he showed her around, she realised that the light came from the kitchen. It had been extended, and glass patio doors led out onto a decking area with comfortable seating. The rest of the garden - little more than a yard, really - was festooned with pots of colourful flowers.

'I wasn't expecting this, it's like a Tardis.'

The modern kitchen had a glass roof, which even in the early evening made the room seem lighter.

Standing in the middle of the kitchen with Ben's arms around her, Julia became aware of some delicious smells assailing her nostrils.

'Mmm, that smells gorgeous! The pasta sauce you made at mine wasn't just fluke, was it? Tell me you're a marvellous cook and I can hang up my apron.'

He laughed out loud, 'I love cooking, and it's been a pleasure to cook for you, because you appreciate it so much.'

She felt sad for him when he told her that Karina hadn't been interested in food, and while he always made an effort to cook something she liked, she would respond with;

'Don't worry about me. A sandwich will do.'

Kissing him on the lips, she said solemnly, 'Well, I can promise you, Ben, that I'll never refuse anything you've cooked for me in favour of a sandwich.'
She also reassured him that she would take her turn with cooking.

'I'm not the best cook, but I can follow a recipe, so neither of us will starve.'

Ben had taken her upstairs they stepped out of the narrow landing into a large whitewashed room, dominated by a king-sized bed covered in a crisp white cotton duvet. Muslin curtains fluttered against the slightly open windows, and two huge seascapes adorned the walls. Ben beckoned her over. He put his arms around her and told her to close her eyes. Pulling the curtain aside, he said, 'Open your eyes. What do you think?'

'Oh, that's beautiful!'

The tide was coming in, and the sea rolled over the beach with a soft whooshing sound.

'We can take a walk along the beach later,' whispered Ben. 'But first we need to eat.'

Lost in thought and reliving every precious minute of her time with Ben, Julia's reverie was interrupted by the phone ringing.

Oh well, back to reality.

It was work. She answered her client's questions then after preparing a salad for lunch Julia spent a couple of hours catching up on e-mails and her schedule for the next few days. Spending those couple of days together had been idyllic. Even so, she was well aware that in order to keep on top of things she would have to work longer days, and some of the weekend too.

Later that evening, she had a long chat with her mum, who reassured her that she had been absolutely fine. 'Your aunt took me out to lunch yesterday, and this morning I had a surprise visitor; guess who?'

Julia laughed, 'Mum, you get so many people popping in for coffee. I'd be hard pressed to remember them all.'

Her mum was so sunny-natured. Although she couldn't always get out and about, people would often visit, and forgetting that her health wasn't that good, used her as a sounding board for their problems. Julia was touched to hear that the visitor was Anne,

'We had a lovely chat, and the time flew. The two of us have really hit it off, and they both love you, Julia.'

Julia was glad; she was already becoming very fond of Anne and Henry

Maria went on to tell Julia that Ben's parents had been quite worried after Karina had gone back to Poland.

'Anne said he went very quiet, and although he was still working at the gallery, he lost his spark for a while. He didn't paint anything for two years.'

Julia knew all about that; the two of them had quite a heart to heart. They learnt that they had both been treated badly by their partners, and had both done their best to keep a flagging relationship going, unwilling to believe that things were not quite right. Julia told her mum about the gallery.

'Mum, you should see it. Ben's got a couple of his own pictures in there, but there are paintings from quite well-known artists too. Billy Connolly had some of his pictures in there recently, and Johnny Depp too.'

She described Ben's cottage and the delicious meal he had prepared for her.

'I bet you're glad I suggested it,' teased her mum. 'If I hadn't got onto you about it, the pair of you would be pining away, relying on your FaceTime calls.'

Julia had to agree.

She was still smiling when she told her mum about how excited Ben was at her surprise visit, and that he was so touched that she would do that for him, that now they were going to take turns with the travelling. One week, it would be her travelling to Ben. Then the following week, Ben would do the travelling.

'I should think so too. Seize the moment, that's what your dad and I always tried to do.'

***

Later on, Julia was pouring a glass of wine for Valerie when Anne rang the bell. Ushering Anne inside, Julia finished pouring the drinks and couldn't help but laugh as they both blurted out, 'Well?'

Keeping a straight face, she said, 'Sorry, what on earth are you talking about?'

Seeing that they were dying to hear about her trip, Julia gave them the censored version. She loved them both, but she had to remind herself that Anne was Ben's mum; she couldn't share everything.

She told them how excited they were to see one another. The lovely meal Ben had cooked for her. How much admired the cottage. She sighed as she recalled the beach walks and the smell of the sea. But she hugged the memory

278

to herself of that first night when they kissed under the stars, of Ben making love to her on the big white bed and how they woke up in the mornings to the sound of the sea and that beautiful sea view.

They loved hearing about the trip to the restaurant. She blushed as she recalled that the owner, who was a friend of Ben's, had brought out a dessert at the end of the meal; A tiny delicious chocolate brownie with a small scoop of homemade vanilla ice cream. And on her plate, drawn with chocolate sauce, was a heart. Underneath was piped, 'Ben loves Julia.' Anne was so caught up in the story that Julia realised she hadn't touched her wine.

Valerie nudged Anne and whispered, 'It looks as though Ben and Julia are going to follow in yours and Henry's footsteps; another pair of love birds.'

Julia couldn't stop laughing. 'A lovely thought, Valerie, but Ben and I are in our forties already. If we're lucky enough to put the time in that Anne and Henry have, we'll be getting on for ninety-four.'

Anne caught Valerie's eye and the three women started to giggle.

The real reason Julia had invited her neighbours round was to show them the posters, tickets and the programme that she had put together for the event. Everything had arrived by courier that afternoon.

'Have you been given a budget for that?'

Valerie was concerned that if they didn't sell tickets, Julia would be out of pocket. Julia explained that she had priced it up, and Sharon had told her that the owners of the pub would pay, so she had invoiced them as she would any job. Julia had included a piece about Anne having her head shaved, with all proceeds going to the charity. She quickly gave Anne a sponsor form that she had made on the computer.

'Have you told Ben and Adam yet?' She hadn't mentioned it to Ben, but she was keen that he should know before he came up on Tuesday.

Anne smiled, 'Actually, they do. I had a chat with both of them before I came over. I Face Timed them together. They both said that they weren't keen, but they were more worried about how I'd feel after it had been cut.' She went on to say that Helen had been supportive, and had promised to get her some nice summer hats. They had all agreed to sponsor her as well.

The conversation turned to the new baby. Anne's face lit up when she spoke about him.

'We've only seen him once, but Alicia and Callum are bringing him over on Sunday afternoon.'
She looked at Julia, and asked if her and her mum would like to join them for tea and cake.

'It's only right that you should meet your youngest client.'

Seeing Valerie's puzzled look, Julia quickly reminded her that she had designed the bedroom for little Henry, and then Callum had given his grandparents Julia's number.

'It's a small world right enough.' Smiling broadly Valerie gathered her things together and hugged them both goodbye. They both took twenty tickets each, and Julia intended to ask everyone else to sell them as well.

'Before you go, Anne, haven't you forgotten something?' Anne looked at Valerie.

'Let's sponsor you, the sooner you start getting sponsors the better.'

With a flourish, Valerie took out a large silver ball point pen and sponsored Anne £20. Julia matched it, then took a photo of Anne and said that she would set up a Just Giving page for her. That way, people could sponsor her online as well.

Chapter 48

Anne was unusually restless this Sunday morning, and having baked the cakes for Callum and Alicia's visit this afternoon, Henry suggested they go for a walk. Even though she hadn't said much, Henry suspected she was getting nervous about having her head shaved. As they left, they greeted Julia and Valerie, who were just coming back.

They often walked together at the weekends, especially when Roger was away. They only stopped for a brief hello as Henry was keen to tell Anne about his worries for Freda's performance.

'She still doesn't come in at the right place on 'Summertime', and that's her song.' Henry grumbled that he thought Freda had got lazy doing karaoke.

'She forgets to listen, and boy, does she hate being stopped and made to start again.'

Anne listened intently she knew that Henry fretted about these things. She recalled how frustrated he used to get playing in a band if one of the members got careless. He was a patient man, but he did think that if you were entertaining people, you should get it right.

'Thanks, Anne, I just needed to get it off my chest. I suppose it's a bit of a responsibility playing for someone who has absolutely no experience.'

Anne pointed out that Freda had only just started singing in public.

'Have a heart, you've been doing this since you were a teenager; Freda's new to all of it. If she messes up, people will understand. And she needs you to be patient, or you'll put her right off.'

'You're right as usual, Annie, I'm sure it'll be alright on the night.'

He gave her a hug, and they continued with their walk.

'What about you?'

'What about me?''

'Anne, I can read you like a book, are you regretting offering to get your head shaved?'

Taking her hand and turning her to face him, he said gently,

'You can change your mind, you know. We could just put a large donation in. I'm sure Sharon wouldn't mind as long as the event raises a decent amount of money.'

Smiling up at her husband, Anne reassured him,

'Oh Hen, of course I'm nervous. But no, I'm not going to change my mind. In fact, seeing someone like Freda who's only just started singing in public, and Florence who up until now has only performed at school events, is making me even more determined. I could never do what you all do and sing in public. This is something that I can do, and I won't back out; not now the sponsors are rolling in.'

When Anne and Henry walked back into the Close, James and Gary were just leaving. Gary waved them over, and they stood chatting for a few minutes. Anne took the opportunity to ask them if they would be willing to sell tickets for the event. They agreed to take twenty tickets each, and assured Anne that if they couldn't sell them, they would return them promptly. They all laughed when Gary said,

'I bet James will sell them at the university, no problem. He could sell snow to Eskimos.'

Anne knew just what he meant; James was certainly the confident one of the two of them. She had been amazed to learn that Gary was in the police force; he just seemed so shy and diffident compared with James. Gary touched Anne on the arm and said,

'Julia says you're having your head shaved, well done. We sponsored you on the Just Giving page, good luck; I hope people give generously.'

Gary and James were heading out to Sunday lunch, and Anne thought she should start dinner for her and Henry so that they would be cleared up in time for their visitors.

As they parted company, they noticed a commotion at Dave's front door.

'Isn't that Dave's dad?'

'Jack, Jack, what's up?'

James and Gary were already making their way over to number four, with Henry following closely behind. As they got closer, they could see Jack pacing, running his fingers through his hair with his phone in his hand. Henry put a calming hand on his shoulder.

'Jack, what's going on? Can we help?'

'It's Dave he was supposed to meet me in the Bull. When he was late, I tried to ring but he's not answering his phone. His van's still in the garage. I've been hammering on the door, but no answer.'

The poor man was distraught. Immediately, Gary took charge.

'Henry, you take Jack to your house, make him some tea. I'm going to see if I can get in.'

Gary and James couldn't see through the windows because of the tightly closed blinds; while Gary got into the back garden, James peered through the grimy glass in the front door. He thought he could see something at the bottom of the stairs, but remembering how cluttered it all was, he couldn't be sure it was a person. In fact, it looked like a pile of clothes. He was peering through the letterbox, calling Dave's name to see if he could get a response, but there was silence. Gary reappeared complaining,

'I can't see a bloody thing. The curtains are all drawn at the back. His phone's there. I rang it and it's just ringing out. I think I'm going to break in, he could be injured or anything.'

Gary used a house breaking tip to pop the double glazing in the back door then he reached through and opened the door from the inside. James stood by with his phone at the ready. Once the door was open, they both walked in, calling Dave's name. Silence, then James caught a glimpse of the hallway. It was a pile of clothes at the bottom of the stairs. All of a sudden, he heard a small moan.

'Gary, he's here.'

Dashing over to the pile of laundry, Gary and James pulled the clothes from the crumpled form lying against the stairs. Looking down, James whispered,

'Oh shit.'

Dave was lying out cold with a huge gash on his forehead, blood dripping down the side of his face onto his blue T-shirt. His make-up was smudged, and Kandy's wig had become dislodged in the fall.

'James, never mind that now, he needs an ambulance. Get onto it.'

Gary assessed the patient, ascertained that he was breathing and that nothing seemed to be broken. Poor Dave would be black and blue, as it would seem that he had tumbled head long down the stairs with a pile of laundry. James said that the ambulance was on the way, and then he spotted Henry at the living room door.

'Henry, we need you to tell Jack that we've called an ambulance, Dave's taken a fall. He's got a nasty bump on the head, and he's unconscious.'

Henry looked upset, he had taken in the situation in an instant, and he knew without being told that they couldn't let Jack see his son dressed like this. He stood in the doorway, not sure what to do. Kindly, Gary patted Henry's shoulder and said,

'Go on Henry. Dave will be fine with us, you look after Jack.'

James quickly secured the back door, he put the glass back. The lock would need fixing, but for now, he had bolted it from the inside. He then opened the front door and stood watching for the ambulance. Gary, meanwhile, was working out whether he could remove some of Dave's make-up discreetly without moving him. In the end, he gently took off the lipstick and removed the wig. He didn't dare remove any clothing; he was just thankful that Dave had chosen jeans and a T-shirt to wear today. He heard James calling,

'The ambulance is here, oh, and Jack's heading down too.'

Gary waited until the paramedics were with Dave, then plastering a reassuring smile on his face, he beckoned to Jack.

'They don't think anything's broken, but they're worried because they've no way of knowing how long he's been unconscious so they're taking him in.'

Seeing Jack's distraught expression, he said kindly,

'The ambulance people need Dave's date of birth and a few other details. If you tell them, then James and I will run you to the hospital.'

Nodding mutely, Jack went inside. Dave was already strapped to the stretcher, covered in a blanket. Jack was too upset to note the state of the hallway or the clothes on the floor, but he did comment on Dave's footwear.

'White trainers, really?'

Shaking his head, he touched his son's hand, murmuring,

'I'll let John know. See you soon, Son,'

Chapter 49

James and Gary took Jack to the hospital. By the time they arrived, Dave - having regained consciousness was waiting to be X-rayed. They told Jack that Dave's blood pressure was low and he would need a couple of stitches in the head wound. James and Gary waited with Jack until John arrived. Jack was feeling happier now that he knew Dave was conscious but they still weren't able to see him.

Dave was in a panic; he couldn't let his dad see him like this. As usual, the hospital was busy. Now his forehead had been cleaned, stitched and a dressing applied and the X-Rays had been taken. He was lying in a cubicle, abandoned on a trolley. He suspected he wouldn't see anyone now until the doctor had the results back.

When he first woke up, he felt as though he had been beaten up, and he had a pounding headache. The nurse had asked him a few questions, and once they had satisfied themselves that he hadn't lost his memory, they had asked him how he had injured himself.

He had a hazy memory of a leisurely morning. He had put on his makeup and was quite impressed as he had completed every step from memory, no longer needing the YouTube tutorial. Reluctantly, he had undergone the torture of trimming his nose hair and remembering to pluck his eyebrows, recalling with amusement Daisy-May declaring,

'No pain, no gain, my darling' in response to his agonised squeal.

He had dressed casually in jeans, a blue T-shirt and white trainers with a pink and blue trim. He set the alarm for two hours hence and even put the phone on airplane mode. Confident he wouldn't be disturbed until it was time to get changed for lunch with his Dad Dave had sat at the table reading the Sunday papers. He had a lovely relaxing morning and before he knew it the alarm was ringing. He switched it off and took airplane mode off and checked for messages.

He remembered going upstairs and thinking that he just had time to wash some of Kandy's clothes before he got changed so he had gathered together a colour wash. A novelty for him, his clothes were all black. He only did one cool wash a week, and then washed sheets and towels every two weeks on a hot wash.

That was it. He stepped down from the landing, missed his footing and tumbled down the stairs in a tangle of clothes. He winced as he recalled cracking his head, and then nothing until he woke up here in the hospital. He told the nurse that he had fallen down the stairs which tallied with the information the paramedics had gleaned from Gary and James.

Lifting the blanket, Dave was relieved to find that his clothes had been removed. Disconcertingly, he was wearing a hospital gown, one of those backless things. When the nurse came in to check his blood pressure, she told him that his dad and brother wanted to see him.

'Do you think I could look in a mirror before my dad sees me?'

Obligingly, she held up a small square mirror. Meeting his eyes, she said kindly, 'We had to clean the wound before we stitched. But we couldn't touch your eyes because of your head injury.'

Dave smiled at her gratefully he was hoping that his dad would not spot the remains of the mascara on his lashes.

John and his Dad came into the cubicle.

'You look like shit.'

Dave responded with a weak smile.

'Thanks, John, you don't need to sound quite so cheerful about it.'

He knew his brother was worried about him. His dad had obviously had a shock. Dave thought sadly that he looked every one of his ninety years today.

Jack told Dave that it was his neighbours who had found him. He explained that he didn't know what he would have done if they hadn't been there.

'They looked after me, called the ambulance for you. Henry and Anne were lovely too. They wouldn't let me in until the ambulance came. Gary checked you out and made sure you hadn't broken anything.'

Phew!

Dave sent out a silent prayer of gratitude to his neighbours.

They were interrupted by the doctor; she drew aside the curtains and explained that the X- rays showed that there were no broken bones. She added that they were going to find him a bed because he had symptoms of mild concussion.

'We need to keep you under observation overnight.'

Turning to Jack, she suggested kindly that John should take him home. Jack cheered up immensely when John offered to get him some food and buy him a pint. By the time they said their goodbyes, Dave's head was throbbing, and there wasn't one part of his body that didn't ache. The nurse came in and did her obs.

'I feel like I've been run over by a ten tonne truck, any chance of some painkillers?'

Dave felt quite pathetic, but swallowed the pain killers gratefully. Gradually, in spite of the uncomfortable trolley and the noise and chaos around him, he dozed off.

A few hours later, John and his dad had eaten some food. Once Jack was safely home, they rang the hospital and were told that Dave had been moved to a ward and was in a proper bed. Even if he did have to be woken up every two hours to have his blood pressure checked, his temperature taken and a light shone in his eyes.

Chapter 50

James and Gary had missed lunch with their friends, so after hanging around the hospital, they realised they were both ravenous. Heading for the nearest pub, they ordered food and started to mull over the events of the day.

'Well, judging by the state of the house, I'd never have guessed in a million years that Dave enjoyed wearing women's clothes.'

'Yes, I could see your face when you realised how he was dressed. To be honest, James, nothing surprises me nowadays.'

He went on to tell James about the big sixteen-stone dark swarthy inspector who had worked at the station where he had done his training. He liked women's clothes. And whether or not he ever dressed fully as a woman, no one really knew. But he wore women's underwear, under his boxer shorts. James had stopped eating, and was looking intently at Gary, his laden fork half way to his mouth.

'How did you find out?'

'He got pissed on a night out, and I had the misfortune to have to take him home.'

Gary started laughing as he recalled thinking he ought to at least remove his shirt and trousers and leave a bowl by the bed in case he was ill.

'That was it he was wearing red satin French knickers. Like parachutes, they were. I was dreading seeing him again, but he just looked straight through me as if it had never happened.'

'What did you do?'

'Not a thing.'

James caught Gary's eye, and that was it, they were both laughing until they cried.

The two of them made their way back to Capulet Close, wondering if it had dawned on Jack what Dave had been doing when he fell.

As they drove into the Close, they noticed that Anne and Henry had visitors, so they decided not to disturb them. They did ring the hospital and were told that Dave was comfortable, and he was on a ward under observation.

***

Alicia and Callum had arrived with what seemed like a removal van full of equipment. Henry made them laugh as he enquired anxiously,

'Are you staying the night?'

Anne had already claimed little Henry, and was sitting cuddling him and exclaiming over how much he had grown in just two weeks. Alicia seemed to be enjoying motherhood. Callum too was very good with the baby. In fact, it was Callum who took the changing mat and all of the equipment into the utility room when it was time to change Henry's nappy.

Henry looked on admiringly.

'Did I change nappies, Anne?'

He really couldn't remember handling the boys much when they were that young, they had seemed so delicate he was always worried he would drop them, but he supposed he must have changed some nappies.

'Of course you did, just not very often. You were good at bath time though, that's because you were dealing with them when they were clean.'

Alicia laughed- her granddad had been very similar.

'Is Granddad alright?' Callum looked anxiously at Anne. 'He seems a bit down. Is it the move?'

Anne reassured Callum, explaining how their neighbour had ended up in hospital and she thought that Henry felt a bit shaken up.

'Granddad was there when Gary and James found him. He had a bit of a shock.'

By the time Julia and her mum arrived, Henry had made tea and everyone settled down to a bit of baby worship. Alicia was asking Julia about her work, and Julia thanked her once again for the positive reviews of Henry's room and told her what a difference the hashtags had made.

'As soon as you posted that, I was getting so much work I was able to give my notice in.'

Callum had gone into the garage to chat to his granddad, leaving the women together. Alicia gazed around the living room and admired the colours and the configuration of the furniture. Anne, of course, gave Julia full credit; saying they couldn't have done it without her.

'She made the move seamless for us. I'd recommend her services to anyone who had to have multiple jobs done.'
Anne looked across and saw Maria gazing wistfully at her daughter. Julia had just picked little Henry up and was loosening his blanket. She was talking to him softly and he was gazing intently at her. Anne sensed Maria's sadness and went over to her. Touching her lightly on the shoulder, she said, 'We're so lucky that our children have found each other, Maria. I feel as though I've gained a friend in you and a daughter in Julia.'

Before Maria could reply, Alicia gestured to Julia and the baby. 'Henry looks as though he's gained an aunty too.'

Julia smiled. Although she was certain she had come to terms with not having children, she did feel a pang of longing when holding Henry, breathing in his gorgeous baby scent and cuddling his compact little body. Ben had said that he hadn't really thought about children, but if Karina had wanted them, he would have considered it. 'If I had met you first though, Julia, I definitely would have wanted the whole thing; mortgage, marriage, babies and a cat by the fire.'

She remembered wishing that she had met Ben first, and she told him so. But realistically, she knew that they were so lucky to have found one another. It really had been a whirlwind and she truly was thankful to have found love again.

Julia remembered the last time she had gone for her health screening. Ali had gone a few weeks after she had, they had both been told that they were premenopausal. Ali had sounded relieved.

'No more periods, no more contraception.'
She had looked at Julia's stricken expression and had put her hand out to her friend.

'Me and my big mouth I'm sorry, Julia, that was so insensitive.'
She had hugged her.

Julia had swallowed hard.

'It's fine, I've known for ages that I won't be having children, I made the decision not to go down the single parent route after it all went wrong with Steve. But being told that I'm at the end of my reproductive life, well, that's pretty final, isn't it?'

Ali hadn't said anything else, but she had sat with her arms around Julia for a while in silent solidarity.

Alicia and Callum left Anne and Henry's at 6.00pm; they wanted to get back for Henry's bath time.

'We are trying to get him into a routine, but it's easier said than done.'

Alicia looked at Julia apologetically as she took the sleeping baby from her arms. They all helped to ferry the baby equipment out to the car and stood on the doorstep waving them off.

Julia was thinking they needed to make a move, she was going to drive her mum home and she still had FaceTime with Ben to look forward to. All of a sudden, they saw James and Gary approaching. Of course, Julia hadn't known anything about Dave's accident. So while Henry made yet more tea, Gary told them what happened.

'Poor Dave, I hope he'll be OK. That explains the woman I saw, then, and the one Freda saw. That's why he was cagey when we mentioned it.'

Anne looked puzzled then smiled as realisation dawned.

'Of course, he couldn't have answered the door without giving the game away.'

'Poor old Dave, he was desperate to keep his secret, and now we all know.'

That was Henry. Turning to Gary and James, he said seriously,

'Can you speak to him and say that we know? I don't want him to feel awkward around us, but obviously Valerie and her family won't have heard. And neither will Freda.'

Gary wondered about Jack. 'I tried to be discreet I made sure that Dave was covered up. The Paramedics never said a word I expect they've seen it all before. I suspect his dad's old-school and wouldn't like it.'

Gary was still puzzling over what to do. Anne asked if Gary had Dave's key. His face cleared and he smiled. 'I do, because I locked up. I could take his phone in to him in the morning; in all the kerfuffle, I left it in his house. When they say he's ready to come home, I could organise that for him too.'

Chapter 51

It was Monday night, and Julia was telling the girls about Dave's accident, explaining that the run through had been postponed until next week. Smiling at Ali and Angie's dramatic groans, she laughed when Ali demanded,

'Did you engineer poor Dave's accident so you could keep Ben to yourself for another week?'

'You'll never guess, but Gary and James broke in and found him out cold at the bottom of the stairs wearing women's clothes, make up and a wig.

'No' Ali and Angie exchanged a stunned glance. 'That can't be right, he is such a scruff and he hardly ever shaves either.'

'Blimey, I wonder if that's why Diane left him.' That was Ali.

'He might have been stealing her clothes, she is pretty stylish.' said Angie with a cheeky wink.

'I know he's the last person you'd think would wear women's clothes, but he must have been doing it for a while,

Gary said there were loads of different outfits at the bottom of the stairs, and so colourful, too. The complete opposite of his usual combats and black T-shirts. That's all he ever wears, isn't it?'

Julia went on to remind the girls that they mustn't say anything, as none of them in the Close wanted Dave to feel awkward when he came home. 'We don't even know if he's told his dad yet. Gary did his best to keep it from him, but I think he's going to offer to speak to Jack if Dave can't bring himself to.'

'Sorry as we are for Dave, I think Ali and I would like change the subject now to hear about your couple of days with the lovely Ben.'

Julia didn't need asking twice, and proceeded to oblige.

Chapter 52

Dave had been woken up every two hours throughout the night, and now it was some ungodly hour in the morning. His body still ached all over, his mouth was dry, but thankfully his headache had subsided to an occasional throb. He really wanted to talk to Gary before he saw his dad again, but he didn't have his phone. In fact, he realised that he didn't have anything with him. He was lying here in a hospital bed, wearing a backless gown and feeling extremely vulnerable.

Something else had been niggling at him, his mind struggled to grasp it. The opportunity was lost as a smiling nurse wheeled a trolley over to him. He introduced himself as Tony. He took Dave's blood pressure, checked his eyes and stuck a thermometer in his mouth.

'That all looks good, now I expect you'd like to freshen up. Do you need help getting to the bathroom?'

He supervised him getting out of bed. When he was satisfied that Dave was on his feet and not in danger of keeling over, Tony gave him a towel and a toothbrush and directed him to the bathroom. He felt glad of the paper pants he was wearing under the gown. Not that anyone was taking any notice of him; most of the other patients were either asleep or were being administered to.

John's right, I look like shit.

He clutched the edge of the sink and examined his face; his eyes looked dark, a large bruise was appearing around the dressing on his forehead. Looking more closely, he realised that the darkness around his eyes must be the remains of the mascara.

He let the hot water wash over him soothingly afterwards as he carefully washed his face, he winced as he felt the tenderness over his eye. Even drying himself was painful, but after dressing once more in the gown and the paper pants he cleaned his teeth and felt a little better.

As he was getting back into bed, he remembered what had been niggling at him.

What the hell happened to my clothes?

After he had eaten breakfast and drank a cup of tea, he asked Tony what time he thought he would be allowed home. He explained the doctor would be round at 11am, and then if everything was OK, he would be discharged. He asked Tony if he knew what had happened to the clothes he had been wearing. He said he would check just in case they had been packed up and left in Accident and Emergency.

Gary, meanwhile, had called Jack and offered to call in at number four and pick up a few things for Dave.

'Thank you, it's very good of you to go to all that trouble. He'll need some clothes and toiletries. Has he got his phone, do you know?'

Gary reassured Jack that he would get the phone and take it in. Jack, having rung the hospital, was pretty sure Dave would be home later that day and really wanted him to go back to his place for a couple of days.

A short while later Dave was relieved to see Gary being ushered into the ward with a bag.

'Glad to see you're awake.'

Dave thanked Gary for all he'd done, and Gary reassured him that as far as he knew, his dad hadn't noticed anything amiss.

'He did shake his head when he saw your trainer under the blanket, though.' Gary grinned as he recalled Jack's face.

'Well, I suppose everyone knows now.' Dave looked so downcast that Gary hastened to reassure him. Gary explained that everyone knew except for Valerie's family, as they were out on Sunday, and Freda still didn't know.

'The thing is, Dave, we're not bothered about what you're doing. It's your business; none of us want you to feel awkward about it. We just felt bad for you because it's obvious you wanted to keep it to yourself; now we all know, there's a good chance your dad's going to know too.'

Dave agreed that yes, he must tell his dad before the run through next week. With everyone there, Gary pointed out that his dad was bound to hear something.

Gary gave him his bag and said that he had used the key to go into the house to get some clothes for him to come home in.

'You could hardly wear the ones you arrived in, could you?'

Dave looked down and mumbled his thanks, and then he had a thought

'Before you go, Gary, could you find out what happened to my clothes? No one seems to know where they are.'

Gary left Dave with his clothes, shoes, his front door key and his phone. Dave was touched to find he had also left a £20 note, and instructions that he was to phone if he needed anything at all.

By the time the doctor came round later that morning, Dave was looking more like his usual self, dressed in black jeans, black T-shirt and black trainers. He was given a list of symptoms to watch out for, instructed to take paracetamol for the pain and told that his bruises would take two to four weeks to heal.

'What about my face, will there be a scar?'

The doctor had smiled reassuringly, told him that it should heal quite well and recommended bio oil which could be bought from the chemist.

Dave decided to ring his brother to pick him up. The clothes still hadn't turned up. Gary had looked but was unable to find them. Dave resigned himself to perhaps never getting them back. It was a shame really, those trainers had cost a bomb, and he worried that there might be blood on his T-shirt as his head had bled quite badly.

John arrived and let him know that their dad wanted him to stay with him.

'No definitely not. He means well, but he'll fuss. All I want to do is go home to bed and get some sleep.'

John agreed that he would tell dad that Dave had been told to rest, and that he would call him later in the evening.

Dave thanked his brother, and he said. 'John, tomorrow when I've had some sleep, can we talk? I want to ask your advice about something.'

Looking at his brother, John was worried. When they were younger, John always looked out for Dave. But as adults, they hadn't talked about their feelings much, and Dave had never confided in him. Not even when his marriage broke up.

'Here, or shall I pick you up and take you to the pub?'
To John's surprise, Dave suggested that he come to the house.

'It'll be easier to explain here.'
John drove off thoughtfully; he just hoped that Dave was alright.

Chapter 53

Dave was relieved to be back in his own place. He noticed a missed call from work. He rang back, explaining that he would need the rest of the week off after falling down the stairs. His boss already knew about it from Jed, but was checking in on him as he knew he lived on his own.

Before Dave did anything else, he checked out the bottom of the stairs. It looked like a massacre had taken place, blood splashes all on the paintwork and up the wallpaper. Grimacing, he filled a bowl with hot soapy water. Although all he wanted to do was fall into bed, he knew he had to get the blood splashes off the wall first.

Afterwards he gathered up Kandy's laundry and put it on a delicate wash, before making himself a hot drink. After the exertion, his head was throbbing. So he took some painkillers and headed up to bed.

He became aware of his phone ringing, it was John.

'I'm outside, open up, I need to talk to you.'

Dave groaned, looking at the time, he realised it was gone five. He had slept for hours. He made his way down the stairs and opened the door.

'John... I thought you were coming tomorrow, is everything alright?'

'You tell me, I just went to see Dad. I only wanted to check in on him, but he had a right go, accusing me of keeping your secrets.

'Looking closely at Dave, he said, 'Is that what you wanted my advice about?'

Not waiting for an answer, he walked past Dave into the house. 'Mine's a coffee, two sugars.'

John sipped his coffee in silence, waiting for Dave to talk. His heart went out to him he looked a sorry sight sitting there with his bruised face and the stained dressing on his forehead. John felt the familiar protectiveness that he had always felt for his younger brother.

'Come on tell me, I can't help you if you won't talk.'

Sighing, Dave said, 'Come with me, it'll be easier just to show you.'

They walked up the stairs. John never said anything, but looking round, he felt sad that Dave had let the place go since he had been living on his own.

Talk about hovel sweet hovel, it's so dark and dingy in here.

Dave led John along the dark landing and opened the door to the small bedroom. The blinds were tightly closed.

But when Dave flicked the light switch and the room flooded with light, John let out an involuntary gasp.

Unlike the rest of the house, this small room was neat and tidy. There was a rail with skirts, dresses, jackets and T-shirts hanging up neatly. Underneath were a pair of low heeled shoes and some long black boots complete with shoe trees. Under the window was a dressing table with pots of make-up, eyeshadows and lipsticks. He even spotted a few pieces of jewellery in a small tray. On the shelf was Kandy's wig, neatly brushed and sitting on the stand.

Dave watched his brother in silence as he took everything in.

'Bloody hell, Dave, have you got a death wish? Dad's gonna disown you, me too if he thinks I knew. In fact, he does think I know, doesn't he? That's why he accused me of keeping your secrets.'

Dave looked stricken.

'I can't help it, John, it started after Diane left.' Looking down, he whispered, 'I used to wear her dressing gown sometimes, it still smelled of her.'

John didn't say a word he just put his arms around his brother.

Back downstairs, Dave told John about how his neighbours had found him, but had managed to take the wig off.

'They must have guessed that Dad didn't know, and covered up for me.'

John looked at Dave sympathetically, and started sharing a childhood memory

'Dad was always hard on you, I think it was because you were a bit more sensitive, more like Mum.'

John reminded Dave about the time when they were still in infant school, they had been playing in the garden and John remembered dressing up as Peter Pan. The little girl next door, Margaret, was fed up of being Wendy. She wanted to be Captain Hook, so John persuaded Dave to be Wendy.

They were having a great time, absorbed in their game, when their dad came home from work. John remembered their dad being absolutely furious, shouting at Dave, and demanding he took off the nightdress. Poor Margaret had gone home very upset. Dave had gone in crying to his mum, and Dad had hissed at John; 'what did you let him wear that for? Do you want to turn him into a pansy?'

Dave hadn't forgotten, but he had pushed it to the back of his mind. He did remember his mum's reaction, though. She had hugged her boys and made them fish fingers, their favourite dinner. Dad had kept out of the way, probably gone down the pub. Then after they were both in bed, he remembered hearing his mum's raised voice, then silence.

The next day when Dad got back from work, he presented them both with a comic. He hadn't said sorry, and it wasn't mentioned again. Sadly, Dave had never dressed up as Wendy again either.

'It's a mess, I'm only sorry you've been dragged into it.' Dave looked at his hands for a few seconds before glancing at his brother.

'I won't be able to stop, you know. However unhappy it makes Dad.' Dave also pointed out that he guarded the secret so closely because of Dad's disapproval.

'I'm not bothered about the neighbours knowing; I'm even ready for the piss-taking I'll get from work, but I'm dreading facing Dad. I wonder how he knows anyway.'

As it turned out, they were about to find out. There was a knock on the door. Gary was there with a casserole dish in his hand and a bag under his arm. Dave invited him in.

Gary started off by apologising to Dave. He explained that he was on his way over with the casserole.

'James thought you wouldn't feel like cooking, so he sent this over, you can reheat it in ten minutes.' He continued that he was just leaving the house when Jack drew up in a taxi.

'He was furious with me, Dave. Just threw this bag at me and said,

'You lot stick together, keeping his dirty secrets.'

'I'm only sorry that he found out before you had the chance to tell him.'

Jack hadn't given Gary a chance to reply either; he had got straight back in the taxi and had left.

Dave made Gary a coffee and took the bag from him. When he looked inside, his heart sank. No wonder he hadn't been able to track down the clothes at the hospital; they had given them to his dad. He showed John the T-shirt.

'That explains it he must have looked in the bag.' Looking at Gary, he thanked him and James too.

'It's me that should be apologising. I should have been up front with Dad in the first place. I can't face him tonight, but I'll go over first thing in the morning.'

When Gary went home, Dave asked John to stay and share his meal. Now John knew about Kandy, Dave felt more able to confide in his brother.

Over dinner, Dave told John about his trip to Brighton. He made him laugh about Daisy-May and her insistence on plucking. He even showed him the photos that Daisy-May had taken of him after the makeover.

'Bloody hell, Dave, you look just like Mum.'

Dave agreed, he had noticed that himself. 'Good job I've learnt how to use make-up, I'll need to cover this scar up.'

John caught his eye and put his knife and fork down.

'Dave, I still don't get it.'

He gestured at the mess and clutter.

'And your own clothes always so scruffy. But then upstairs, there's that neat and tidy room with top quality clothes.' John merely shook his head, shrugged and continued to eat.

Chapter 54

Dave had spent the rest of the week recovering from his fall. It was interesting watching his bruises change colour from red to dark blue, the one on his face was looking less angry now.

He was looking in the mirror on Friday morning thinking about his neighbours, who he had to admit had been amazing.

They had all popped round with offers of help in the house, which he had politely refused. He had, however, been happy to accept the many small gifts of food.

He had eaten better this week than he had since Diane had left him. Homemade casseroles, cakes, and on Tuesday, a loved-up Julia and Ben - walking hand in hand - had popped round with a curry as they were on their way to the pub. She had also cut the lawns, even though it was really his turn.

The only person he had really dreaded meeting was Valerie, he couldn't imagine sympathy coming from her in verbal form. He winced as he imagined her crushing him to her. Her hugs were bad enough when he was feeling one hundred percent, but he dreaded to think what damage she would inflict on his battered and bruised body.

In the end he needn't have worried. Thursday evening, Valerie and Florence had called by with a music magazine, some homemade lemonade and a small pot of arnica that Valerie assured him would ease the bruising. She had passed on Roger's regards and had whispered sympathetically that she was sure that his dad would come round and accept things soon.

'Just give him a bit of space, I bet he'll have calmed down by Tuesday.' She had contented herself with a kindly pat on the arm, and reminded him to use the arnica every night before bed.

Freda and Freddie had called round with a couple of bottles of beer. Unlike the others, she didn't skirt round the subject, but said quite bluntly,

'I knew it! I said to Maisie you were up to something. That was you that time, wasn't it?' She nudged him playfully and said,

'Sister indeed, no wonder your dad looked at me gone out.'

Barely pausing for breath, she said, 'How's your dad taking it? Not well, I'd think. He's that generation isn't he? My dad would've been the same.'

Giving him a pat on the arm, she said that she hoped he felt well enough for the rehearsal on Tuesday. Dave realised as she turned to leave that he hadn't actually said a word. He did thank her for the beer, though.

He went back inside and sat at the kitchen table. Anne had made him a roast dinner, it was heating up in the microwave and it smelled delicious. Henry had dropped it around earlier and they had talked about music. Dave had confessed to Henry that he wasn't at all sure his dad would want to play at the fund raiser.

'He can't bear to look at me, never mind being on the same stage.'

Seeing how upset Dave was, Henry offered to come in for a minute or two. 'Do you want to tell me what happened when he realised?'

Dave discovered that although Henry was a man of few words (and up until now they had only really chatted about music), he was a very good listener. He sat at the kitchen table and just let Dave talk, and what a sad story it was too.

Dave explained that his dad had been given the clothes that Kandy had been wearing. If he had gone back to his dad's, it probably wouldn't have happened. But because Dave decided to go home, his dad thought he may as well wash the clothes.

'I found out when I spoke to him that he presumed he'd been given the wrong bag at first. He was about to phone the hospital and complain when he recognised the trainers.'

Dave looked visibly upset as he looked at Henry and said, 'He's not only angry at me; he says I've shamed him in front of his friends. But he blames James and Gary, he doesn't approve of their relationship anyway and now he thinks they covered up for me.'

Dave recalled that Jack had said something like, 'You lot are all the same and now you're keeping his dirty little secrets.'

Dave thought his dad was probably thinking that crossdressing is the same as being homosexual, hence the 'you lot.'

Henry asked Dave if Jack had actually given him a chance to speak. Dave shook his head, explaining what his dad was like. Jack had always been strict. And of course, because of the band, it did feel as though Dave and his dad were close. Dave, however, had just started to realise that their closeness relied on him agreeing with his dad.

'He said something derogatory about James and Gary a few weeks back. He didn't like it when I challenged him. I'll be honest, Henry, I've always been scared of him. And I hate disappointing him.'

Henry reassured Dave, saying that he was sure his dad would come round.

'When he sees that you're still Dave, going for a Sunday pint, playing that piano and trying out new songs he'll come round. Just give him time, it's a lot for him to come to terms with.

Chapter 55

Dave had spent the rest of the evening playing his beloved piano. He was wearing his wig, and dressed casually in a floral skirt and a long sleeved jumper. It was the first day he had been able to shave, he still wasn't able to wear makeup as he still had the dressing, and the stitches weren't due to be removed until Monday.

As he played, he felt a lot calmer, and also hopeful that his dad would come round. After dinner, he had chatted to Heather. As usual, she was on the move, and the conversation was peppered with traffic sounds and her slightly raised voice. Eventually, she found a quiet spot and they were able to chat properly. She was alarmed to hear about his accident and was thankful that his injuries weren't too bad. She was reassured when he told her how kind his neighbours had been.

She had promised to call her granddad just to find out if he would talk to her about it.

'Don't worry, perhaps if he realises I know and I'm alright with it, he might calm down.'

He had asked her how her mum's visit had gone, and she laughed as she said that they had both enjoyed themselves.

'You know what a culture vulture Mum is, she was easy to entertain. She loved the Gaudi buildings and the park.' Heather made him smile when she mimicked her mum criticising her appearance.

'She's subtle about it, but she says things like, "Heather, you're looking very pale today! Why not put some lipstick on, here, borrow mine." When what she really means is that I'm scruffy like you, Dad.'

There was a pause in the conversation before Heather, realising that probably wasn't the best example, started laughing. Soon, Dave was joining in. Wiping his eyes, he said,

'I bet she wouldn't have believed you if you'd have told her there was more chance of your dad borrowing her lipstick than you.'

They were just saying their goodbyes when Heather said that she thought he ought to tell Diane about what was going on.

'She does call in on Granddad occasionally, and he'd be bound to tell her. You need to keep her onside, Dad; you do know she worries about you.'

Dave knew that his daughter was right. He hadn't really given Diane's reaction a thought, but it wasn't fair to expect Heather to break the news. Or worse than that, ask her to keep it a secret.

The next morning was Saturday, he decided to text Diane to see if she was free to talk. She rang him straight back. She told him how pleased she was that he was making more effort with Heather.

'I know we've had our differences, Dave, but I could never fault you as a father. You had miles more patience than I did..... Heather adored you when she was a little girl, do you remember she followed you everywhere?'

Dave apologised, saying that he appreciated what Diane had just said, and he felt bad that he had neglected his relationship with Heather.

'The thing is, I want to tell you something before you find out from somebody else.
Dad knows, and he's furious with me.'

With that, Dave launched into the edited version of his secret life. He also told Diane about the accident, his neighbours finding him dressed as Kandy and doing their best to keep it from Jack.

Diane was very quiet, and then said calmly,

'Dave, I don't care about any of it, it's your business, but I'm going to ask one question. And I want you to be absolutely honest, will you do that?'

'Yes, fire away.'

'Did you ever, all the time we were married, dress in women's clothes? Or worse still, wear any of my things?'

'No, honestly, it didn't start until after you left.' He explained about the dressing gown and how he had found her scent comforting.

'Oh Dave; I wish you'd always been this open with me. I hope your dad comes round, if anyone can persuade him, it'll be Heather.'

After their chat, he sent Heather a text.

Mum knows; all fine.

The next morning, Dave got up feeling a lot more comfortable the bruising on his body seemed to be getting better. He wondered if the arnica had done the trick, he had applied it every night since Valerie had given it to him, and it did seem to be very soothing.

In a fit of enthusiasm, he decided to clean his hall. Since various people had been calling in, he had begun to see the grimy hall through their eyes. He started by sorting the post then he washed the paintwork and cleaned the glass in the front door. Cleaning done, he swept and vacuumed the dusty carpet.

As he switched the vacuum cleaner off and looked around the hallway, he felt pleased with his efforts. He wasn't as worried about the rest of the house as he rarely invited anyone in, but at least now the glass in the front door had been cleaned. And with the sun shining through, everything was looking a lot brighter.

At that moment, he heard his phone ringing. Seeing his dad's name pop up, he felt a flash of hope. Would his dad let things go, or was he going to have another go at him? Answering the phone, he waited for his dad to speak.

'I'm coming round; I need to talk to you.'

'I'll put the kettle on.'

Dave couldn't settle, he did think about inviting John over as well. But on reflection, he thought that it would be better to face his dad on his own. He did wonder if Heather had managed to talk to his dad, although he would have thought she would have let him know if she had.

By the time the doorbell rang, Dave had made coffee, laid out a plate of biscuits and made a rudimentary effort at tidying the kitchen. Inviting his dad into the kitchen, he noticed him scrutinising his clothes. Nothing to complain about there, as Dave was dressed in his usual outfit of black tracksuit bottoms, an old black polo shirt and black trainers.

His dad didn't say anything for a few minutes; instead, he waited until Dave joined him at the table. Avoiding his gaze, Jack cleared his throat.'

This is it, he's going to apologise... good old Heather.

'The thing is, Son, I've been talking to Heather. She explained what you've been up to, the clothes and everything.... I've been thinking, you stop all this, get rid of the clothes and all that nonsense. And we'll say no more about it.'

Dave swallowed hard, took a sip of his coffee, and looking at his dad, said,

'I'm sorry, Dad, it's not as simple as that. I could agree just to please you, but I'd be lying; I can't stop. Actually, I don't want to stop.'

His dad stared at him. Pushing his chair back abruptly, he responded through gritted teeth, 'Don't expect me at the pub then. And tell Sharon that the Stompers will be short of a guitarist. I'll leave you to explain why.'

With that, Jack stormed off, and the door slammed after him.

I'd better offer to call him a taxi; I don't suppose he'd get in the van with me after this.

As it turned out, he needn't have worried. He followed his dad outside, and saw a car draw up; it was his dad's neighbour Jim. Dave couldn't help but wonder what his dad had told him.

Dave sat at the table finishing his coffee, and tried to work out how he was feeling. He was pleased that he hadn't just gone along with his dad; it was a relief for it to be out in the open, and he felt glad that he had stuck to his decision. He supposed that was what had infuriated his dad. It had always been his way or no way. And at the age of ninety he had just had a taste of losing control.

He was hoping that his dad would come on Tuesday, he wasn't holding out much hope. But this new assertive Dave was already wondering if Henry could learn the set in two weeks and be an honorary Stomper for the fundraiser.

Chapter 56

At 2pm the following Tuesday afternoon, Ben drove into Capulet Close. His face creased into a smile, and his heart beat a little faster as he took in Julia's neat front garden and the colourful flowers in the pots that flanked the front door. He couldn't wait for her to get back from work so that they could spend a couple of hours together before the run through tonight.

Last week, he had been secretly glad it had been cancelled. Not that he wished poor Dave any harm, but it did give him and Julia a bit more time to themselves. He smiled as he remembered her sending him over to his parents'. Giving him the key, she had kissed him on the lips and had whispered that she would be waiting for him.

'I'll give you an hour, we can take your parents out to lunch tomorrow, but I want you to myself this evening.'

Julia was indeed waiting for him upstairs. They had spent the rest of the afternoon making love, and lying cuddled up together intermittently talking and dozing. When they were hungry, Julia had gone downstairs and brought up bowls of curry that had been simmering on the stove.

When they had eaten and were enjoying a glass of cold beer each, to her amusement he had said,

'Mmm Julia you were telling the truth, you can follow a recipe.'

That evening, they dropped off a portion of the curry to Dave, and then went off hand in hand to the pub, where they spent the evening making plans for their holiday.

***

Ben spotted Anne waving to him. He got out of the car, and ran up the path; giving his mum a bear hug that almost lifted her off her feet. He popped his head round the garage door to find his dad wrestling with the Stompers' set. Henry explained what had been going on and how Dave didn't think his dad would play.

Henry took a break while Anne made bacon sandwiches, and they sat and ate them, waiting until Julia arrived home. Ben noticed that unusually, Henry looked a bit stressed, and asked him what he was worried about.

'It's the music, Ben. They all read music and can't jam. I can write music, but can't read; I tend to go by chord charts.'

Anne gave Henry a hug. 'You'll be OK, Dave's just thankful that you'll be there to help out. He doesn't expect you to get it spot on, I even heard him say that if there was anything you weren't happy with, to stop playing.'

Ben patted his Dad on the back. 'Dad, take your own advice. You always used to say to us,

'You can only do your best.'

It's going to be difficult to learn a whole set in just over a week, so you can only do your best.'

Henry smiled up at Ben and agreed.

'Hopefully, Jack will come to his senses, and I'll be off the hook. Imagine disowning your own son; I could never do that.'

Anne and Ben exchanged smiles; Henry really was an old softie. Ben spotted Julia's car outside number two and said goodbye to his parents. They agreed to meet at the pub; Henry had offered them a lift. But Anne had smiled knowingly and said,

'I think Ben and Julia would rather walk, Henry.'

Chapter 57

Valerie and Anne were at Julia's on Thursday evening. It had become a regular thing since they had been involved in the fundraiser, but Julia could see it becoming as important as her Mondays with the girls. In Valerie and Anne, she felt she had made two lifelong friends.

The three of them were delighted with the ticket sales; they had sold over one hundred tickets, and Sharon had been amazed. Usually on a Tuesday, Sharon just left them to it, but this time she had been there from the beginning. She was treating it like a dress rehearsal and had instructed everyone to be on stage in the right order, just as it would be on the day.

She was compering the event and wanted the timings just right, as she had to allow for the barbecue and the raffle as well as Anne's head shave. Anne was pleased to be able to let everyone know that the Just Giving page had passed £2,000 already.

Valerie had noticed that Anne touched her hair anxiously whenever it was mentioned, and had an idea to make the whole thing less of an ordeal for her.

'Would it be easier, Anne, if you asked your hairdresser to cut your hair and then shave it for you?'

Julia agreed, 'Yes, it would make more of an occasion of it. There could be collection buckets near the stage so you'd be collecting sponsors even right up until the event.'

Anne smiled. 'That would definitely make me feel better; Henry too. He's really bothered about me going ahead with it, he thinks it's brutal.'

Valerie complimented Henry on stepping in for Jack. Julia said how impressed she was, saying that Henry was going to be working harder than anyone. She pointed out that he would be there with The Stompers to open the event. He would have a short break when Lary and Luke played, and another for Florence's set.

They all knew how hard he had worked with Freda.

Anne made them chuckle when she described the blood, sweat and tears that Henry had put into those rehearsals.

'Freda says she doesn't think she'll ever sing those songs again after Saturday. Henry said that he didn't think he could play them again either.'

Anne went on to say that Freda didn't quite know how to take Henry sometimes.

'Her face, she wasn't impressed. It's been worth it though she sang all three songs really well at the rehearsal.'

They were all in agreement there the run through had gone really well although Jack's absence had cast a bit of a shadow.

Julia offered them both a glass of wine. Valerie refused, saying she would stick to coffee as she had to pick Florence up, but Anne accepted. As they sipped their drinks, they recalled the awkward moment when Dave arrived, and Jim started asking Dave where his dad was.

Jim had spoken to Dave as though he was a naughty child. 'You've really upset your dad, what have you been up to? Just apologise, he is your dad after all.'

Anne had felt proud of Henry at that moment. He had stepped in and spoken to Jim calmly.

'With respect, Jim, this is between Dave and Jack. Let them work it out on their own. I'm helping out until Jack feels able to play again.'

Julia was thinking about Ben. He had enjoyed the evening, the music and meeting her friends and neighbours. She smiled when she remembered him whispering that he didn't care where they were just as long as they could be together. She made Valerie and Anne laugh when she told them that she had received Ali and Angie's seal of approval.

'They think Ben's gorgeous, and are satisfied that because he cooks and respects my work, he's my ideal man.'

Valerie and Anne agreed with her wholeheartedly.

The talk turned to Dave, and they wondered if he would ever have the courage to go out dressed up. None of them wanted to be the first to say it, but they were all secretly thinking that Dave was the last person they would imagine would dress in women's clothes. It was Anne who voiced what they were all thinking.

She piped up, 'I know people cross dress for all sorts of reasons, but I can't believe that someone like Dave who has such terrible dress sense as a man would not only wear women's clothes, but make-up too.'

Valerie and Julia agreed that the same thought had crossed their minds. Valerie had received a lot of diversity training as a teacher, and said

'Dave might never go out dressed up. He might only ever do it at home. His dad's old-school, he probably thinks it means he's gay.'

They all agreed that they felt sorry for Dave, he was between a rock and a hard place; they just hoped that his dad would come round. Valerie said she remembered Jack's reaction at his birthday do when he saw Gary hug James.

'I think I diverted a homophobic rant there, I whisked him off for a dance.'

The other two giggled at the picture this conjured up for them.

Chapter 58

At number eight, Freda was on the phone to Maisie, she was bubbling with excitement. She was telling Maisie that her sisters and brother were coming on Saturday. She had bought the tickets and given them to Phil. She refused to take any money for them as she wanted to demonstrate how much she wanted them there.

'Once this is over, we can start going out on Sundays again.'

Maisie winced; it had been a nice break as far as she was concerned. The last few Sundays, instead of the teatime jam session, Freda had invited Maisie round to listen to her go through her songs. Maisie gave a non-committal murmur in response, and asked Freda about the grandchildren.

Freda could talk about Hannah and Archie all day, and Maisie was happy to hear that her friend was making more effort with Mandy. She told Maisie that she had picked Hannah up from nursery two Wednesdays running. She had loved having her. Freda smiled as she recalled Hannah's excitement the first time she picked her up. She had taken Freda's hand and had told all of the nursery staff,

'This is my nanny, we're going to go home and sing.'

Freda told Maisie that one day Blake had called in with Hannah, something that seemed to happen more regularly lately, and she had been singing the songs. Hannah had been keen to sing too, so Freda had given her the microphone. She had stood her on a large box, and there she was on her makeshift stage, singing her heart out.

Freda and Blake had reminisced about when he was little and he and his brother would pretend to be in a band in the garden, banging on pots for drums and strumming on their dad's old guitar.

'That's nice, my lot like it when we talk about when they were small.'

The two of them said their goodbyes, and Maisie said she would pick her up on Saturday. It dawned on Freda that she had often put Blake off coming round before.

He probably didn't feel that welcome.

She could already see the difference in him even in this short time, so she was hoping their relationship would continue to improve.

One thing she had done, though, was to stop seeing Jan. The free trial with Match Makers had finished, but she really only had to renew that if she wanted to meet new people. She had gradually stopped seeing the other young men. Jan was the only one she was getting any pleasure from. When she realised that things had stagnated and that the relationship wasn't going anywhere, she did try to move things on.

'Lovely Freda, let us enjoy, come.'

She did her best to spend some time chatting, she wanted to find out more about him, but his English just wasn't good enough. He would apologise charmingly, but that was it. Conversation between them was a non-starter.

Things came to a head on the day he offered her the promised ride in the sports car. He turned up at the house. Freda was waiting for him dressed in her most glamorous outfit. He drove out into the countryside. The car stopped in a deserted layby, and Jan tried to engage her in one of his fantasies but she had staunchly refused. It was one thing massaging him all over with baby oil in the safety of her bedroom when she was dressed for the occasion, but quite another in the back of a very small sports car wearing her best pencil skirt and some very expensive stockings. Anyway, she had to think of her back, it was murder some days.

Jan had been positively huffy, and they had driven to the pub in silence. However, once there, he turned on the charm. He handed her out of the car, said she was beautiful, took her in and bought her a drink.

Freda had never told this to another living soul, it was humiliating. But when Jan went up for another drink she thought he had been a while and decided to let him know she would have coffee instead. He had to go through a little archway to the bar so she couldn't call him from the table, she followed him out. In perfect but heavily accented English she overheard him chatting up the young lady behind the bar, and she caught him just as he said,

'I will take my grandmother home, then I can come back; we can go to a club.'

Freda felt a hot flush suffuse her body; swallowing hard, she returned to her seat. But the feeling of rage she felt was intense. He returned, smiling, to their seat with their drinks. She didn't let on that she had heard, but just said that she wasn't feeling well, and could they go?

'I am sorry, lovely Freda.'

They drove back in silence, Jan glancing at her now and then. But when he dropped her off outside her house, he made to follow her inside. Stopping him with a raised hand, she repeated word for word what he had said to the young lady in the pub. Before he could protest, she had looked him in the eye and said slowly, accentuating every word,

'Your English seems very good to me, Jan.'

Leaning forward, she whispered in his ear,

'Now fuck off, take your baby oil and shove it up your arse.'

Freda felt a great sense of satisfaction as she stalked off, leaving Jan staring after her open- mouthed.

Chapter 59

The day of the fundraiser dawned bright and clear. Sharon and her staff were out very early setting up the stage and making sure the electrics were available for the equipment. They had set up a small covered table where the raffle prizes were displayed. Ben's picture, which was quite a large canvas, was displayed on an easel and had earned quite a lot of interest from everyone that had seen it. Sharon was very taken with it herself and wondered if they might have earned more money by auctioning it off.

Anne and Henry were getting ready. Anne, to Henry's amusement, paid exactly the same attention to her hair as she always did; styling it carefully and even spraying it to keep it in place. When she caught a glimpse of him standing there smiling she said,

'So! I'm not having it cut until 3pm I refuse to look a mess until then.'

Henry enveloped her in a gentle hug, kissing her lightly on the top of her head.

'I get it, I really do. And Anne, I know I tried to talk you out of it, but I'm very proud of you. You do know that, don't you?'

Anne smiled up at him, a lump in her throat; he really was such a lovely man.

***

Julia and her friends Ali and Angie had arrived early, and decked the place with banners and posters. They had been joined by Valerie, who had asked her pupils to decorate some bunting triangles.

Valerie and Florence had spent the morning threading them onto string, and now the four of them were hanging them up between the trees that lined the pub car park. They fluttered in the light summer breeze, and they all agreed that the decorations added a festive feel to the place.

Valerie was going back home to collect Florence and Roger, while Julia and her friends took a seat and had a quick catch up on their week. Ali and Simon had taken Jake to Bristol last weekend. He was heading to university there in September, and he wanted to get a feel for the place. Angie was telling them about her couple of days in London, her and her husband had been to see a show for their wedding anniversary.

'What about you and Ben, Julia? Still all loved up?' Ali teased.

Julia beamed, and went on to say that they were going away on Monday. Ben had surprised her with a couple of days in Paris; flying out Monday, coming back Thursday. Then he would return to Cornwall on Friday.

Julia fiddled with the edge of her blouse. Looking down, she confessed to her friends that she was finding running her business and the travelling up and down very difficult. She and Ben wanted to be together, but they had to find a way to make it work for both of them.

'My instinct is to pack up and go to Cornwall, give everything up for love. But I did that for Steve, and I was left with nothing, I never want to be in that position again.'

Her friends nodded sympathetically but pointed out that Ben could not in any way be compared to Steve.

'For a start, Julia, Ben would never expect that of you. He wouldn't want you to give your business up. You only have to see you two together to see how much he loves you, and he's so proud of your work too.'

Hugging her friend, Angie reassured her, 'These things have a way of working themselves out.'

'I know, it's not just that, and thanks for not pushing me. It's sort of been the elephant in the room for a while, but Stacy's had the baby.'

She went on to say that they were proud parents of Elijah Steven; he was a couple of weeks early, but doing well.

'Steve let me know yesterday, quite sensitive of him really. He pointed out that it would be all over social media and he wanted me to hear it from him.'

When her friends noted her matter of fact tone their expressions cleared.

'You really are OK with this? You've moved on so much, and we did worry that it might bring that upset back up again.'

Her friends exchanged an anxious glance.

'Honestly, girls, I didn't think I would be! As it got nearer I was steeling myself not to be upset but really, I'm fine. You'd have been proud of me I congratulated them and wished them well. But I didn't feel anything much, really, it was like hearing about someone you'd known at school. Glad they're doing well, but no emotional attachment.'

***

Back at number twelve, Ben was helping his dad pack up his gear before loading it into the car. Ben tittered to himself. It was like a military operation. Henry was so organised, counting in his leads for his amplifier and his microphone. He had a music stand and a microphone stand, a case of harmonicas and two guitars. He also had his iPad with his set list on, his backing tracks and Freda's songs too. Henry thanked Ben and asked him,

'Am I squeezing you in the car with us or are you heading off now?'

Ben told his dad that he was heading off to find Julia, who was already at the pub with her friends. Giving his mum a quick hug and wishing her luck, he set off in a hurry to catch up with Julia.

He couldn't wait to surprise her in Paris. She didn't know, but they were staying in a five star hotel near the Eiffel Tower and he had booked a dinner cruise on the Seine where they would have a sumptuous five course meal, wine and there would be a live band.

He could tell Julia was struggling with the travelling, he did understand. It wasn't as difficult for him, he had regular hours and was able to swap days off. Julia was still establishing her business and couldn't really afford to take time out; hence the three day trip to Paris. He would have loved to have smoothed the worry lines from her face and whisked her away for a week of luxury, but that would not have been possible. She had to work late into the evenings, and the weekends they weren't together; he knew that she worked to free up time for them.

Ben had been so deep in thought that it was with a start of surprise that he heard voices and realised he was at the pub. He started to hurry as he spotted Julia's animated face smiling at Callum, who was holding little Henry in a sling against his chest. Ben walked up silently with his finger to his lips: Callum grinned at his uncle and carried on talking to Julia. Ben slid his arm around Julia's waist, and his heart thumped as she turned to him and snuggled closer.

'Look at Henry, Ben, he just smiled.'

Julia stroked Henry's soft downy cheek and shared a smile with Callum over the top of the baby's head.

They were joined by the rest of the family. Helen and Adam had found them a table. Alicia and Julia went to get some drinks and Ben and the others all sat down. Anne was pleased that they were so near the stage, Henry could join them in between his performances.

Chapter 60

Dave and Henry were setting up. Because of the age of the other members of the band, Dave always set their gear up and none of them came up onto the stage until it was time to do the sound check. Henry had checked in on Dave regularly since his dad had refused to play. To Henry's surprise, he seemed resigned to his dad's silence.

'The thing is, Henry, I know he's alright. John's taken over where I left off. He checks in on him every day, and takes him to the pub or to his house on a Sunday.'

Dave made Henry laugh when he said that John was struggling with his dad.

'According to John, Dad hates going to the pub with him because he doesn't drink. He doesn't want to have Sunday lunch with them because he prefers a pub lunch.'

As they were setting everything up, taping down leads and generally making sure everything was set up safely and performers had room to move on and off the stage, John turned up. Dave stepped down to speak to him, leaving Henry to keep going.

'What's up?'

John was running his fingers through his hair, and a slight narrowing of his lips indicated all wasn't well.

'It's Dad, sorry, Dave. I just had a go at him.'

Dave raised his eyebrows, and John continued to explain what had happened. Jack had been moaning about Sundays.

'Why can't we do Sunday lunch in the pub, I've been going every Sunday with your brother since we lost your mother.'

Exasperated, John had just let Jack have it.

'I told him that he was lucky that you'd been willing to spend every Sunday at the pub, but that wasn't how we spent our Sundays. I told him that he was welcome to join us for Sunday dinner, though.' John looked down, misery etched on his face, and said in a lower voice:

'Dave, I told him that if he hated Sundays with us so much, then maybe he should apologise to you for the way he's treated you.'

'What did he say?'

'Nothing, so then I said that Mum hadn't liked the way he was with us either, and reminded him of when he scared us to death that day when you were dressed up.'

John went on that he told his dad he was coming today, but his dad sat there, not saying a word.

'I hate being at loggerheads with him, but sometimes.....' Dave patted his brother's arm consolingly but indicated that he had to get on. He told John they would talk later.

Maisie and Freda were just buying a drink. They had stopped briefly to chat to Anne and her family, and had wished her luck with the head shave. Freda had a pang of doubt when she saw them all together laughing and chatting,

Would her lot even turn up?

'Nanny, Nanny.'

Freda heard Hannah before she could see her. Oh, there was Blake and Mandy! Freda smiled delightedly as she caught a glimpse of Hannah sitting on Blake's shoulders. Dragging Maisie over to her family, she hugged them all. By now, Hannah was on the ground holding her nanny's hand. Archie was nowhere to be seen, but Blake assured her that he was somewhere about, and he had teamed up with one of his friends.

'He won't go until he's heard you sing.'

Mandy pointed at the board where the performers were listed. Freda felt a flutter of excitement, or it could have been nerves as she saw her name on the board. The Soar Valley Stompers, Larry and Luke, Florence. And then, just before Henry, it was her name. 'Freda.' Bold and clear.

At that moment, Blake started waving. 'It's Uncle Phil, Mum.'

To Freda's relief, it was Phil striding towards them, followed by her sisters. She hugged Liz and then they all started talking at once.

Liz whispered in her ear;

'What a pair of sillies.'

Within five minutes, it was as if they had never been apart. Mandy and Blake went and found them a table. Liz was bossing Phil, and he was arguing with her good naturedly about something. Freda fell easily back into the role of older sister. Settling them at the table with Mandy and Blake and sending Phil off to get the drinks. She introduced them all to Maisie, who joined the family party as if she had known them all her life.

Chapter 61

Sharon looked around happily, the place was buzzing. Gary and James had offered to sell raffle tickets and it looked as though they were doing a good job. She smiled as she overheard James. He expertly reeled off the prizes and made a huge show of saying that the painting was done by a 'famous' local artist, and pointed Ben out to them. Gary was content to take the money and let James do all the talking.

The Stompers were doing their sound check and were almost ready to go. She did wonder what had gone on between Dave and his dad there had been some sort of rift. She had heard some gossip that Dave had been crossdressing and it had caused a huge family row.

She had taken that with a pinch of salt she couldn't imagine Dave dressed as a woman. A bag lady perhaps, but definitely not a womanly woman in smart clothes and make-up! He was just too careless of his own appearance. Having said that, he was a lot smarter today. He had abandoned his combats and black T-shirt in favour of the band uniform of black trousers, white shirt and a thin black tie. His face was healing nicely, and he was clean shaven for a change.

She shook her head, who knows and even if it turns out to be true it's up to Dave what he does in his own time.

Oh well, let's get this show on the road.

Sharon picked up the microphone stepped onto the stage. She was very articulate; outlining the work of the charity, talking about her niece and the effect her illness had had on the family and finally expressing her gratitude to everyone who had come together, giving their time and expertise for free.

Julia got a special mention for her efforts with the publicity, and Anne blushed as everyone cheered when Sharon mentioned the head shave. She drew attention to the hairdressing chair with the buckets next to it and the poster with the QR code for the Just Giving page. Anne's smiling hairdresser Kirsty was also introduced, and she had offered to go around with the buckets if people wanted to donate cash.

The Soar Valley Stompers were introduced to cheers and claps. Anne and Julia exchanged amused glances as they usually did when they heard the name. Anne was looking at Henry; she knew stepping in for Jack had caused him a lot of worry, but he had rehearsed enough that he was confident of doing a good enough job.

Just as Sharon stepped away, there was a kerfuffle. Julia nudged Anne and pointed. It was Jack. John was following closely behind carrying a guitar. And a young woman was walking beside Jack, holding his arm and speaking to him.

The audience was fascinated as they watched Henry step aside and unplug his guitar. The young woman beckoned to Dave, several emotions crossed his face simultaneously. He smiled at the young woman but greeted his dad cautiously. Craning her neck, Anne could see Jack reaching into his jacket and removing what looked like an old comic. He handed it to Dave and looked up at his son. Dave smiled hesitantly, shook his dad's hand and started to set his dad's guitar up.

Henry was back at Anne's side. Kissing her cheek, he said, 'Well, that's a relief! I'm not sure what that was all about, but it looks as though I'm no longer an honorary Stomper.'

Henry turned to John and Heather, who had bought Jack to the stage.

'This is John, Dave's brother and Heather, Dave's daughter.'

John said he was sure Dave would fill them in later, but he gave Heather full credit for talking Jack round.

'She flew in this morning. Dave didn't even know she was coming.'

John and his niece exchanged smiles as the band started playing. It was just like the first rehearsal all over again, thought Dave, as his dad's friends Jim and June started jiving on the grass in front of the stage.

Valerie and Roger had arrived, they were enjoying the music. Valerie had found Anne and wished her well for the head shave. Anne pointed out her hairdresser, and squeezing her hand, thanked Valerie for thinking of it.

'She even has a proper chair, cape and everything. I'll almost be able to convince myself I'm at the hairdressers.'

The Stompers finished the first set, and introduced Lary and Luke. James and Gary asked Julia and Ben if they could join them, and told them the story of the open mic and Freda possibly pinching Lary's bum. They all laughed, especially when Ben asked if Lary realised that Freda was there.

'Yes, he knows, but he feels safe. Look at her, in her element with her family.'

Sure enough, She was happily chatting with her siblings, little Hannah on her knee; Freda looking every inch the family matriarch.

Gary sought out Henry. Nodding to Dave and his small family, he said, 'Not sure what went on there, but I'm so glad that Jack came to his senses. I bet you were relieved too, weren't you?'

'Yes, it was worrying me to death, although I was willing to help out. It's a relief to be off the hook.'

Lary and Luke sang their usual Beatles set, and then they performed one of their own songs. Florence by this time had joined her parents by the stage, and was very impressed with the harmonies the boys could do.

She was feeling surprisingly confident. Dave had offered to let her use his piano so that she didn't have to bring her own instrument. Lary and Luke introduced her, and she went up on the stage to the applause from her proud parents and The Capulet Close contingent.

Valerie and Roger were sipping their drinks and listening as their daughter played two classical pieces on the piano. She then announced that she would play a song she had written herself. The buzz of chatter stopped as the audience became aware of Florence's melodic voice as she sang her ballad. She finished to rapturous applause. Then Dave, in a fit of enthusiasm, had a quick word with Florence, asking her if she would like to do a repeat performance of the duet that they had played on the curry night.

Freda, aware that it was almost time for her performance, kissed Hannah and sent her back to her dad. She waved to her siblings and walked over to the stage with Maisie.

Dave and Florence were doing a great job so much so that Freda was rapidly losing confidence.

'What was I thinking?' she wailed as she saw the audience tapping their toes and smiling. 'I'll never measure up to these two.'

'You'll be fine. Henry knows what he's doing. And you, Freda, do have the voice.'

Maisie went on to point out that Florence had only sung the one song. She sung it beautifully, but it was sweet and gentle to go with the song that she played.

'Your voice is powerful, and the songs you sing suit your voice.'

Freda didn't have any more time to worry. Dave and Florence were graciously accepting their applause. Dave gave Florence the microphone, and she introduced Freda and Henry to the stage.

When Henry began playing the introduction to 'Summertime', Anne and the rest of the family began cheering and clapping.

Freda's nerves seemed to be getting the better of her, so much so that at first her voice to her own ears sounded quite shaky and tremulous. But as she caught sight of her family all gazing towards her, she remembered Henry's advice, which was to focus on something or someone in the audience. She fixed her gaze on her family, and sang it just for them.

After that, time passed in a blur. Two more songs, and she was leaving the stage to the enthusiastic applause of the audience. Archie was standing there with his friend, and he kissed her cheek and mumbled,

'Well done, Nan.'

As she walked back to their table, she was transported back to childhood. She thought to herself,

Well, I did it! I've actually sung at an event and in front of a big audience, too.

As she walked across the grass to her family, Hannah ran towards her for a hug and Freda just couldn't stop smiling.

Chapter 62

Gary and James were having a great time. James had sold most of his tickets to students and staff at the university, so he knew quite a few people. The two of them wandered around chatting to colleagues and friends. They were enjoying the music too.

They both agreed that Freda was far less scary when seen in the context of her big noisy family. In fact, she had hardly given them a glance apart from when she graciously accepted their congratulations when she left the stage. James had grinned at Gary and given him a nudge.

'Do you feel safe now, Gazza?'

Gary had laughed out loud. 'Yes, I think I'm OK. Valerie just told me that Freda thought we were housemates and that's why she kept flirting.'

James roared with laughter.

'Oh dear, I think we may have been a bit too discreet!'

With that, he gave Gary a big hug and kissed him on the lips before linking arms with him and heading off to the bar.

There had been a short break for food and the raffle, and now Henry was heading up to the stage for his set. Julia motioned to Ben to sit with his Mum as she was looking quite nervous, so they shuffled around the table. Julia took little Henry for a walk in his pram, leaving Ben and Adam to sit either side of Anne. Callum was there keeping them company, and Alicia and Helen were getting everyone a coffee.

Henry, as usual, did them proud with his set. Anne was soothed by the familiar music; she smiled as she heard Valerie whooping her appreciation as Henry launched into his last song which he announced he was singing to his wife of nearly fifty years. It was his favourite Dusty Song; "The Look of Love". She felt the blush rise in her cheeks as she heard the familiar words.

All of a sudden, she noticed the Capulet Close contingent all gathering round her, clapping and cheering. At that moment she felt truly blessed, surrounded by her family and to have moved to a new area and been welcomed so completely by everyone in the Close.

Anne waved to Julia as she approached with the baby. Helen whispered something to Alicia, who smiled and agreed.

'We think we should take some photos of you, Anne, with little Henry.'

Anne looked puzzled and then started laughing. 'Oh, while I've still got hair, you mean.'

It really was very thoughtful of Helen and organised too. Anne knew she would have regretted it if most of the photos of Henry's first year were of her holding him with a shaved head.

Everyone bustled about, tidying the table so the glasses were not visible. Someone lifted Henry out of his pram and settled him onto her lap. He was already beginning to smile, and it did seem as though he understood that this was a momentous occasion as Helen snapped a photo of the baby smiling and cooing at Anne as she gazed into his little face.

***

As Anne sat there sipping her coffee and waiting to be summoned to the hairdressing chair, Dave was sitting a little further away with John, Jack and Heather. Thanks to Heather and her enthusiasm for the event and her ability to chat and keep the conversation light, there was no awkwardness. Tactfully, she sent Dave and John to get some food from the barbecue and some drinks from the bar.

'Well, did he apologise to you?' John looked at his brother curiously.

'Don't be daft, John; Dad wouldn't say sorry.' Reaching down, he pulled something from his rucksack. 'He gave me this.'

Taking it from his brother John exclaimed,

'The crafty old sod, he made out he didn't remember what he was like when we were kids. This is the Beano that he bought you the next day, I had a Dandy.'

The brothers exchanged a look.

'It's the nearest thing to an apology I'll get, so I'll take it.'

Looking over at Heather and Jack deep in conversation, John told Dave that he thought it was Heather arriving that morning that made Jack realise he had to back down.

'She swept in there and gave him a real talking to. Said he was cutting off his nose to spite his face, reminded him he was missing out on the band and his Sundays in the pub with you too.'

Heather had told her granddad that she would take the guitar and wait ten minutes. If he didn't join her, she would leave the guitar at the front door and go off to see her dad play. Good old Heather, Diane was right; she had said that if anyone could persuade his dad, she would.

Chapter 63

Although outwardly calm, Anne was dreading the moment when it would be time for Kirsty to use the razor. But by the time she had been led to the chair and the cape had been draped around her shoulders, she was ready.

Everyone had gathered round. In some ways, she felt a little like the performers must have felt today - all eyes on them with everyone waiting to be entertained.

The first part was just like having a short haircut. Kirsty had whispered reassuringly that she would cut her hair first. Anne was touched that she was making such a ceremony of it and talked the audience through what she was doing.

Anne began to relax as she saw her hair fall to the ground.

Ouch, it's a lot greyer than I thought.

James and Gary had started to take the buckets round in order to collect more donations.

All of a sudden, Anne had an idea. Stopping Kirsty, she turned to the audience and announced,

'Anybody who wants to can put in an extra donation and shave some of my hair.'

Some people took her up on it, and queued up to put cash in the bucket before taking the razor and running it over her scalp. Poor Henry had nearly been in tears and had been unable to look. She smiled as she noticed the whole family in turn added a donation to the bucket, but not one of them would use the razor.

Afterwards, Kirsty took charge of the razor and tidied Anne's scalp. She brushed the hair from her neck and whispered,

'Do you want to take a look?'

With a lump in her throat, Anne nodded. Looking in the mirror, her first thought was that she hadn't realised what a small head she had. She did feel a little odd, and also very surprised at how chilly she felt; it was a lovely day. But she shivered slightly as she thanked Kirsty and turned to everyone who started cheering and clapping.

A young lady approached as Anne was heading off with the family; she was from the local paper. Introducing herself as Amina, she said,

'I took some photos, it's such a great fundraising idea; will you talk to us for a minute?'

Anne was only too pleased to chat, and then pointed her in the direction of Sharon, who Anne was sure would be delighted to share her story in order to drum up interest in her charity.

People were just beginning to head for home. Alicia and Callum wanted to get little Henry back home for his bath and bed. He had been fussed and cuddled all day, and was getting a bit fractious. They kissed Anne goodbye, and Callum noticed with concern that she seemed to be rubbing her neck.

'Are you cold, Nan? You could do with a scarf.'

Before Anne could reply, Helen - who was saying goodbye to Alicia and little Henry - hurried over with a bag.

'Oh, Anne, I meant to give you these.' Smiling at her mother-in-law, she handed over a large bag.

Anne was touched to find three stylish summer hats inside, and promptly put on a little straw boater adorned with a blue ribbon, which happened to go perfectly with the blue dress she was wearing.

Henry, who had never quite known how Helen felt about him, warmed to her a little more.

'Helen, that was so thoughtful, Anne's definitely a hat person.'

They all agreed, and Helen flushed with pleasure.

Praise indeed coming from Henry!

Anne hugged her daughter-in-law gratefully. She felt much better, less exposed and a lot warmer too.

Sharon was delighted that the event had been such a huge success. She took to the stage to let everyone know that so far, the head shave alone had raised nearly £3,000; the final total wasn't available yet as the money from the buckets still had to be counted.

Chapter 64

The next morning, Julia and Valerie were just coming back from their walk. Valerie made her laugh when she told her about Dave asking Florence to perform at the fundraiser.

'He is still wary around you, then?'

Valerie laughed. 'As you know, I'm very tactile it's the French in me. But Roger says I need to lay off now that I know Dave isn't comfortable with it.'

Julia smiled at her friend.

'Asking you not to hug is like asking Ben not to paint, it's impossible.'

As they were walking back into the street, Julia started telling Valerie about Paris.

'Is he going to propose at the top of the Eiffel Tower?' teased Valerie.

Julia laughed delightedly, 'Early days yet, we've only been together six weeks, give us a chance.'

Hugging her friend goodbye, Julia hurried off to wake Ben. She had some work to catch up with, her mum to visit and packing to do. But she thought that she could spare another hour in bed with Ben.

Kicking off her shoes, she tiptoed up the stairs. Taking off her clothes, she slipped into bed beside him and snuggled into him, waking him with a soft kiss.

***

Next door at number four, Dave had made tea, and Heather had joined him at the table. Looking at his daughter, he smiled. She had used the shower, her hair was wrapped in a towel and she was dressed in a pair of ripped jeans and one of her oldest T-shirts. She really was her father's daughter.

They hadn't had much chance to talk at the fundraiser, but to Dave's delight, Heather had asked if she could stay for a few days.

'I'll go and see Mum, but I'll feel more comfortable here, especially now she's with Alan.' Heather went on to say,

'I can come to the pub with you and Granddad if you like, and go and see Mum later on this evening.'

Dave smiled at her gratefully.

'I know I'll have to be on my own with him at some point, but it'll be easier with you there. Thanks, I appreciate it.'

Heather was sleeping in the middle room that had been hers when she lived at home but her curiosity about Kandy's wardrobe couldn't be contained. Once they had arrived back Saturday evening, the piano was back in place and they were settled in the living room with a beer and a takeaway, she had asked if once they had eaten she could take a look.

Dave agreed. Like John, once the light was switched on, she looked around amazed. He saw her run her fingers over the fabrics of the dresses and jumpers. She looked at the labels and said, 'Wow! I have to say Kandy's got miles better taste than you. I reckon even Mum would like some of these outfits.'

***

Over the road at number six, Gary and James were eating breakfast. They had offered to help Sharon count up the money in the buckets so that she could put her final tally of ticket sales, raffle money and sponsors on her Facebook page.

Gary had cooked this morning, and they were eating a big fry up. All of a sudden, they heard Freda through the wall shouting at Freddie.

'You little sod, every time I go to put the music on, you start. You'll have my toe up your arse if you don't shut up.'

Gary caught James' eye and laughed.

'Good to see fame hasn't changed her, still yelling at the poor dog.'

They both agreed that it had been good to see Freda with her family. It was hard to think of the woman they met yesterday - doting grandma, parent and big sister - as the predatory neighbour that Gary had first met.

'I don't think she can be seeing anyone, although a few weeks ago I did see a red sports car outside so who knows?'

'I don't care if she's got toy boys queueing down the street, so long as she never flirts with me again.'

James laughed as he saw Gary shudder at the thought.

Meanwhile, the subject of their conversation was on the phone to Maisie. She was really glad that her friend had come along yesterday, but even more so that she had got along so well with the family.

Freda confided in Maisie that she hadn't renewed the subscription to Match Makers and she didn't intend to either. Freda had another plan; one which she thought Maisie would approve of.

'You remember Jeff at the Sunday jam, don't you?'

'Yes, the one you sang "I Got You Babe" with? He was nice and he's got a good voice.'

Freda went on to say that he had given her his number, but she had never rung him as she didn't really fancy him.

'Yes, I do remember. You found out he was ten years younger than you and you thought he was too old.'

Freda went on to tell her friend that maybe she had been a little hasty.

'I rang him earlier he wants to go to the Sunday jam. Do you fancy it?'

Maisie took a deep breath. She wanted to say, 'Freda, you've got a bloody cheek! And no, I'm not going to ferry you about and then play gooseberry to you and Jeff.'

What she actually said was,

'That would have been lovely. But I'm babysitting tonight. Why don't you ring him back and ask him to pick you up?'

Freda put the phone down feeling wrong-footed, she was used to Maisie falling in with her plans, and now she wasn't quite sure what to do. After taking Freddie for a quick walk around the block, she came back inside. Before she could talk herself out of it, she made the call.

Ten minutes, later she put the phone down; she had a smile on her face. Jeff had agreed to pick her up, and he had even suggested a song that he said would suit her voice that he thought she should try. Bending down to stroke the dog she said, 'What do you think of that then, boy? Your mum's got a date.'

***

At number twelve, Henry was watching Anne putting on her make up. He still felt a pang each time he saw her smooth scalp. She was wearing a red summer dress with matching jewellery, and had perched a red beret on her head which was one of the hats that Helen had given her.

'Annie, you look so stylish, like a model.'

Anne accepted the compliment graciously, and gave him a kiss. Henry would think she looked wonderful if she wore a bin liner. He was taking her out for Sunday lunch, but first she wanted to look at the photos that Helen had sent of the head shave. There were two lovely ones of her with the baby, and one of her and Henry - Henry cradling little Henry and Anne talking to the baby.

'Look Henry, let's get this one printed off and framed.'

He agreed, saying, 'Anne, promise me you won't have any photos taken of you without hair. I'm OK if you've got a hat on but it'll be really upsetting to look back on them later.'

Anne agreed. Smiling at Henry, she said, 'I've been thinking. Don't you think it's a shame to waste all this talent in Capulet Close? I think we should start planning for Christmas.'

Not waiting for a reply and ignoring his startled expression she grabbed his hand and said,

'Let's go I'm ravenous.'

One Year Later

Julia slid the quiche out of the oven. She was hosting Monday night with the girls. As she set the table and made a salad, she marvelled at how much life had changed for her over this last year.

It was a warm summer evening, the kitchen window was slightly open and the blinds moved gently in the breeze. The fragrant smell of warm pastry hung in the air. Looking around, satisfied that everything was ready Julia took off her apron and went to get the glasses.

This year had flown by; after the success of the fundraiser, the final tally including the head shave had been nearly six thousand pounds.

The following Monday they had flown out to Paris. Ben had thought of everything. They had stayed in a beautiful hotel with a four poster bed. She smiled as she remembered that they had made full use of that bed. That first morning after breakfast, Ben had given her a wicked grin as he put the **Do Not Disturb** sign on the door, picked her up and had taken her back to bed saying cheekily,

'It would be a shame to waste it.'

They had been on a river cruise and they'd drunk champagne, eaten delicious food and had danced to the band under the stars. The next day, they had walked hand in hand over the bridges on the Seine, looking at the thousands of padlocks that couples had romantically attached to the bridge.

As she was looking and reading the messages, Ben had whipped a padlock out of his pocket and had shown her that he had inscribed it with their names and the date they had met. He fastened their padlock to the bridge and had kissed her before throwing the key into the river as per, *la tradition*.

Hearing a tap on the front door, Julia greeted her friends with a hug. They sat at the table; she poured drinks and served food as they caught up on their news. They were keen to hear about her latest project.

Children's bedrooms and play spaces were her bread and butter, but she was excited to tell the girls about a project that she was working on with Ben.

Ali interrupted to compliment her on the quiche. 'This pastry's delicious, so light and crisp.'

They both turned to look at their friend before Julia burst into peals of laughter.

'Come on, I'm not going to lie, you know Ben's the cook in this house! I'm a one pot wonder kind of girl.'

They nodded; they loved Ben's cooking, but they knew he respected their Monday night get together. Like Simon, he usually left them to it. Since he had moved in, he had a workspace at the bottom of the garden, grandly called the Studio, but Julia and Ben privately referred to it as 'The Shed.'

Excitedly, Julia started telling them all about their joint venture. Although Ben had been working in a gallery in the City, they wished that he could have his own space where he could display his paintings as well as work by local artists.

Recently, they had been talking to Julia's mum, and she had drawn their attention to an old building. It had been empty a while, and Maria recalled that it had once been an old fashioned teashop.

'I do know it's got a flat above it, but no idea what sort of condition it's in.'

Julia got her laptop and showed her friends the sort of thing they were planning.

'We went to see it and we both think it's a goer, just waiting now to see if we'd be allowed to make the alterations.'

She showed her friends the room at the front of the building which could be a café. It had space to seat about twenty-five people comfortably. There would be room for a toilet with two cubicles and a separate disabled toilet with a baby changing area. A small awkward room behind could have bookshelves and comfy chairs.

Julia enthusiastically outlined her idea for the café to allow people to sit in the back with a cup of coffee and just relax and read. They could host story-telling sessions, possibly book clubs could meet there.

'What do you think, girls? Is that something you would have liked when your children were small?'

'Definitely, I'd have loved somewhere to take Jake where he'd have something to do. Unless it was a toddler group, I always felt about as welcome as a fox in a chicken coop.'

They all laughed remembering Jake, he had been a bundle of mischief right enough, but lovable none the less. Bringing the girls back to the plan, she pointed out that the top floor would be where Ben could paint and create his own gallery.

He had loved the idea that it was south facing, telling her that it reminded him of the quality of light that he enjoyed in Cornwall.

Julia was just pouring them another glass of wine when they heard Ben's tread on the landing.

'Sorry girls, I'll be back in a minute, chat amongst your selves.'

Angie and Ali exchanged a glance, smiling as Julia left the room.

'We know where you're going,' they hummed in unison.

Running lightly up the stairs, Julia smiled to herself. She knew what the girls were thinking but she didn't care. She could hear Ben speaking softly. Pausing for a second, Julia quietly opened the bedroom door. Her heart contracted as her eyes took in the sight of her two favourite people.

Ben was sitting in the rocking chair cradling three month old Amélie in his arms, her brown hair just a tuft at the top of her head, eyelashes resting like half-moons on her flushed cheek. With fierce concentration, she sucked the last few drops of milk from her bottle.

Julia crept over to the chair and bent over to kiss them both. Ben looked up, blue eyes crinkling as his face broke into a smile.

'She's nearly off, little monkey's fighting it though,' he whispered.

Julia nodded her hand briefly caressing Amélie's soft cheek and headed back downstairs, leaving Ben to wind their daughter and settle her into the crib.

As she joined her friends, they burst out laughing.

'We knew it, Angie and I both said you wouldn't be able to stay away from Amélie even if she was asleep.'

Julia smiled, she knew they were right, but Amélie was the baby she thought she would never have. She couldn't be more grateful to have been given this chance of motherhood.

When they returned from Paris Julia and Ben had come to a decision, he was going to move in with her.

He had quickly established himself, building his garden studio and getting a job in an art gallery locally. Her life had just got a whole lot better and easier so why was she so darned tired? It was Angie who had wondered if she might be pregnant.

Julia thought that her tiredness might be menopause symptoms. Her periods had been so irregular for a while now that she was hoping she could stop using contraception. Her Mum however reminded her that your period needs to be stopped for two years before you can consider that you are through the menopause and a quick google search confirmed it.

She had taken a pregnancy test which was negative so at Ben's insistence she had made a doctor's appointment. She remembered with a smile that they had left the surgery stunned.

After examining her Doctor Dhillon announced that he thought she was about two months pregnant. She didn't know whether to laugh or cry but when she looked at Ben all she could see was excitement. He had mouthed 'Paris' at her and thinking about it they had been in the most romantic City in the world so no surprise that if she was going to conceive it would be there.

In spite of the worry about her age it had been a text book pregnancy, early on they decided that this was a gift neither of them had expected and had agreed not to have any tests, they would love this baby no matter what.

Amélie, their precious daughter, she just had to have a French name. She was a lucky little girl, two doting parents and three loving grandparents all living close by. Angie and Ali were her honorary aunties. She had her big cousin Henry and his family. Julia hoped that the two children would become close as they grew up, especially as Amélie was definitely going to be an only child. Coming from a small family; she believed in the African proverb,

'It takes a village to raise a child'.

Ben joined them for coffee, and they sat chatting about work and family until it was time for the girls to leave.

'Don't forget there's music at the pub on Saturday night. Dad's playing, and I think he's going to get Freda to sing a few songs.'

'What about Dave's lot?'

Julia explained that recently, the Stompers hadn't played as much. At first, they had wondered if the rift between Dave and his Dad was still an issue, according to Henry, the drummer and the saxophone player were just too frail now. Henry said that Dave and his dad still played together sometimes at his dad's, but that was about it.

Florence was going to be playing duets with Dave, so it should be a good night. Ben and Julia would be coming along, as Maria was keen to babysit now that the baby slept well through the evening.

'She takes a bit of settling down, but once she's asleep she's out for the count.' Ben and Julia exchanged proud smiles.

In the time it took Julia to say goodbye to her friends Ben had already started loading the dishwasher.

'Go on up, I'll finish off here.'

He kissed her and turned her towards the stairs.

'Ali and Angie are right you really are the ideal man.'

Yawning, Julia tiptoed up the stairs. When Ben came up ten minutes later he wasn't surprised to find that she wasn't in bed. He knew exactly where she would be.

He gently opened the door to Amélie's bedroom and paused for a second enjoying the sight of Julia gazing down at their daughter He joined her by the crib and slipped his arm around her waist holding her close. He couldn't wait to see what the next year would bring.

If you enjoyed reading Capulet Close

Follow Suzy Edney: on Instagram

Visit my website www.suzyedney.com

And read a new short story every week

Printed in Great Britain
by Amazon